PEARL

PEARL

A Romance

CHRISTOPHER BIGSBY

Weidenfeld & Nicolson
LONDON

For Bella and Ewan,
who travelled from Colney to America

First published in Great Britain in 1995 by
Weidenfeld & Nicolson

The Orion Publishing Group Ltd
Orion House
5 Upper Saint Martin's Lane
London WC2H 9EA

A catalogue record for this book is available from the British Library

ISBN: 0 297 81533 4

Typeset by Deltatype Ltd, Ellesmere Port, Cheshire
Printed in Great Britain by Butler & Tanner Ltd, Frome and London

All stories are connected.
How could it be otherwise?

What is life but repetition,
living, throbbing repetition?
Always the same. Only different.

Prologue

On an April afternoon, long before the present age of confusion and despair, a bird flew out of the sun and into the grey-silver of a window pane. It snapped its neck on that invisible divide. For a second or so it fluttered in a circle of dust and feathers as though it still flew. It had dived into a silver pool to meet its own reflection and had met death instead, death being the moment when at last we do see ourselves for what we are. The bird was a cardinal. To the pale face which stared out from within, it was a splash of deep scarlet, a sudden wound in the tangled grass, an omen. Something had ended, something was about to begin.

Boston, in 1660, was a settlement of some two thousand souls, some of them saved, some doomed for eternity. One of the doomed, or so it had been supposed, was a woman known as Hester Prynne who had travelled to the Massachusetts colony twenty years before. Her sin was to have known a man not her husband, and certainly she had lived to learn that dark deeds will have their consequence. A child was born who was christened Pearl but she bore no other name besides that of her mother and was therefore thrice cursed: once by conception, once by birth and once by the loss of a name and hence of true identity.

As for Hester, she was required to stand forth before the world with the mark of her sin in her arms; and emblazoned, too, on the clothes she wore, a scarlet letter A shining in the dim light of the market square as she stood upon the scaffold ready to pay her penance. These were unforgiving times and unforgiving people. They saw but the outward world and took it for an image of that within.

To be sure, Hester had been joined in marriage, in the England she left behind, to one who called himself Roger Chillingworth, a dark and private man who sought to understand the human soul as a man of science will analyse a sample of rare mineral: by crushing it and seeing how it will react when put to the test. He and Hester met when he went riding one winter's day and his horse stumbled in the river by her home. Brought together by chance, they discovered that chance further decreed that a kind of mutual fascination would be born and from fascination what might pass as love. There followed nuptials which proved cold indeed, for the sacrament was denied by the man to whom she had so carelessly wed her soul. Older far than she, he had refused her the passion which she sought and begun, instead, as she believed, to plot against herself and others too, perhaps, for civil war was fast approaching like the tide across a bay. There were those who saw his twisted body – one shoulder higher than another – as token of a spirit no less deformed.

Hester was not the first to escape her fears by taking ship for western skies nor yet shall be the last. But on that voyage she met another, and from that meeting was bred a love as warm as that which went before was cold.

And her lover? None in that heartless colony ever knew, for he was one they believed must be without sin, a man who preached of God and retribution each Sabbath in the church. Thus, when her deed became manifest, the very minister charged to urge her name her fellow fornicator was he who had lain with her in the dark and whispered there what he lacked courage to speak aloud before his congregation. His name was Arthur Dimmesdale and though she breathed that name in the

2

privacy of her chamber, with love, and, yes, with desire too, all others spoke it with respect for his seeming purity.

But if the sheep did not suspect the shepherd there was another who did, for Chillingworth followed on behind and set himself to destroy the man who had won Hester's love from him, as she had won love from God himself. And so they wrestled one another to the grave, the alchemist who practised his dubious skills on the human heart, and the minister who had learned that love must have a human face or remain forever simple piety, disdainful and remote as a distant star.

The years went by, as the clouds move across the face of the earth. Dimmesdale was hounded to his grave by private guilt and by the subtle yet poisonous ministrations of the man he had wronged, though less man than devil as the cleric came to feel. Whichever it might be, his vengeance complete, he too slipped from this life, his passing noted by few and regretted by none. Such is the way of things: yesterday's wound fades by degree to the merest scar. There came a time, indeed, when few remembered what had passed before.

The colony itself was no longer what it had been. The Boston of 1640 was a kernel from which had grown a firm-rooted tree. And Hester, too, had sunk her roots. Remembered sin had become no more than a window opened on the transgressions of others, the source of true compassion. And if there were those who had not forgotten and whose eyes were still drawn to the scarlet letter on her breast, even they saw meanings never meant by those who thought once to entrap her forever in their own alphabet of sin.

But yesterday's story is done and another is about to be told for if there was a mother there is also a daughter, and each generation begins with a page which, if not blank, bears only the faint impression of another's writing which will disappear once a good pen and clear black ink begin the job of telling what must be told.

Chapter One

Descend from a hill called Beacon, as an eagle will swoop down through the liquid air, and below you will see houses, standing together like mourners around a grave; ahead, the ruffled sparkle of Massachusetts Bay. It is a bright day. Sea-birds ride the wind, the very wind which brings the smell of seaweed into carpenter's workshop and magistrate's court. It is an odour which seeps up King Street, along Cornhill and even into the new Town House, like some invisible spirit risen from the ocean deep.

There are times when seaweed can smell of decay and putrefaction but there are others when it seems to freshen the air as though it would drive out dust and mould and the winter's grime. And this is how it was this March day. People sniffed the air and knew that spring was on its way. Pure white sheets hung between trees while carpets were beaten out of doors. The ice had begun to melt on the Charles River, jostling and turning in the current, while on land the snow had retreated and there was a pause before the first shoots of new growth showed green against the sullen earth.

In a certain lawyer's office a young man nervously prepares for his first clients, re-reading the papers before him and rehearsing the speech he will make in a few minutes' time. The task ahead is a light one. He has only to tell a woman of her good fortune, but first times are never easy and his heart beats a little faster than it might.

Up the street, in the direction of the Common, two women walk together in the spring air, the one an echo of the other save that one has black eyes, the other blue, while the one with black eyes wears a dress which bears a scarlet emblem at the breast. She walks a deal less willingly than her partner, from time to time stopping in the street only to be urged on again by her young companion: Hester and Pearl on their way to an appointment, on their way to a moment of fate.

Outside the lawyer's office a sign hangs squeaking in the wind. Inside, everything is bright red cloth and new-hewn oak. The lawyer himself looks scarcely older than the young woman he now addresses. Indeed, it is with difficulty that he looks to the documents before him.

Hester draws her chair back when he explains further the reason for the summons, as though the ghost of a dead man has risen up before her.

'No,' she says, abruptly. 'I will none of that. He is nothing to me nor I to him. Let it be.'

'That may be so, mistress, but the law must take its course. You may do with property and money as you will but I must discharge my responsibility. Nor is the bequest to you but to your daughter.'

'She will have none of this, neither.'

'Mother, permit the poor man to do his duty. As he says, we may do as we wish when he has completed his speech.'

'Indeed. I thank you. To tell the truth, this is the first such duty I have performed since setting up my sign. The first of any kind. The other name written there is a deal more practical than I and has permitted me this pleasant duty, or pleasant as he assumed. I should never explain it to him were I to fail in such a simple task.'

'Very well. Continue. But your duty done, we shall leave.'

'And it please you.' He turns to the documents before him, tied with a red ribbon and, it seems to Hester, with a scarlet letter upon its first page. 'This packet was left in the charge of these chambers some years since, on the death of a client, with instructions that it was not to be opened until a certain day should come. This day. And I see that I have a cause to congratulate you, mistress, for it states that the reason for this occasion is your eighteenth birthday.'

'If you please,' says Hester impatiently.

'Even so,' says the young man, his face reddening, his collar suddenly tight about his throat, 'I will read what it says here.'

'May we not do as much ourselves?'

'I am instructed to read to you.' He shrugs his embarrassment. 'Mine is a profession in which instructions must be obeyed.'

'Please, sir,' says Pearl, 'continue.'

'I am required to state that there is a certain property in the county of Norfolk in England and in the village of Colney.'

Hester flinches, as though struck.

'The said property comprises a hall and the land which surrounds it, including a wood and meadowland, down to a river and marked on a map which is contained within the packet. This hall and this land is to be yours, provided that you return to claim it. There is, too, a matter of thirty sovereigns which is itself only a part of what shall be added along with the property.' He pushes the papers from him and looks anxiously from mother to daughter.

'Mother,' says Pearl, turning in her seat.

'And are you done?' asks Hester, her face severe.

'There are details as to how the claim is to be completed and the whole is signed by one called Roger Chillingworth.'

'You are done now?'

'I am done,' replies the young lawyer, with a deepening sense of failure.

'Then we shall go. You have performed your duty in speaking and we in listening. I thank you.'

'And your instructions?'

'I am not your client.'

'But there is money. And, as instructed, I have prepared a

letter for colleagues in the city named as specified in the document.'

'I have no need of such.'

'But, begging your pardon . . .' – the poor man's embarrassment is growing by the moment – 'the document is not directed to you but to your daughter.'

'And so?'

'And so I must take my instructions from her.'

'Then do so.'

'Mistress?'

Pearl looks from her mother to the papers in front of the young lawyer who by now appears to wish himself anywhere but in this office confronted by these two women. 'We will consider further, sir. I should be grateful if you would await our decision. There is no hurry, I presume.'

'Indeed not, except that you must make your claim before you reach one and twenty years. There is time enough, as you see. I am sorry that this news was not as happy as I thought it must be.'

Hester turns and steps out into the bright light of a Boston spring which has suddenly lost its joy. Pearl smiles at the young man before following her. In those moments she has made a decision she will not rescind. She will leave this place where she has never felt at one with those around her. Another place and another time beckon her. Hester senses her daughter's mood. Has her old adversary, then, won a final victory? Has he reached from the grave to destroy her life anew?

Nearly two years passed before Pearl sailed on the *Revenge* (an odd name for a vessel not a ship of the line). She had been commissioned to replace another which had foundered with all hands. Her owner, who himself had never set foot on sloop or brigantine, nor even a rowing boat not securely tied to a quay, offered the name as a gesture of contempt for the sea. Happily, the sailors, who otherwise would have shunned her to a man, took it as a sign of his military profession. The

7

ship that was lost was the *Hope*, broken by the force of a nor'easter, her tracery of ropes trailing about like the hair of a drowned woman as she dwindled in the depths. It was twenty years since she had sailed one November with two people who began as strangers and ended as one another's destiny. One was Hester, in flight from a husband as cold as his name, the other a man who loved her as he had vowed to love God alone.

Pearl looked up at the same changing sky as had her mother, listened to the same tinkling melody of bubbles, the same harsh smack of wood on sea. But her mind was not full of the past, nor yet tortured by guilt and fear. There was no shipboard romance, though there were those, officers and men returning from an adventure not quite to their taste, who watched her with a mixture of desire and regret. She moved against the current of history for she chose as her future what others took for a past.

The destination of the *Revenge* was not Plymouth or Yarmouth but London; in her hold not Norfolk cloth but skins of beaver and seal. For ballast she carried some ton or more of stones taken from a Boston sea wall built along the marsh and abandoned by its builders. Half of her rigging had been renewed by Boston shipwrights so that she was as much a cross between old world and new as the woman on the edge of life whom she now carried towards a home she had never seen and which had once been a prison to her mother.

The leave-taking of Hester and Pearl was a blend of pain and joy. Whoever has parted from their own children, grown into men or women and anxious to be on their way, will know something of what passed through Hester's heart that day. There can seem a cruelty in those who so carelessly break bonds which once were as strong and vital as the cord which gave them life and tied them to their origin. Certainly for Hester it was as though this daughter were being torn a second time from the womb. Theirs had never been a gentle pairing. There was a wildness in Pearl that would never be tamed, an independence born, perhaps, as much of their frontier world as of the exile from human sympathy which they had felt in her early years. And yet Hester had thrilled to see her grow so straight and proud, to watch her walk the town with a step so light and firm that there was nothing but love in her heart, that and regret for years that would never return, for childhood days slipped by. Pearl was that part of Hester which had never bowed and she saw, as in a forest pool, her own reflection yet somehow stronger than herself because not burdened by her history.

That Pearl should go she had no doubt. For though Hester, once shunned for loving unwisely, was now fully a part of this community of souls, the memories of some were long. Her daughter had a right to be the heroine of her own story and not a coda to her mother's. Nor was this a nestling, trembling on a branch. She was a young colt which eyes the fence rail and prepares to jump. And if the fortune she returns to claim, a fortune left to her, as Hester supposed, out of guilt, seems tainted by its origin, yet what mother would not feel a kind of pride that a daughter should return in triumph to a place which she herself had left in fear and virtual penury? Yet to lose her was so close to losing her own life that she hardly imagined she could survive the day.

And so they stood at the harbour front, where the *Revenge* waited with a dozen other vessels along a wharf which reached out into the bay, and held one another at arm's length: mother and daughter. On the very edge of her own future the daughter saw the past, proud and clear. For her mother still wore a scarlet letter A, the badge of her adultery, small and entwined with silk but so much a part of her that it seemed as natural as her smile or as the tears which now traced down her face, as sun and rain contend on an April day. The mother saw that past, too. For what mother does not see herself in her daughter's eyes, recall what once she was when she set off to command the world? So the tears she shed were partly for a daughter lost and partly for her own lost self; one of those reminders of mortality which drift across our consciousness like a cobweb across the face. Neither spoke but stared at each other to fix the face, to imprint a memory. The years ahead would be full or empty but never again would they see one another, they who were flesh of one flesh, though each promised that it would be otherwise.

And why did Hester not accompany her? Because her life was here and her death prefigured by one whose last resting place must prove her own, the man whose love she claimed but whose weakness, perhaps, and divided loyalties had left her all alone. Why did her daughter not stay? Because she had witnessed a drama played to its conclusion and must be about her own adventures; because she now had the means to travel to her destiny. Nor should it be thought that Pearl had been unhappy in this place. There was a wildness here which echoed that of her own spirit. The forest, now driven back, felled and burned, to make space for the growing town, had been her natural home. She took delight in the Indians who wandered through the streets, bodies uncovered in a town wrapped up even in the fiercest heat. She had followed them to camps and eaten by their fires, quite unafraid though the ordered citizens of Boston saw them as demons in their cold cosmology. But for her there was another wildness, beyond the sea, a place where she would be more than Hester's child, daughter of the scarlet letter. Besides, there were but two directions in which to proceed: westward, towards the setting sun, or east, towards beginnings, where the day itself began. She chose the east, perhaps because by retracing the path her mother took she might the better find herself.

Neither mother nor daughter could hold back tears, clinging to each other as though they were one, Pearl pressing her face to her mother's breast and Hester stroking her hair in a distracted way as she had so many years before. So tight was their embrace that when Pearl at last released her grasp and stepped back, the embossed letter on her mother's dress had pressed an indentation on her cheek and for a moment, as the sun rose across the cobalt-blue waters of the bay, this mark turned from white to red and blazed with a fierce glow before cooling to invisibility. Pearl knew nothing of this but her mother stepped back in alarm, raising her hand as though to fend off some threatened evil. But as it disappeared she pulled her close again and gently kissed her on her way.

And so separated two parts of the same person, pulled asunder by forces they could not understand. Around them the world continued unimpressed. Labourers rolled barrels of salted fish, men, with documents fluttering in the morning breeze, strutted fitfully back and forth while the people of Boston raked cold ashes from their fires and looked through windows to judge the coming day. The city went about its business, which it presumed to be identical to that of God. But I fancy God had greater interest in these two souls who so unwillingly relinquished each other's hands and turned aside, one to return to what even now she forbore to call her home; the other to walk along a rutted gangplank towards a future she could not yet read.

Pearl was not the only one of Boston's citizens to choose east over west. There were those whose dreams had died in the winter chills and fetid heat of a New England that had little of England about it. And failure was felt more keenly here, for if such a dream could die where should hope be born for those who had travelled so far, following a star which faded with the dawn? Resignation is a poor fuel to warm the spirit. When a door slams on the future nothing remains but a thousand todays and then a thousand more.

There were two such who took up station on the *Revenge* as, with a sudden wind from the shore, she swung away from the quay, her sails filling like a wet nurse's shirt. They stared silently at the city they had failed to make their own. Husband and wife, neither touched the other for this new-found land had found them out and they no longer held hands to form confederacy against ill fortune but stood, side by side, sentinels to guard over their own disappointment and despair.

Pearl watched, too, long after the figure of her mother had shrunk from view. For all her independent spirit and the excitement which comes with new ventures, she saw the scene refracted through a tear which so distorted her vision that a single cloud which drifted above the town seemed to her to take an angel's form, with hands outstretched. Then, contrary winds dissolved the shape until it became no more than a cloud again, floating above a city which was itself merely a dark design against a green hillside, though the sun sparkled on glass and metal so that a thousand points of light shone from that shade and signalled some message to the world.

I have said that there was no shipboard romance, but there was a man who wished that it were otherwise. He wore a kind of uniform, though one that seemed fashioned by anyone but a regimental tailor. There was some blue in it and a little green but mostly it was a bright red, while the whole was sewn together with such care that it was evident someone shared sufficiently in his ambition to clothe him in a magic garment. He sailed to purchase a commission and sought to anticipate what it should feel like to serve the new king and shine a little in the world. Nor was the effect as strange as it might sound, for he wore his soldier's clothes with a certain pride, if also some embarrassment. To be sure it caught Pearl's eye, as should it not. It would be a strange young woman who did not look more than once at a man dressed in scarlet with a silver sword, if not a silver tongue, and a still stranger young man who would not be drawn to a woman of nearly twenty years with the bluest of eyes and dark hair which blew in the wind.

'Mistress.'

'Sir.'

'You are for England?'

'Unless this ship be headed for some other port.'

'Ah! Exactly. Quite so.' The words were clipped, precise, if the thoughts they expressed were not. Nor did they quite seem to belong to the man who uttered them. It was as though he tried on a language along with his uniform.

'And are you,' he looked about the now empty deck, 'alone?'

Pearl smiled at his discomfort. 'And it seems,' she replied, herself looking about the vessel and even up into the shrouds. 'Yes, entirely, so it would appear.'

'Indeed.'

'Indeed.'

'And are you come from Boston?'

It occurred to Pearl that several weeks of such questioning must send her quite mad so that she resolved to put an end to it then and there. 'I am, indeed, sir, since we are only three hours from leaving it. Is there any further you would know?'

A lieutenant, in prospect if not yet in fact, might be thought to be made of durable material, not steel, perhaps, but iron at least. This particular would-be lieutenant, however, more closely resembled a puppy smacked for bringing mud indoors and the conversation would have ended there had Pearl not taken pity.

'You are on an errand for your regiment, sir?'

'No. I go to purchase a commission. There is little for a soldier in Boston. I go in search of war.'

'And why should you do so?'

'Because that is a soldier's duty, mistress. There is no honour or fame in idleness.'

'No, nor in killing your fellow man.'

'It is not killing. It is fighting.'

'I see.'

'Should I show you my sword? It were my grandfather's.'

'Indeed no. And you will forgive me, I must go below.' She dropped him a mocking curtsey and turned on her heel, her hair blowing across her face. She threw her head back to release it in a gesture which came close to breaking his heart, as it seemed to him, though he had only seen her a few minutes since.

The soldier watched her go and, when at last she disappeared below, struck the deck rail with his fist in frustration at his failure to impress. He might have felt otherwise, however, had he witnessed that selfsame woman below deck open up a small sea chest, take out a mirror and smile as she looked into it, as though she looked to find what a young soldier, in his new-found finery, might have discovered in one who wore only her workday clothes and looked for nothing but a moment's conversation.

Yet Pearl sought no liaison and distrusted the breed called man. She had seen little in her life that would lead her to admire those who believed their sex gave them natural authority. To her they seemed to lack precisely those qualities necessary to life: compassion, understanding, intelligence and natural human warmth. From her earliest days she had seen men declaim their truths from platform and pulpit and seek to determine the limits of her life. She had sensed their cruelty and suffered their disdain. She was a woman, with a woman's needs, desires and dreams, but she had seen how dreams can ensnare, how desires and needs turn a free soul into a disregarded supplicant. She stared into the future and saw no man in it who would brand her with his shame or make her subject to his will. The scarlet soldier must tread his path to glory on his own. She sought other destinies; and if these remained as yet a mystery, she was content, meanwhile, to greet each day with a smile, even if each night was heralded with a tear, for it took courage to cross such an ocean and courage to change one's life by doing so.

Twenty and more years before, Hester had sat in her cabin and confided her thoughts to a diary. It was a way to make them real, to examine each day for its meaning, to interrogate herself. Beyond that it was a confederate she could treat as a friend. Pearl had a diary which she kept in her sea chest alongside a package in which were wrapped brushes and paints, the tools of an artist who is not content that the world should remain as it is but must work to transform it into what it may be. She opened that book her first night at sea and, in the swaying light of a lantern, and to the sound of a woman retching into a bowl as the Atlantic took the ship into its rolling embrace, wrote her first entry.

My dear mother is gone. She would not come with me, though I begged her to. She tends a grave and that is all there is to it. She will not leave him who was happy to leave her. There is much I do not understand, and chiefly that. How can her life have become subject to that of another, whoever it be, and how subject to one who in denying her denied himself as well? I will plough a different furrow.

My cabin is simple and I share it with a Mistress Quigly who returns, with her husband, to the England she left but a few years since. Her unhappiness is writ on her face and is doubled now as she has been sick these last hours since we cleared the Cape.

An hour ago I heard a man sing. There were none who accompanied him, just his voice rising and falling with the sea. He sang of one he left behind. The sky is clear and the stars a bright shine from horizon to horizon. I could almost believe I were alone and that voice within my very soul. The sea is black and throbs with a steady pulse and, as it does, so the stars swing in a great arc as though I were at creation's centre. I, too, have left behind one whom I would that I had not. There, he sings again. There is such sadness in his voice.

At that moment a particularly violent shudder ran through the length of the *Revenge*, accompanied by a sifting sigh such as a sledge makes in sliding down a hill. Pearl's quill broke, sending a small explosion of green ink over what she had written as though the stars of which she had spoken had come down onto her page.

Unbeknown to her the vessel had found a sandbank it did not seek. But this was the last hand which reached out to grasp them to the land. The sound ceased and they were free again to rise and fall, to pitch and sway under a tumbling sky until at last they should come to safety in England's green land, if safety it should prove to be.

When Hester sailed to Boston she had followed the sun, with the wind at her heels and, for all she knew, a vengeful husband, too. It was winter and storms lay in wait for travellers who chanced their lives, and merchants their cargo, amidst December ice. Pearl headed for the rising sun, each day making her way to the prow and there waiting for a thumbnail of gold to break the line of the horizon.

For the first few days the young lieutenant stood beside her, his uniform glowing in the morning light. He greeted her stiffly but then seemed to lose either his courage or his tongue. After no more than a week, though, the soldier abandoned his uniform and the lieutenant his pride. Two days spent being sick in a bucket will have such an effect. He learned quickly

what common intelligence should long since have acknowledged, that beneath the scarlet we are all alike in our distress.
Thus, stripped of his finery and his manly conceit, he also
found, what other men have found before, that a young
woman who shuns the braggart may be drawn to the clown.
And so sorry for himself did he become, slumped across the
galley's rough table or leaning over the ship's side, as though
death among the fishes might be preferable to life on a ship
which never ceased its rolling motion, that there was something of the clown about him. Whatever the truth of that,
Pearl, who had repulsed his first advances, now sat beside him
and set herself to restore his spirits. There is, after all, little to
do on a voyage in which each day seems much as the one
before.

'And where is your uniform?' she asked, when at last she
judged him capable of conversation.

'In the cabin. Soiled,' he replied bitterly and endeavoured
not to look at where the horizon swayed with such deliberate
and disturbing regularity.

'And are you fully recovered?'

He was silent for a moment as though he had not quite
understood. Then at last he nodded and turned aside.

'All are sick when they first venture on the sea. I myself . . .'
she hesitated a second, 'have suffered likewise. It passes. The
motion . . .'

He raised a hand as though to ward off the word as much as
the reality it expressed.

'. . . is one to which you will grow accustomed.'

He groaned.

'Walk on the deck. Take the air.'

He turned to her, his brown eyes sunk in pale cheeks. 'I am a
soldier and I have no strength. What good can I be? I should
have stayed where I was.'

'You have been sick. As to staying at home, at least there
you would have done no injury to anyone. My pity is for those
you might kill, not for one so easily turned about by wind and
tide.' She regretted her speech immediately. 'Yet,' she added

quickly, 'if there is ought I can do you have only to say. We all sail together and must be friends to each other.'

'Friends?' he asked, turning towards her.

'Friends,' repeated Pearl and in such a tone as to suggest that there could be nothing more. 'And what is your name? We have stood side by side and still I know nothing of you.'

'I am Lieutenant . . .'

'I would know who you are, not what.'

'I am Matthew Borrow.'

'And I Pearl Prynne.'

'That is a name I have heard and I think on it.'

Pearl stood up and looked at the man whose age she judged to be much as her own but to whom she felt herself senior. 'I cannot say as much of yours,' she said sharply. 'But what is a name, which can be so easily changed? Look to the person. I think you live too much with appearances.'

So speaking, she turned around and walked steadily towards the stern, though the ship rolled in the swell and the deck was slick from washing. Matthew Borrow, meanwhile, looked after her in amazement, unaware what offence he might have caused.

Pearl, then, was not free of arrogance herself who treated as a schoolboy one whom others might presume her superior. But in truth her anger had been sparked by his wayward memory of a name which in Boston still tied her to a history she would escape. Was she never to be free of their catechising rule? They dealt in symbols and took them for simple truth, sought to spell out what they saw as offence, oblivious to the life which they would castigate as sin.

The scarlet letter which her mother wore was still to some a mark of shame. But who was Pearl but the living consequence of that shame? Hence she could never accept the meaning they would give to it. Even now she remembered a time in the forest when her mother had unpicked the letter from her clothes and thrown it away from her. To Pearl it had been as if she had sought to unpick her daughter with that gesture. She remembered with what fast-beating heart, what sense of betrayal and alarm, she had jumped across the stream to recover the letter from the brambles where it lodged; remembered, too, the panic she had felt until it was once more pinned in place over the heart of the one she loved most in a world where few offered themselves for love.

Beneath the stern the water tumbled and turned while a widening V marked their passage, as though they sliced the living flesh of the ocean, opening a wound into the icy depths. Far behind, beyond the horizon, pale men and women in dark clothes sought salvation along the shore of a land they took for Eden but corrupted with their severity. She needed no reminder of her past. Where Hester had fled from memories she feared would prove present facts, as a cold husband pursued her over a still colder ocean, Pearl looked for tomorrow's grace and, turning once again, made her way past a man who looked towards her but said nothing, until she found herself at the bow of a vessel which rode up onto a ridge of water as though it would take wing.

Silence at sea is not as silence on land. There is never true quietness in either realm but I have exchanged for the rasp of crickets and the vulgar croak of frogs a kind of music. The passage of the sea past the hull creates a constant hushing, like a mother with her finger to her lips who bids her child be quiet. Along with that comes a noise which defies my skill to describe. It is like a brook passing over rocks, liquid yet sonorous, a distant sounding of muted bells. Beneath that I sometimes seem to hear a crying which the sailors, who hear it too, say is the mermaids calling them to their arms but which I believe must be leviathan sounding in the deeps, for I saw one such this forenoon turning slowly in the ocean before seeking out the depths. I painted its portrait but made a poor job of it, as it seems to me, though my scarlet lieutenant expressed his wonder that it should live on my canvas as on the sea. And I think perhaps that it did for I feel a deal in common with a creature which finds itself far from shore with no compass but the stars and no knowledge of what lies ahead but ever greater depths and a day's new dawn.

★

As Pearl had predicted, the lieutenant recovered both balance and temper with a few days more at sea, such is man that he may accustom himself to vicissitude and place. He quickly forgot his self-pity and tried once more to convince his companion of virtues which might otherwise prove invisible.

'You are alone.'

'As you see.'

'It is not good that a woman should be so.'

'Indeed. And why may that be?'

'Why, because she may not know what will befall.'

'Neither we may. But why, pray, should this prove less true of a man?'

'A man is born to bear such burdens and so may meet challenges with a strong arm and heart.'

'And women?'

'They must tend the hearth and keep the home.'

'Whence this wisdom?'

'Mistress?'

'Is this your own opinion or another's?'

'It is the opinion of everyone I ever met. The minister in the church. The teacher at school. It is no more than a truth to which all subscribe. Do you doubt that it is so?'

'How could I doubt a wisdom of such pedigree? You, sir, and forgive me, are a fool and have found a fool's vocation.'

The lieutenant was for a moment unable to speak, looking at his companion with genuine perplexity.

'Do you call soldiering foolishness?'

'Do you count it wisdom to kill others or to make your own life be forfeit?'

'For king and country. I fight for the new king Charles and country.'

'For anyone at all, Matthew. There must be those that love you, though I can discover little enough reason, to be sure. Were they glad to know that you had your heart set on death at so young an age?'

'I shall not die.'

'Not ever?'

'Mistress, you sport with me.'

'A little, perhaps. But you sport with me who thinks that I would join my fate with one who treads a proud path to his grave.'

'Join your fate? I never said so.'

'No. Indeed. Yet I think some such thought occurred to you.'

'No, mistress, truly. I were but . . . there be no . . . it were a courtesy, no more.'

'For your courtesy I thank you, then.'

'It is nothing, mistress.'

'Indeed. I had already measured it at that amount.'

There could be cruelty in Pearl, as in any woman of twenty years who knows her own beauty and the power it may bring for a season.

Unlike her mother, Pearl sailed at a gentle time of year and though the wind blew and the sea offered reminder of its power it was a rare day which did not dawn with blue skies and white clouds. Such weather has a healing power. It warms more than the skin, and so it proved with those on board the *Revenge*. The soldier once more put on a uniform which was a kind of barometer of his spirits, and stood each day on the deck to perform with his sword, a scarlet figure within a blur of flashing silver. The husband and wife, whom failure had infected with despair, could be seen arm in arm together, while Pearl sat at an easel, made for her by the ship's carpenter, and sought to find enough varieties of blue to do full justice to ocean and to sky. What she had once struggled to accomplish with needle and thread she now perfected with beaver hair and subtle pigments. No Leonardo, yet she had a skill which surpassed that of a casual dabbler. More than one home, in a Boston suspicious of images, was warmed by a picture she had painted and sold to keep the larder full. She had a natural sense of colour and of form and amused those on board by sketching the faces of passengers and crew. Even the captain, who liked to keep himself aloof, stood close by her one afternoon, as though by chance, until it occurred to Pearl that his pose was too self-conscious not to be offered as subject for her art.

There are those who can describe some acquaintance with such vividness that their words seem to summon up the very person they invoke. There are likewise artists, though few, who can, with a piece of charcoal or a pencil, capture not the outward form but the inward spirit of those they survey. This was Pearl's skill. When she had done with a sketch those who looked on it would stand for a moment, as often as not, in silence, and then nod slowly in recognition of a truth which lay far beyond mere verisimilitude. Nor was this so only for those who looked on the image of a friend, for she held up a kind of spiritual mirror, as it seemed, and when her subjects looked on themselves thus rendered by her hand they, too, were oftentimes reduced to staring and acknowledging, though perhaps to themselves alone, that she had found them out in their secret selves. For some this was a kind of pleasure, for others hardly so, for who is there who would not be shocked to find displayed to the world what we scarcely acknowledge to ourselves and assuredly would prefer to remain closed to our acquaintances?

The captain, who would perhaps have stood for ever, a hand raised, seemingly casually, to the lanyards, had not Pearl released him from his pose, was one of those who saw what he would not. Strolling past his picture, as though he had no knowledge that she had been drawing him this forty minutes, he stopped and looked over the sloping shoulder of a girl who could have been his granddaughter. Who can know what he saw there, but when Pearl at last turned towards him, sheltering her eyes from the brightness of the spring sun, this bluff authoritarian, who strode the deck alone and had done no more than glance in her direction, had a tear in his eyes. He, too, nodded and for a moment looked in puzzlement at the woman who had offered him a vision of himself which must have stirred a memory or regret or perhaps a guilt he must otherwise never articulate.

We so contrive to deceive with our smiles or scowls, so

dedicate ourselves to adjusting appearance to match the impression we would give, that it is a shock to think that there might be those with some secret knowledge who can read us as simply as a mother reads a story to her child. Yet it was only in her art that Pearl was granted such insight, nor could she read the meaning in her own portraits for that required a recognition which could come only with the combination of image and knowledge, a knowledge to which only the subject of her sketch could be privy. Were it otherwise, were she blessed with the skill to read the human heart on mere acquaintance, she would never have trod the path she was to tread. But if things and people were truly what they appeared, would we really be content? Mystery is what urges us on and if disillusion will breed despair, revelation may light our lives as never yet did the noonday sun.

A mystery of sorts awaited but a few days' sail away for, at the mid point of their journey, Pearl was witness to a scene which seemed to defy both faith and reason alike as life and death were brought so close together as to seem part of the same experience. She committed it to her diary not simply for itself but for the meaning which she felt it must convey, being sufficiently a child of her time to know that there are lessons in the day's events if we should but learn to look aright.

In the late afternoon, still under a sky so blue that nature seems to have abandoned the rest of her palette, there came a sudden rushing of sound. I had just gathered up my paints having tried once more, and again failed as it seems to me, to create a portrait of my mother, when all began to look about them. Though the noise was loud and shrill, none, it seemed, could discover where it might be coming from. It was as though sound had converted itself to light and shone all about. Then there was a cry from the rigging and a sailor, who had been mending the ropes with a wooden stave, pointed off the starboard bow. In common with others I ran quickly to the side and looked down into a sea whose green was flecked with white. None knew what we sought but all looked about to see what might be there. At first there was nothing to be seen but some drifting jellyfish whose glass-like clarity was tinged with a subtle pink. Then, of a sudden, the sea seemed to rise to a swelling point, its green turned black as though a great rock had been uncovered by our passing. At such a moment the mind tries several interpretations as though meaning was inchoate and undecided how to resolve itself. Then, all became clear and I was filled with nothing but a sense of wonder as from the depths there arose a creature so great and yet so lithe that for a moment it seemed more an animal of the air than of the sea. Indeed, time seemed to slow, for I fancy I saw every particle of its being, every sparkling drop of water which hung about it, as it soared into the sky. Its great black streaked body was furrowed with ridges as though some celestial carpenter had scored them with a router, while along its length were studded barnacles like rivets along the hull of a ship. As it rose so it turned, gently, as though it sailed in the wind like ourselves. It was so close to us that its eye was turned directly on me and when, at last, it returned to the sea, its tail never entirely leaving it, so a great folding sheet of spray rose up like some great waterfall reversing its direction.

The would-be lieutenant was quite overwhelmed by the wash, his scarlet uniform turning black with the water. I myself saw my mother's face washed away and my canvas float across the deck and disappear into the waves.

'Stand clear,' came a voice from above but truth to tell I pressed to the rail to see what so great a creature should look like close to. Thus was I witness to a great mystery which became a greater tragedy.

The whale had once more disappeared from view and for several long minutes all scanned the water for sign of her return. But one piece of sea looks much like another and after a moment or two it was difficult even to detect our forward motion. Seabirds no longer skim the waves and what is far and what is near become confused. Then, with a rasping rush of air she breached once more, not this time rising to the sky but settling alongside as though she sought to sail in our lee.

Again I noted the barnacles which grew about her head, giving her a distinctive look so that she appeared to wear a cap against the cold. They seemed, indeed, to form a kind of pattern, though what it might signify was beyond my comprehension. Despite the order from above none did stand clear but lined the ship's side. There was, to be true, little enough to disturb the day's monotony but even should we have been sinking we would, I think, have spared a moment for this wonder.

She swam for a while beside us, and with no effort that I could detect. It was almost as though the ship itself drew her along. The Revenge creaked and swayed, as it made its passage through the turquoise sea, but leviathan sailed as silently now and as gracefully as though on an inland sea. Then, with a vent of air and a plume of spray she turned half on her side and I saw what few have seen before and why I refer to this creature as 'she'. Towards the rear of this sleek black creature there appeared, as it seemed, a small growth as though she had grown an extra limb. At first I hardly noticed this at all until it began to bend to and fro like a worm on a fisherman's hook. For a while I puzzled over what it might be until, with a pulse of scarlet which stained the icy water, a young whale slipped backwards into this life and in a cloud of blood began to swim as though the exchange of warm waters for cold was as agreeable as life itself.

I have seen mares foal and sheep give birth to lambs but this nativity was both strange and moving as none before that I have witnessed. I felt my pulse race. So, I thought, God ordains we multiply our kind even here where there is none to know. Yet what are we to make of this solitary beast whose labour is observed by no other of her sort and whose offspring breathes its first in a world of water where there is no respite for those new-born? How fragile its grasp on life I could not know nor how short a time it was fated to spend under God's blue heaven. The red blood turned pink then thinned to transparency and was swept away astern while the young whale swam so close to its mother that it was all but invisible.

So it continued for the best part of an hour. The crew returned to their work and soon there was only myself and the lieutenant to watch. He had withdrawn to his cabin to remove his uniform once more, having yet to learn how unsuited it is to shipboard life. But he returned and took up his post like a sentry, as eager as I to watch the drama of new life.

Then there came a cry. It sounds still in my mind. I looked up into the yards. A sailor pointed behind, neither did I hear what he cried. He called again: 'There it be.' There what was? It did not take long to resolve that question, either. One letting of blood, it appeared, was *not sufficient, or sufficient only to whet appetites which I guess will never be satisfied, a thirst never quenched by a thousand sacrifices. Before I saw it, fin angled up and slicing the water like a knife, the whale began to turn, her great flukes lifted high. She slapped them down on the water as though to signify her power. The sound was that of a cannon and it echoed round the ship. But still that dark triangle of death advanced, scything through the water. Once again all were at the rail but only as observers of what befell. There was nothing we could do but watch and lament, if we may so regret the ways of God on earth.*

The new-born whale slid out of sight beneath its mother who began to turn slowly but, as a ship must needs take time to come about, so, too, with a creature as great as this, and before she was halfway towards facing it the shark was on its prey. For a moment longer it was unclear if it should relent or no. Again came the cannon shot and then the waters opened and she slid downwards, her eye, so small and crusted about, staring blankly as she sank. Nothing disturbed the surface of the sea except where the wind lifted flecks of white foam into the air. Then the waters themselves began to bleed. There was a flash of sleeked blackness as the shark spun round and round in a flurry of white spray and scarlet blood before it turned about with half the new-born whale in its throat. The moment of birth had provoked its end. Somewhere death had lurked for the smell of life and then come looking for its prey. And though I came straight below deck for fear I should cry for the mother whose child was thus still-born, granted no more than a few minutes of grace to breathe in the cool spring air, it is impossible to dwell on such a scene without remembering the fate which must await us all. Without birth there is no death, without death no birth? But what is it to be a mother who gives birth to death? The cold waters await.

As the voyage continued, so the lieutenant lost more and more of his martial spirit. The determination which had set his feet on the gangplank in Boston's harbour seemed to dissolve in the warmth of an early spring. Each day softened his resolve, as it seemed to Pearl, and, insofar as it did, she warmed to this young man whose certainties seemed to have slipped away in the wake of a merchantman which followed an invisible path across the ocean. His father had been of some minor nobility in England but rank and money are not always partners and though a certain piety had directed that father towards the American colony yet he had hoped to make salvation pay a dividend. And so it had. Several of the warehouses which fronted the harbour were in his ownership. His son, though, yearned for the rank and station his father had left behind and persuaded him to purchase a commission that he might have a touch of glory yet. That lust for glory was principally what had disappeared. Though he polished his sword each morning he no longer gave display of his skills each noon.

'Why do you go to England, Mistress Pearl?' he asked one morning, as Pearl tried to capture his face with pencil and paper.

'Because I had lived long enough where I was.'

He nodded, who perfectly understood such an answer. 'And do you have family there?'

'I do. It is to them in part I go.'

'In London?'

'No, indeed, though there is one who meets me there. No, I go east, to the county of Norfolk where my mother's brother still lives in a place called Colney.'

'Even so,' he replied, listlessly.

'And you?'

'London first, where I must report, and then wherever God decrees.' He fell silent and watched as a small ball of paper, with which he had tried his own hand at sketching, rolled to and fro with the movement of the ship. 'I am not sure I have taken the right course.'

'No?'

'No. It is a brave life and there will be excellent company and a soldier is always something in a town, yet I am not certain, not . . .' he grasped for a word and did not find it, 'not certain it is the life I should lead.'

'Do not lead it, then.'

The young would-be, would-be-not, soldier lifted his eyes to hers. 'But what should I do, then?'

'Why, anything you wish. We are free to choose, are we not?'

'Free? With a little money, perhaps.'

'But your father . . .'

'Has given me money to purchase my commission. Beyond that he will not go and I will not have him go. He saw me for a merchant and will give me nothing more unless I should return to him and stain my fingers with ink and my brain with reckoning.'

'Then you must make your own way.'

'That is very well to say, but you must be provided for, else how should you make such a journey as this?'

'Sir!' replied Pearl, somewhat shocked and perhaps not a little guilty. 'Well, it is true. I do travel with expectations but freedom is a matter of the spirit and not the purse.'

'Forgive me, Mistress, but that is a faith principally held by those whose purse is full. Where would your freedom be without the means to purchase it, without the funds to exercise it?'

Pearl, who had been sitting on a rough stool put on deck specially for her benefit, rose and stood for a moment looking down at a man she had pitied for a fool but who asked her questions she might have asked herself had she only thought for a moment how chance had seemed to enter her life and transform it without her will.

'Matthew Borrow, for a man who seeks his fortune by separating others not only from their fortunes but their lives with what, for all its shine, is no more than a butcher's knife . . .' She had quite lost her logic and did what young women of twenty will do in such circumstances: she stamped her foot, shouted 'Oh!', quite as though he had dedicated his life to irritating her, and walked swiftly across the deck to where steps led down to her cabin. He, meanwhile, looked on in amazement, again unsure what should have fired her anger.

Below deck was a constant gloom. A lantern hung from a beam but it shed little light and that unsteady. Down here there were other noises than above. The wash of the sea was louder and she could hear another sound, too, as water in the bilges slopped from side to side. Talk of money and expectations made her want to see again the documents she carried, as another's loss will send our hands to our pockets lest we should also have suffered theft. She took from a leather pouch a small key wrapped in a piece of cloth and turned it in the lock of her chest. There, beneath a dress whose colour was dulled by the uncertain light, her hand closed on a small packet. She drew it out and placed it on the table which divided the two bunks from each other. She unwound the cloth and revealed two further packets, one sealed with red wax, the other unsealed but with no address. The latter, as she knew, was a copy of the will with its promises and conditions. The other was for the lawyer who would deliver all into her hands. She picked it up and held it to the light. A name and address were written there in the youthful hand of the lawyer whose first day at work must have proved a greater burden than he had hoped. She moved it closer to the lamp as though she might in some way read what lay within but all she could see was the address: James Simple, Esq., Opie Street, Norwich, in the County of Norfolk, England.' She savoured each word. 'James' sounded strong and spoke of reliability. 'Simple' suggested a lack of guile. Opie was a strange word, to be sure, but who is accountable for the name of their street, while Norwich and Norfolk had a familiar ring, she having heard them a thousand times from her mother who spoke often of the family she had left behind and of the city which was her own.

She turned the packet in her hands, ran her fingers over the raised letters of the seal and knew that she held her future in her hands as few others could be said to do. And if the wayward lieutenant were correct and there was a connection between freedom and gold – and in that same chest were thirty gold sovereigns tight packed against the light – then this was merely a recompense for freedoms earlier denied. For had not the man who now sought to set her free been content before to see her mother and herself banished from the company of men, and her true father, if true he was, driven beyond endurance and life itself? This were justice, she argued to herself, not advantage, and the scarlet soldier as wrong as those who placed the scarlet letter on her mother's breast.

'And if there be a God in heaven, mistress . . .'

'Master Borrow, you doubt it?'

'And he has the making of our lives . . .'

Pearl began to smile, having experienced his ponderous logic before.

'And sees all and knows all and directs our path through this life to the next . . .'

'Even so.'

'So that all that comes to pass must be in His plan and nothing that is not pert . . . pert . . .'

'Pertinent?'

'. . . to that plan, then it must follow, must it not, that this encounter twixt you and me must be writ in the stars.'

'The stars, even!'

'I believe it must be so for there is an order in all things.'

'And what was the order which rendered a new-born creature into the jaws of its enemy?'

'Why, hunger.'

'Then why the effort of birth if it be rendered meaningless at once?'

'Not meaningless. It were food. Do we not have chickens on board to feed us? Were they not born?'

'Not a bare few minutes before they were devoured.'

'And does time make morality, then?' he asked triumphantly.

'It is not morality I question, but logic,' replied Pearl, who was somewhat impressed in spite of herself, having not previously suspected him capable of consecutive thought.

'All creatures feed on others. That is the way with things. Even we contend for supremacy.'

'But if the outcome be determined, as it seems to me you believe, then where is the purpose of such contention? It is not God you believe in but simple fate.'

'Perhaps these are but one.' He leaned forward eagerly, his brow furrowed. 'We may walk hither and yon on this vessel but we do not have the governance of her course.'

'The Captain does.'

'Exact,' he half shouted, 'and that be God who has directed you and me to meet so that our journey might be together.'

'And are we no more than pieces on a chess board to be moved around? And what should our meeting signify? We encountered a whale. It has sunk deep and far behind. Hail and farewell, whale. Hail and farewell, Master Borrow.'

'Mistress Prynne, how may we know God's will?'

'I do not know, lieutenant. There are times I doubt He knows himself.'

'Mistress! If this were Boston . . . there would be those who would . . .'

'There would, which is perhaps why I am not in Boston.'

'Is England so different?'

'That we shall discover, shall we not?'

'Mistress, I cannot decide whether I am destined for a soldier or no. My father believes I should be by his side. Obey thy parents, he says, and there is such an injunction in the Bible for he has shown it me.'

'There are many injunctions in the Bible. If you were a woman you would have had certain of them recited to you many a time.'

'Yet in consulting my conscience . . .'

'Your conscience? In Boston? Take care.'

'Ay. Not conscience, to be sure. Consulting, then, what might be His will, I decided on the king's shilling.'

'And you have your father's blessing.'

'Not blessing, more agreement. But what is right, and how should we know it?'

'How, indeed. You ask of the wrong person.'

'Why did you leave?'

'You have asked that question before, as it seems to me.'

'You are a woman and alone.'

'So it would appear.'

'Were you free to make such a decision?'

'I see that freedom is on your mind. I heard it on the lips of many whence we come but saw little evidence it were believed. I am here because I could no longer be there. I am here because there you are a saint or a sinner and which you are is determined not by God but by man. I am here because I do not know what I might have become once I had broken with their liturgy. As for you, soldier or merchant, I think you will make your way.'

'And God be willing.'

'The question is whether your way will be in accord with the plan in which you place so much faith.'

'And you, Mistress Prynne, and me?'

'Hail and farewell, Master Barrow. Is Ovid known to you?'

'Ovid? I do not believe I am acquainted with such a person, if person it be.'

'No. Perhaps not. He is not fitting for your new profession, it is true. And speaking of such, where is your uniform?'

'It has been stained with sea water. I have put it away until we land. They are very costly, uniforms.'

'Indeed. I know the price of scarlet.'

Pearl was not an unbeliever. Few were, then, and few, in their hearts, are now, for faith is composed of little more than hope seasoned with a touch of wonder and a deal of fear. The wild sea is a missionary. It has made more converts than the most zealous minister. Prayers are heard often on a ship and some, I dare say, are answered since vessels do make port and crew and passengers, white-faced and wild-eyed, still step onto shore to tell of storms and the terrors of the deep. Nor do we need to venture on the ocean to know the consolation which comes from knowing or believing that there is one who will reach out a hand to us when we should be in need. Consult your heart and, since none can hear, say boldly if you who read these words have never, in distress, offered up a prayer, for health, for safety, for love, for deliverance or success. If this be no more than a superstition then superstition must have a true longevity.

There is that in us that will not be alone. There is that in us that may not face the truth which daunts us most: that our days are numbered and that our journey has a destination, be it one we would deny. Always be travelling, never arrive. And do not travel alone who can find a companion to share the road. And if that companion should never falter nor turn his face from us, so much the better.

Pearl was not one who went to church, as did her mother, nor recognised the rituals and rights observed therein. Yet she did not doubt there was a God, who saw the evidence of His works around her, from the forest's grandeur to the perfection of a flower. And if she was perplexed at sudden death in the midst of beauty and worried at the extent of the freedom she would claim, but whose particularity she could not identify, she was scarcely alone in that. Yet she trembled on the brink of a doubt which might yet grow into a deeper scepticism and already she asserted a liberty of behaviour and of mind that most would scarcely acknowledge in one of her sex or yet in any but the most radical of beings. Even the Levellers, who thought all equal before God, were not so sure when it came to women whose voices seemed too shrill to speak with true authority.

Pearl had been an elfin child who had seen a woman marked out for punishment by a church whose power she grew to see was tainted alike by hypocrisy and cant. If she was a woman of tomorrow, then it was because she would not be a woman of yesterday. Nor was the word 'Father', with which we are taught to begin our reverence for God's authority, one which she could utter without a hesitation born of experience. She spoke the words she had been taught but there are other lessons that we learn than those in school or at our mother's knee. We watch and see and draw conclusions. Nor had Pearl yet done with learning. Why else voyage into the unknown?

A voyage is a passage of time, a space between two places whose power is suspended for a while. It is a chance to discover who we may be, free of the demands of custom and decree. To pass each day under the sun and each night beneath the stars with nothing but our own thoughts, stripped clean of civility, is to make discovery. Yet all life is a voyage and the sky always above. There are those who recall that truth no matter the tumble of incident and the noise of event. But what meaning can there be which remains uncontaminated by our fellow men, what true identity which is not born of its forfeit as we blend our lives with those of others? All stories are connected. How could it be otherwise? The connection is all. The problem is to know what the nature of that connection might be. History is so many stories jumbled together. We think its plot simple to decipher and cling to that simplicity, preferring narrative to a broken text. Yet in truth it is no more than a kaleidoscope. Shake it and another pattern will emerge. Truth lies in fragments. Better to distrust completion as a lie. So with our lives. The moments are true; the meaning we give to them, as we place such moments side by side, no more than a fiction which gives us contentment and relief.

So we exist within God's eye, within a greater text than that supplied by our confusions. Or, like Pearl, we go in search of meaning believing the search itself an evidence that meaning must exist. Or, perhaps she is braver still than this, venturing to transform herself with each new day.

The only event, thereafter, to interrupt the daily passage of the *Revenge* through the green depths of surging seas, came when a call from the masthead brought the vessel about into the wind, the sails throbbing as the ship luffed. Practical eyes had seen two shapes amidst the waves, like swimmers struggling to keep their heads above water. Obviously it could not be such here, far from land and with no other sail in sight, but it was impossible to continue without they should know who or what these mystery swimmers should be. Thus, though it lost them time, what was time to these who might wait a week for want of wind or drive before a hurricane and be in port early, if at all? They lowered the boat.

Pearl watched, her hand to her eyes as she looked towards the west, where the sun would set within the hour. The boat pulled away, its crew moving back and forth in their seats as she had seen Indians bow and straighten as they prayed to their alien spirits. What would they find? Bodies stripped of flesh, corpses committed to the deep as her mother had told her she had herself once seen? The rowers ceased, as in the prow a man reached out with a boathook. Whatever it was he sought, it disappeared in the downward sinking of a wave; its companion likewise. The longboat swung between her and those they sought to bring on board. Ship, boat and mysterious forms floated on the same sea but each appeared to move to its own rhythm, one rising, another falling, the others invisible to the eye and perhaps dwindling in the deep. Like sun, moon and earth they were held together by some force yet had their own motion within it.

The sun itself, meanwhile, touched the softly curving rim of the past, so that those in the boat seemed to float of a sudden on liquid flame. Then, as the returning boat closed on the *Revenge*, so that same sun slipped out of sight, one last gold coin of light resting for a second on the distant edge of the world before disappearing, draining colour from the sea, except where a slight pink glow reflected a sky streaked with vermilion. They had thrown a rough tarpaulin over those they had rescued from the waves, a shroud to cover the modesty of their humanity, perhaps.

Ropes were sent down, coiling and straightening in the air like dockside eels thrown from ship to basket. Men stood and braced bare feet against wooden deck, leaning back, ready to pitch muscle against gravity. The boat rose darkly against the crimson sky, then swung inwards as others pulled at still more ropes, until it rested in a kind of cradle, a child newly delivered by the ship, its mother. And certainly the crew seemed like new fathers, proud as fathers are who have done nothing but obey nature's easiest command. And if it seemed to Pearl a behaviour strangely out of tune with recovering the dead she was swiftly disabused, for in drawing back the cover they revealed not two ravaged mariners but two stout kegs, wooden barrels encrusted with shells.

The cook was summoned and a mallet and spigot fetched from below. All watched as if this were a rite of the church – and if this was, as they suspected from certain markings burned in the wood, French brandy why, then, perhaps, those who rowed and rocked back and forth had indeed been worshipping alien spirits. One blow and a fine mist sprayed like a liquid wheel until a second blow sealed the breach. But with that spray came the smell of brandy and a cry of satisfaction was followed by a certain stillness. The captain permitted that each should drink a cup and Pearl, too, anxious not be omitted, drank her fill.

So are we deceived as what we take for one thing proves another. Here, presumed death had rendered up a cordial which warmed the heart. And, locked within brandy, though not to be seen by the eye, are there not grapes and the sun and much labour? And, within these, sweetness and heat and an ache of health? And within these? There is nothing like a cup of brandy, drunk by one who has never tasted it before, to send the mind ever further outwards in search of meaning.

But there was something more in that barrel, for from that moment on there was no barrier of custom or position between passenger and crew. Friendship, or its like, it seems, may be plucked from the sea or perhaps, more truthfully, drunk from a pewter cup. Nor did any question the fate of those who perhaps had followed their cargo into the ocean, for, as the ship at last turned about and the sky became first indigo and then velvet black, they were warmed within by more than a golden liquid drawn from a strong oak cask. Every voyage a lesson; every life a truth.

The *Revenge* was only a day or so from the English coast. The air itself smelt different, as it seemed to Pearl, danker, like soil after rain. Black-headed gulls rose and fell, twisted and turned in the churning wake of a vessel nearing its destination. It was a special day, and that not simply because soon she would pick up the story her mother had put down. It was her birthday.

She told no one, wanting, suddenly, no company but her

own, being denied that of the mother who had shared all other such anniversaries. Instead she set herself to write a word or two in her diary. But on opening it she had a surprise, for instead of falling open near the beginning – her entries, though frequent, having proved brief – it did so at the middle. And there, like the fragment of a faded rainbow, was a butterfly, long since pressed to thinnest gauze. The mere gesture of opening the book, however, had stirred the air and, in doing so, stirred, too, the weightless wings so that for a second red and blue and velvet purple rose in the air, mimicking a summer beauty, before spiralling downward again to settle on the pure white page.

The diary had been given to her by her mother and the butterfly, therefore, likewise, perhaps so that it might, in rising as it had, recall she who had been the last to see the wonder of its dying flight. Whatever the truth of that, its wings seem to have stirred a memory not her own for Pearl stared at the page as though she read words there invisible to the eye. Then the moment passed and it was as if nothing had happened beyond an insignificant event, one of a million such which fill our waking lives and whose meaning may not be understood. She looked at the thin transparency of the creature which still moved gently, trembling in a sudden draught, and then slowly closed the book on its faded shimmer before re-opening it to note the day whose passing would leave her on the very brink of her new life.

Birthdays are the striking of a clock. They mark the time so we may measure what is past and prepare for what is to come. Yet there is something in twenty which seems separated by more than a twelvemonth from simple nineteen. For in this year, as I know, will be made decisions which will last beyond year's end. Childhood, when we bear the mark of others, is past. Now I am myself alone.

She paused, lowered her pen towards the paper, paused again, then, without noticing she did so, as the ship swayed first one way then the other, as though nothing were certain, not even which way they should proceed, repeated the word she had already written: '*alone*'.

★

As they entered the lower reaches of the Thames, a thick low mist rolled towards the ship, like the boiling smoke of a gorse fire. The tide was on the turn and a rill of grey-brown marked the point where two currents intertwined. For a minute or so they drifted backwards, as though the ship yearned for a deeper sea; then they were still, held perfectly by contending forces, before one current gained supremacy. At the same moment a pale sun rose behind them so that a faint shadow of the ship was cast on the now pink-tinged mist, a ghost which they pursued through a strange miasma.

Pearl shivered at the bow, desperate, as all sea passengers are, for her first sight of land; but land seemed to have dissolved into a dense cloud which parted only slowly, as they advanced, and filmed her face with water. There were no sounds except, somewhere far ahead, the faintest hint of a tolling bell. Beside her in the bow were two sailors who stared before them, like her wiping cold tears from their eyes. High above, invisible to all, was another who shouted to the deck from the whiteness, an angel whose voice, disembodied and unreal, seemed to come first from one quarter then another, quite as though he flew around the cope of the invisible masts. All looked for signs, lost, for a moment, as it seemed to Pearl, on the very path to their front door.

Then, slowly, as the sun rose in the eastern sky, a perfect disc seen as though through cataracts, a breeze began to fill the sails and the mist started to thin, imperceptibly at first, then at a gathering pace until every detail of the river stood out with the clarity of a mystery resolved.

The land seemed all but invisible, so wide was the river which opened its arms to embrace the sea. But then a cloud of seabirds launched into a sky which seemed to fragment with their flight into a thousand pieces of light, and below them she could make out the mudflats, only just catching the pink light of dawn. To Pearl this, not the bustle of Boston's streets, was the New World. She drew in a deep breath, as clean and fresh as the day itself, and watched the river's surface sparkle as

37

though it were winter ice. Now, tide and wind together drew them on.

'And is the water fresh now?' asked Pearl of a sailor by her side who straight away threw a bucket on a rope into the torn silk of the water and drew it up again. He set it on the deck, took a small metal cup from his leather belt and dipped it into the slopping water. With a smile no less bright for its gap-toothed menace, he presented it to Pearl, indicating with a nod of his head that she should drink. And drink she did and spat it out again. Though they had sailed several miles inland, as it seemed, the sea had yet to lose its supremacy.

'The tide still flows here,' he explained. 'It is a great river but the sea be greater still.' With this lesson in comparative power he returned the cup to his belt and spat over the side as though to add a little liquid of his own to that which flowed beneath their hull. If this was England's water and she a lost child now returned, she was offered little yet to quench her thirst.

As she had drunk, so, out of the corner of her eye, she saw a sudden hint of scarlet and a flash of silver as the soldier came on deck. The early sunlight made his uniform glow and the man himself scarcely less so. He had surely decided on his destiny for he held himself erect as though he played his new role with true conviction. Indeed, determining to display all his skills, he saluted the young woman who had stood with a cup lifted towards a brightening sky.

'Lieutenant,' she said, in spite of herself impressed by such military splendour, or perhaps even by the young man who wore it to such effect.

'Mistress Prynne.' He bowed a little and smiled.

And so they stood, side by side, as their separate destinies came ever closer on the flood tide and a world they had imagined became palpable and alive.

The low banks began to close on the ship so that Pearl could make out greater detail. She could see a curious tumble of buildings with a thin plume of smoke rising into a pale sky before bending as the wind caught it like the torn edge of a ragged cloth. Further still, a man, muffled in a tangle of dark clothes, sat fishing on a clump of grass. She felt a sudden impulse to wave and did so as they passed. For a few moments he remained so still that she wondered if he were awake, but then he raised an arm. So close were they now that she could make out the pipe he carried. She waved again but he was staring once more into the moving water.

The sharp cold of dawn was already easing and as the sun rose higher in the sky so the deck began to steam gently, as if spirits were returning to the heavens. The air smelled sweet. Sailors scurried round the deck, coiling ropes, preparing for their arrival, there being no captain who does not prefer to sail into port as though he were merely returning from a saunter down the river, with his vessel in the best of order.

The river was so tumbled together with ships that they seemed an extension of the buildings which now rose up on either bank. Those at anchor, with bare masts, swayed gently in the wind; those under sail manoeuvred with a grace which, to Pearl, made them seem like skaters on a New England pond. They were nearing the city now. A few years later she might have smelt the burnt bodies of those who fled before a great fire, but what she detected on this morning breeze was spice: nutmeg and cinnamon and pepper. And though Boston had changed and grown, even in her brief life, the London that she saw was less a town than a whole world. As far as she could see, beyond the timber warehouses, were streets of houses, close together. And above them was a haze of grey smoke, as though the city were itself aflame.

There was a distant murmur in the air, not the grating sound of cicadas, which had sounded through her twenty summers, but a low and constant buzz as though field upon field had been filled with hives. It was some time before she recognised it for the sound of humanity, the bustle and gossip and daily intercourse of a city greater than any she had imagined. As the ship slowly closed towards the quay she thought of that city as opening its arms to her.

It opened something else, too, for, at spaces along the bank, a foul and stained liquid, which was not quite liquid, discharged into the river and the smell of spice was quite overwhelmed by other odours which told her that she was returned to the company of men, indeed. Such is the way with ports, which have something of the elemental about them. They are a place for taking in and sending out. They are already intermediary. And yet there are truths to be discovered here for as cargoes are displayed for all to see so appetites, concealed by custom or controlled by decree, are here given licence. Men return from an unforgiving ocean and women are sometimes drawn to the smell of money and the evidence of need.

For Pearl, though, as at last her journey was complete and the *Revenge* settled against the quay, all was excitement and possibility and beginning, nor was any aspect of human life repugnant. She looked about her as though she would devour everything she saw. This was her new England, her destiny.

'Mistress Prynne.'

'Lieutenant Borrow.'

'You have been kind to me.'

'Have I so?'

'Indeed. Oh, indeed. When I first stepped on board I scarce knew what I was doing.'

'If that was so I knew nothing of it.'

'No? Perhaps it were the sickness. But without your company . . .' He did not finish the thought but held out his hand. She clasped it readily enough. 'If you should ever be in need of help,' he said, with such solemnity that Pearl could not help but smile, 'I shall hasten to your side.'

'Then let us hope such need should never occur, for I understand that desertion is not encouraged by His Majesty.' Then, relenting her irony, she pressed his hand in hers. 'Good luck to you, lieutenant. May God protect you. Do your best to serve your king by spilling as little blood as possible; none at all if you but think of me.'

'I shall think of you.'

There was an earnestness which could not be misinter-preted. Pearl withdrew her hand, which otherwise might have stayed entrapped until all others had disembarked the ship.

'You are your own man, Matthew Borrow.'

'The king's man, mistress,' he corrected, then added, blushing as scarlet as his uniform, 'and yours.'

Then he was gone, unable, perhaps, to bear such a parting one moment longer, and Pearl saw him a minute later on the dockside where there were many colours to be seen but scarlet was otherwise in short supply.

So, shipboard alliances dissolve in a moment and those brought together by the hand of fate go their separate ways as though they had never met.

Pearl looked down at the dock to see if she could identify the man who was to meet her, but one stranger among many can hardly be distinguished at a glance so that, at last, she took leave of the *Revenge* knowing that whoever awaited must have little difficulty himself in finding a young woman who travels alone and steps onto England's soil a solitary in need of help.

So, no sooner had she set foot on shore than a man of pleasant looks, though somewhat large and red about the face, waved vigorously at her and made his way through the crowd. At last he was by her side and straightway seized her hand.

'It is Pearl, is it not? Tell me it is Pearl.' He shook her hand up and down as though it were the handle of a water pump. 'I saw thee on the ship and knew thou must be Hester's child. It is Pearl, is it not?'

If it had not been, whomever he should have greeted thus must have felt alarm, for he continued to pump her hand as though this must eventually force an answer from her.

'It is, it is,' replied Pearl, smiling at such a warm welcome to a strange land. 'And thou must be . . .'

'Indeed! William Prynne, of course.' At last he released her hand but only to seize her by the elbow and begin to pull her through the crowd.

'My trunk,' cried Pearl, looking behind her where already men had begun to unload the cargo.

'Will follow, my dear. All is arranged. Come. This is a noisome place. We must go.'

And go they did.

Chapter Two

Like all those who have been at sea, she found the land at first more treacherous than the ship. Indeed, she felt decidedly ill as she was conveyed, on a cart which swayed and lurched far more than the *Revenge* had ever done, to a Cheapside inn. Her companion, a relative stranger – both a stranger and a relative – was a Prynne, a second cousin, as her mother had explained. His business took him not only eastwards to Amsterdam but south to London, from which Norwich worsted had begun to reach distant parts of the world. This day it took him first to meet a ship fresh arrived on the morning tide and then to a hostelry which can have had few equals on either side of the ocean, which was perhaps as well.

William Prynne had nothing of the severity of the Boston merchants she had encountered. His face was a kind of mottled purple, the colour of September plums, and there was a sweet smell about him as though he were gently fermenting his own brandy, while the ground seemed to play him as false as it did Pearl, for he stumbled several times as he led her through the low doorway of the Swan and crossed a sawdust floor to a wooden hatch on which he rapped with the silver head of his cane.

'Mistress Nibbins! Mistress Nibbins, if you please!'

There was no reply, except for the strangled screech of a cat somewhere beneath her feet. Outside, a cart rattled and ground its way along the cobbled street.

'Mistress Nibbins! Where is the woman? It is I, William Prynne.' He announced himself, so it seemed to Pearl, as though he were the king.

'And so it is,' said a voice from the gloom behind them, and the strangest creature that Pearl had seen slowly got to her feet, as it were in sections, like some vast caterpillar which had decided against the butterfly state. First one hand rose, then another, each clutching a heavy stick. There followed a chest which seemed likely of itself to prevent an upright stance and which in turn raised into view a kind of vast round appendage which was her lower half. This was all accomplished with many a grunt. She had a tortoise-like head, topped with a mop of orange hair. Nor did she rise and walk so much as fall forwards, relying on gravity to pull the rest of her bloated body behind her. When she took a pace it was with the grace of a swan mounting a slippery river bank.

'And if that be you then who is this?' she enquired, in a voice which made the glasses ranged along a wooden plank rattle and sing.

'This is my cousin or niece. Or some such.' He glanced at Pearl as though genuinely confused as to what she might be doing in such a place and he with her. 'We spoke of her.'

'We did, that we did,' Mistress Nibbins commented with absolutely no sign of remembering. 'We 'av a lot of nieces 'ere. You would be surprised. Sometimes I thinks the world be full of them and you have my meaning.'

William Prynne did not. William Prynne was looking instead at a small barrel mounted decorously alongside the glasses. 'She has just stepped from a ship and would be grateful for some food, I dare say, as would I.'

'Ah, food is it? Well, food it is to be, I suppose. Assumin' there to be such, as there ain't, seein' as 'ow I'm on me own as shouldn't be.'

'If it be any trouble,' began Pearl, with a strong desire to burst into laughter.

43

'Trouble? Trouble? Be this an inn?'

Both uncle and niece, or whatever they might be, assumed this to be a rhetorical question but evidently the woman, barely four and a half feet tall and swaying like an oak half sawn through, did not, for she repeated the question several times, turning it over in her mind as though genuinely perplexed until at last there was nothing to be done but reassure her.

'It is, most certainly,' assented Pearl's cousin.

'Why yes, and a most charming . . .'

'And if it be an inn would food be found in such a place?'

Pearl was very tempted to remind her that she had denied as much only a moment since, but thought better of it and settled, like her cousin, for a brief nod of the head.

This Socratic dialogue might have continued for some time were it not that a cat shot up vertically from a dark opening in the corner of the room, as though it had taken it into its head to try life as a bird for a while. As all three sets of eyes turned in its direction it executed a half turn in the air and landed facing them, one eye blind, the other gleaming like a signal fire. With a surprising show of speed and a display of coordination and balance for which nothing had yet prepared her guests, the woman stepped forward and neatly kicked the creature back into the hole. All three waited for the scuffling thud as it hit the cellar floor below. The whole exercise was conducted with such a practical skill that Pearl realised it could only have been a regular feature of the Swan, and certainly her cousin showed no hint of surprise. It did, however, have one beneficial effect for it seemed to release their hostess from her linguistic hall of mirrors and permit her to wave her two guests to a table by a fire, newly lit, it seemed, since a large mound of grey ash and black charcoal were piled in the brick hearth and the flames were yellow in the gloom.

'Eggs,' she stated rather than asked.

'Eggs?' said William Prynne, raising an eyebrow generally in the direction of Pearl.

'Eggs,' she replied.

44

'And ale,' added William Prynne firmly, as though expecting an argument.

'Before, after or with?'

'Yes,' he replied, settling himself agreeably into a capacious wooden chair, which nonetheless looked as though it could have done with being yet more capacious.

'Thought so. An' 'er?'

'I think not. A little water, perhaps,' said Pearl incautiously.

There was a squawk of genuine merriment from her hostess. 'Water! Oh my God! Water!'

'I would advise not,' said her cousin, with some seriousness. 'I had some once. I cannot at the moment recall why that should be but I do remember it was unpleasant both during and after, especially after. The ale is tolerable, in quantity. Or try a little wine. But water, never.'

'Water!' shrieked Mistress Nibbins, who was clearly a woman of great humour for she repeated the word to herself amidst cackles of laughter as she propelled her various segments through a door at the back of the room.

For the first time William Prynne looked at his young cousin, as far as he could in the flickering light of a Cheapside inn. This, then, was the girl he was charged to deliver back to Norwich as soon as his business should be done. There was something in her face which recalled a long forgotten past.

'And how is thy mother?'

'She is well, sir, and I thank thee,' said Pearl, and then found her eyes filling suddenly with tears.

'It is the fire after the cold air,' said cousin William, looking vaguely about him as though someone might save him the embarrassment of his life.

For a moment or two the tears ran down her face, reflecting yellow-red in the firelight. Then she brushed them away with the back of her hand.

'She sends her love and remembrances.'

'Even so,' he replied, as though considering this intelligence with interest. He leaned forward to inspect a row of white clay pipes whose blackened bowls faced into the room like the eye

45

sockets of a line of monkey skulls. He reached a hand towards hers and when she grasped it looked down in astonishment quite as though it had moved without his volition. He enclosed her pale fingers in his own and then snatched back his hand and inspected it in an abstracted way.

'It is kind of thee to meet me, sir.'

'I am William to thee, and it please thee, or uncle or cousin or whatever . . .' He subsided into a kind of vague bewilderment as if the whole business of relationship defied logic and memory.

'Yes, cousin. But it is kind, indeed. Without thee I should not have known where to turn.'

'Thou art Hester's child and though . . .' At this point he seemed quite to forget his stock of language, his mouth half open. He might well have remained so had his hostess not shuffled up behind him and banged a tankard on the dark oak table with such a force that a spittle of foam flew in his face.

'Ale,' she announced, speaking as though to a foreigner who might have entertained his doubts. 'Ducks' or chickens'?'

Pearl looked at her cousin and he at her.

'Eggs! Ducks' or chickens'?'

'Ah, chickens'.'

'Ducks',' she corrected him and swung her body, in its various articulations, back in the direction of the rear room.

'Cousin,' began Pearl.

He held his hand up as though in benediction and then, with a studied concentration, lifted the tankard slowly to his lips. No popish minister has raised the communion cup with greater gravity. He slowly closed thick lips around the cool metal and tilted his head back, eyes reverentially closed. Pearl watched in fascination as his Adam's apple rose and fell. Evidently he had, over the years, devised a method of drinking and breathing at the same moment or else suspended breathing in favour of the more important motion, for he did not pause until all the ale had gone. At which he slowly lowered the tankard to the table and stared for a full half minute into the fire, contemplating, as it seemed to Pearl, the mysteries of meaning and being. Then, coming out of his reverie, he turned back to her and as though there had been no interruption to their slender conversation, replied, 'Yes, my dear.'

For a second she could not remember what she had been about to say, so struck had she been by the ceremony. 'I hope it was not I alone who brought thee here. It is over a hundred miles.'

'Business,' he responded. 'Wool is a demanding master. It has a will to travel. If thou dost not watch it will fly off quite by itself. I but follow it.'

'And is all well with thy business?'

'All is never well with business. That is the nature of business. If it were there would be no need to stir from Norwich; but worsted is in demand and so I travel the London road and the Yarmouth road and the Ipswich road. To tell thee true, I am more often to be found at the Swan than in my own home. Ale!'

This last was shouted into the void, for the caterpillar woman was nowhere to be seen. 'And for my niece as well.'

'Niece!' A cackle came from the distance and a sound as though someone were strangling a cat as, Pearl supposed, was more than possible given what she had seen since her arrival.

'And how long will we dwell here before travelling to Colney? My mother has spoken of it so often I feel I could find my way around it on the darkest night.'

'There's plenty of those. Here there be light at all times. Walk the streets at midnight, if thou durst, and there be torches flaming up and down, though I'd not fancy to be wandering abroad myself. The Swan is world enough for me.'

The inn began to fill with the smell of cooking eggs and a dozen other smells besides, all mixed in with that of sawdust, ale, smoke and the reassuring smell of humankind.

'Thou wilt like it here, my dear. Odd fellows, to be sure. Nay, many are quite out of their minds but they make an agreeable company. At times. Though they do drink.' As though reminded he half turned in his seat and shouted vaguely to an empty room, 'Ale!'

A faint echo came back from the distance.

'No ale where thou come from, I dare say.'

'Indeed, sir. Too much at times.'

'Really,' he replied, as though he found such an idea difficult to comprehend. 'Is it so?' There was a stirring of interest in his eyes. 'And I had thought them a dreadful sober lot. Well, maybe there is something to be said for them, after all. Never trust a man who does not stagger. It is an old wise saying.' He wagged a finger at Pearl, like a father instructing his child in the ways of God and man. 'Never trust a man who does not stagger a little by nine,' he added, revising a wisdom of centuries in a second.

Whether he meant nine of the morning or nine of night was not clear to Pearl since another pewter mug with a white ruffle of foam was set before him, and another before her, but this time by a diminutive figure in leather breeches. Cousin William clipped him familiarly around the head as he turned to leave.

'Ow!'

'Morning to you, Sam,' he said benignly, as the recipient of his friendliness ruefully rubbed his hair. 'Eggs?'

'Comin'.'

Few words, it seemed, were wasted in the Swan. Pearl tried again as the boy retreated, still rubbing his head. 'And when shall we take the road to Norwich?'

'Road? No road. We sail at the week's end.'

'Sail?'

'Ay. They are unloading cloth now. When it be done we shall sail to Yarmouth.'

And so, had she but realised, she was fated to reverse her mother's progress of those years before, retrace her mother's steps, searching perhaps for what she had fled.

Through the doorway came the eggs. And a wedge of pork. And some devilled kidneys. And a black pudding. One plate was carried by Mistress Nibbins, a stick under each arm, shuffling sideways. The other was held by young Sam, for whom the plate seemed like the world on Atlas's shoulder.

'Eggs,' announced their hostess with satisfaction.

'Cousin,' said Pearl, with some trepidation, 'I do not think I can do justice to this.' In truth, her hunger, increased by the smells five minutes before, had diminished on sight of a dish half aswim with grease on which a large piece of pork fat sat, its outer skin prickled with hairs turned quills by baking, like some final adornment on the scalp of a cannibal.

'No matter,' he replied, his lips already smeared, 'eat what thou canst. The rest I'll assist thee with.'

Out of the corner of her eye Pearl saw the inn's remarkable hostess, queen of pork fat and ale, take a clay pipe from the rack and collapse, in stages, onto the grimed brickwork which formed a seat within the wide mouth of the fireplace. There was, it seemed, a practical sequence to the lowering of such bulk in such a space and Pearl watched, in spite of herself, until this small feat of primitive engineering should be complete. Two grunts of satisfaction followed, one from the woman whose own fat now settled around her like egg white in a pan, and one from her cousin. And as a rolling ball of pipe smoke came towards her she realised that she was indeed hungry and set to, if not quite with the enthusiasm of her new-found relative, at least with a commitment which seemed at odds with the slender form of one whose beauty reflected even in the gloom of a London inn.

So Pearl spent her first hours in the England of which she had heard so much and the city which for so many was the centre of power and the very emblem of earthly delight. And though she longed to go abroad into the streets and see the wonders which they should offer yet she readily agreed to her cousin's suggestion that she should retire, for she had indeed known little sleep in the last days at sea, so many thoughts crowding out the peace which unlocks that sleep.

She allowed herself to be led up a small winding staircase to an upper room, smaller than the space which had been hers on board the *Revenge*. Though the ground still seemed to move disconcertingly beneath her feet, once in bed she found the gentle movement urged her quickly to the very edge of slumber. But as she seemed to float once more at sea so she thought of her mother and of the place to which she would go by the week's end. Then, all thoughts died away and, amidst a shifting array of images, she slept the clock around, waking the next day to the smell of breakfast being prepared and the unmistakable cry of her cousin, echoing through the inn.

'Ale!'

Dressed and breakfasted, this time on plain bread and fresh milk, the latter brought, so she was assured, straight from the cow in the street beyond, though tasting more than a little of ale, she accompanied her uncle on her first tour of London. Everyone, it appeared, was in the streets, and most seemed intent to sell each other goods. Hot pies, lavender, a small bright bird in a cage, a length of rough cloth were all held out towards her. There were shops aplenty – pepperers', tallow chandlers' – and, in a great thoroughfare, a tall stone tower which he told her was called Eleanor Cross.

Above the mauve-grey wood smoke from a thousand chimneys rose the spire of St Paul's, with but a few years more to reign before fire would be its undoing, and which to her eyes seemed to soar so far above her that it made her giddy to contemplate it. Her America was contained and low, its buildings hesitating to reach into the heavens. Here was a kind of arrogance, even, it seemed, in worship. Then the smell of spice reached her again. It seemed to emanate from the buildings themselves, to breathe with the city.

'Where are we going, cousin William? To the church?'

'The church? 'Tis not the sabbath. The docks, girl. Business calls. Mind thy feet.'

The advice was good, though late, since a whole herd of dairy cows seemed to have passed that way before them and the smell of spice gave way to quite other aromas. Pearl quickly found herself jumping from one dry cobble to another, like an eight-year-old playing hopscotch. And, to be sure, there was something of a child about her. Just turned twenty, she greeted life with open arms, if not quite open heart, for there was a shadow there which she would soon confront. But, beyond that, life was at the full and every sight and sound was a delight.

For her cousin, things were quite otherwise. Having warned her of the menace underfoot, he himself strode straight ahead through the still steaming slurry so that as he walked so every piece of discarded rubbish stuck to his boots which soon seemed like two exotic animals coated in fur and feathers, potato peelings and other substances impossible to tell.

Pearl was dressed simply in New England homespun but even so stood out from those around her whose clothes seemed oddly improvised while there were those who went barefoot. By contrast she seemed to glow with health and her simple beauty turned many a head. At last they rounded a corner and there ahead of them, at the end of a pinched street, was a ship. Barely a third the size of the *Revenge*, it nonetheless appeared to fill the sky and because it blocked off all sight of the river seemed to float in the air, so out of place that it disturbed her sense of the real.

'The *Nancy Jane*. Friday,' said cousin William, having, it seemed, exhausted his day's allotment of air.

Pearl, who had come to realise that words to him were as acorns to a squirrel, nodded once, a gesture lost on her companion, who had affected to disappear. She stood, bemused. The crowds which had pressed upon her were gone, as now was cousin William. There was just herself and the hovering ship, itself deserted. For a second the world seemed to have disassembled itself into separate fragments and then come together in a new order. She felt confused. Then a head poked out of the wall beside her.

'In here,' he wheezed, and disappeared again.

She passed through a narrow doorway into total darkness. A hand gripped her wrist and pulled her onwards and through a still narrower door into a room in which a man sat at a tall desk. He could have been dead for all the notice he took of either of them. Together they passed through yet another door

51

into a room whose lattice window looked directly onto the river. To the left was the prow of the *Nancy Jane*, to the right the flat, iron-coloured river. It could almost have been a painting, certainly to one such as Pearl who had a painter's eye. Something about the light made each element stand out sharply and at first the river seemed quite still, a cul-de-sac of time, everything fixed as though placed to please the eye. Creation seemed to hold its breath and life to shape itself to the demands of art. Then a figure appeared on the ship, looping a thin line around his elbow and hand, and, as a sudden memory of winding wool into skeins before a distant fire passed through Pearl's mind, the world re-animated. The river began to flow; a wherry, with dull red sails, tacked at an angle across the current; a pigeon exploded out of the sky, teetered on the narrow window ledge, then fell away, its wings two fans shedding feathers in the air.

'There she is,' he said, sinking gratefully into a chair which, by its groans, seemed not to share his gratitude.

And there she was, indeed. Pearl, who had not yet stood on firm ground for twenty-four hours (and the ground, she realised with some relief, had ceased to move), was, it seemed, to be invited back on the sea again. But to her surprise there was a pleasure in the thought, and not simply because it would complete her journey, bring her at last whence her imagination had already travelled. It was that she had grown to like shipboard life where there was none to chide her, none to contain her free spirit, and all knew that they clung together not for advantage but because they recognised their mutual need. She was not made for habit, discipline or order and if there were elements of these on board the *Revenge* they had been born out of necessity. The *Nancy Jane* was a poor relation of the *Revenge* but relation she was and she would not always lie thus, sleeping through the morning hours.

'And shall we be going aboard?'

'Whatever for? She's no more than a place of storage. Perhaps a glass of something to keep out the chill.'

'Because I should like to,' she replied, with that implacable logic with which every child secures its desires.

William Prynne had no children of his own and had never regretted it, having seen the noise and mess which seems inseparable from their existence, but he recognised implacability when he heard it. He grunted. She took the sound for assent and with one regretful look at the table, ringed with the stains of a thousand glasses, he rose unprotestingly to his feet.

The *Nancy Jane* was half unloaded. Bales of cloth for transhipment were piled in irregular mountains on the dock. Further along the quay were two other ships in a similar state, so it seemed to Pearl, of undress. The masts were bare, reaching up nakedly over the rooftops. Hatch doors were swung wide while the steady removal of cargo had the appearance of the disembowelling of some creature which had been snared by the ropes which slackened and straightened in the ebbing table. Some of the bales were carried on carts through the open doors of the warehouse or raised on squeaking pulleys to what looked an attic store, a jutting beam holding each bale away from the wall until it was rocked and swung into the darkness. Still further in the distance was another ship, twice the size of these others, a mother, so it seemed, fed by its children, for carts were delivering goods to the end of a gangplank along which men passed, some with black leather caps and shoulder pads, others stripped to the waist and glistening with perspiration.

Pearl longed for her brushes and an easel, aware that life which goes unrecorded is life lost, life blown away in the dust which even now spun in eddies, lifting the remnants of a dozen cargoes – lint from cloth, a powdered film of pepper, ground corn, mingled with the grit and grime of Cheapside – into a cloudless sky. It was the same artist's eye, however, which could abstract her from her youthful enthusiasm into a cool detachment as she reduced event and scene to contending planes and countervailing colours. For a brush stroke, like a word, denies the reality which it purports to express, transforms quicksilver life to stasis, denies the pain it would acknowledge. So these men who laboured became for a moment so many figures in a landscape, splashes of colour, vertical lines against the horizontal planking of the ship's side. But when one of these shouted out to her and others turned to admire her beauty they became no more and no less than men on a dockside. That too, though, is perhaps the essence of art which exists both within and without, creating imagined moments in a landscape sharply real.

'Shall we go on board now?' she asked of her cousin, who showed no signs of doing so despite her earlier request.

'I should have thought thou had seen enough of ships yet awhile.'

'But this be thine.'

'Mine?' He opened his arms wide, then looked at the vacant air enclosed with a quizzical smile. 'Why, I never owned even a paper boat. They do no more than carry my goods. Ships are risky, having a tendency to search out the bottom of the sea.'

'Cousin!'

'Oh, thou wilt be safe enough,' he said, blushing. 'All I meant . . .'

She smiled and placed a hand on his arm. 'Can we not go on board, then?'

'Of course thou may, and the captain be willing, but I have business which needs my attendance here on shore.' He smacked his lips, perhaps in anticipation of the business to which he would return.

He stepped out of the shadow of the warehouse and raised his stick above his head, waving it in irregular circles. After a moment or two a man with auburn hair, who was leaning on the gunwale, raised a finger to his forehead and strode purposefully along the deck and down the gangplank. His hair, caught by the breeze and sun, seemed to flicker with flames and when he spoke his face lit up with pleasure.

'Mr Prynne, sir. 'Tis good to see you. Will you come aboard and join me for a . . .'

The same Mr Prynne cut him off in mid-sentence, perhaps none too anxious to betray yet further evidence of his social habits.

'This is my niece, Captain McCarthy. She is to be your passenger on Friday.'

'Mistress Prynne.' He inclined his head towards her and gave her the benefit of another of his smiles. 'It seems that all my passengers are paying me a visit today. Yonder gentleman has just been loading his boxes.'

Only then did Pearl notice that another had followed the captain down the angled gangplank. He had turned away from them to walk past the other vessels with their masts like so many crosses carried on a pilgrimage. She watched as he picked his way carefully among the bales and bundles which squatted in the dust. Then he paused for a second and turned back to face the *Nancy Jane*.

'A cleric,' the captain added with a smile, but it was not that which caught Pearl's attention, indeed that word alone was not one she favoured. Nor was it the manly build or dark and tousled hair. There was something more which she could not name: the grace, perhaps, of his movement, something even in the tableau of man and ship and river which appealed. Time and place brought suddenly together have an alchemy. There are, besides, moments, known to all, when something invisible may leap across the spaces set between us. So was it now. I cannot say that their eyes met, for they were a hundred paces apart, but she stared past the captain's now faltering smile and would have remained a statue had a hand not closed around her wrist.

'Here, captain. Do me the kindness of showing Mistress Prynne around your vessel.'

Pearl, though, brought back to the present from wherever she had been, shook her head.

'No, cousin. As thou sayest I have perhaps seen sufficient of ships for the moment. I look forward to seeing you on Friday, sir.' This last she addressed to the captain, who half bowed in response, his smile restored. Pearl turned away, afraid that some family trait might make her own cheeks glow red like her cousin's.

It must not be supposed that Pearl thought much of this moment when once the trap of time was sprung. The moment came, the moment passed and she was once more intent on devouring London, if not whole then in a series of healthy bites. Her cousin, appalled at the thought of being required to walk the streets so far from his worsted cloth and from the inn which, for all its peculiarities, he plainly favoured, secured a companion, wife of a fellow merchant, to effect the task for him on the following day. And since the idea of two women abroad on their own stirred some doubts he enrolled the services of another of his landlady's endless family.

'Jack!' had shouted the woman mountain, descending from herself, as it seemed, as she collapsed into a chair. 'Jack!' No one spoke in anything but a resonant bellow in the Swan. Jack duly emerged from the trap door, blinking even in the dull light of a day whose presence, within the inn, was itself apparent only by inference from the grey sheen on the dust-grimed windows.

'This be Jack,' she indicated.

Jack nodded vigorously and edged backwards as though seeking some yet darker corner of the room until he should be permitted to return to the obscurity of his cave. And, indeed, he seemed something of a night creature, his eyes being abnormally large and his clothes those of an undertaker.

'Jack is a gentleman as knows his London and his place. He gives no offence nor yet receives none, I dare say. He will protect the ladies should they be in need as they won't be, nor never was a gentler nor more welcoming place than this we live in which is the envy of the world.' She spat casually into the fire, which hissed its approval, then lifted one section of herself as though about to rise before sinking back, exhausted, no doubt, at what might have been the longest and most eloquent speech to which she had ever committed herself.

Jack smiled, as it seemed to Pearl, most alarmingly. 'And it is just as Mistress Nibbins do say and ever shall be,' he observed to the room at large.

'Pray do not bother yourself, sir. I am sure we shall be perfectly safe,' observed Pearl, none too sure that she welcomed such an escort.

'It may not be,' said her cousin, for emphasis setting his

tankard down with such a jolt that the contents slopped over its side.

The landlady nodded her agreement, then, after a pause, shook her head vigorously, a little confused as to how to show assent to a negative.

So, Jack it was, Jack and Mistress Tubbs. The one had a disconcerting habit of walking backwards, as though under the impression that his two charges were visiting potentates. As a result his passage through the streets was marked by a succession of collisions, dull and painful thuds, and a growing sense on Pearl's part that time itself had perhaps begun to retreat. The other, a woman of quite remarkable plainness but evidently the best of hearts, insisted on breaking off their conversation with disturbing frequency to clasp her young charge to her bosom with still more disturbing vigour.

'Poor child. Poor child.'

'Poor, Mistress Tubbs? Why poor?'

The question hung suspended for a second as the attentive Jack had trodden on a goose and killed it, or at least so it appeared from the vigour with which the owner thrust a bunch of hazel twigs in his face and screamed in a torrent of words which Pearl found unintelligible and her companion affected to ignore.

'To have left your mother, my chuck. Mother and daughter must never be separated. Men are very well in their way and have their uses, I dare say,' though what they might be was hardly apparent from Jack who, in stumbling backwards in the face of assault had evidently trodden on another goose, this one, however, proving more than capable of defending itself, 'but a mother and her daughter . . .' Words failed her and she brushed a tear from her somewhat pitted cheek with the back of a hand which was far from clean. 'There be the gibbet where they hanged three men together,' she added, brightening considerably. 'My husband and I were to see it, though it rained so much we were hard pressed to stay.'

'So they hang men here, too,' said Pearl gently.

'No, my chuck. 'Tis more usual at Tower Hill to use the axe.'

57

Something stirred in Pearl's heart. Somehow she had imagined that the cruel severities of her Boston home had been a product of its own impieties, of a fierce climate which bred an unforgiving soul. But here the gibbet stood, a broken cross in the very heart of life. Nor, despite the bubbling foolishness of the woman who once again, for no apparent reason, crushed her to her breast, could she fail to wonder at such a casual attitude which could turn death into mere play.

Ahead of them, as they climbed the gentle incline of Tower Hill, itself bright in the sunlight, stood the crenellated walls of the Tower itself, with the river running hard by to sweep it clean of blood. Boston had no such monument to death. Its prison house was dark enough and Pearl was tied to it by history, but this, not without its beauty, was pain transformed into stone.

Nonetheless there was an energy here in the jumble of humanity, in the exultantly aimless pattern of the streets whose houses reached out to one another so that it was possible to shake hands across the narrow space between, if shaking hands should be what neighbours had in mind. She felt, as once she had in the forest and the marshes of New England, a thrill of freedom. She was not of this place but felt she could command it. It lay before her, awaiting her desire. Her very anonymity meant that she could pass through its streets as freely as she had through the fields and deep woods of her youth. It is a natural and necessary article of faith for the young that the world exists only to be shaped to their will and, were it not thus, what world would there be for us to inhabit? Pearl felt that thrill now as she descended into the mud-grimed streets with Jack seemingly bowing like a courtier as he retreated before her.

'We are to dine with you this evening, mistress,' observed her companion, looking as though she might launch herself once more.

Pearl smiled brightly at such intelligence. It would take more than this news to take the excitement from her heart.

'At the Swan,' she insisted.

On the other hand. If in America she felt that she sometimes acted in an over-solemn drama, here, in England, she seemed fated to perform in a farce.

Certainly, that evening there gathered together such a cast of characters as can have been unrivalled in the hemisphere. Her cousin presided, at the end of a great table, with one leg, in which he suffered pain, pointed towards the fire and resting on a stool. He smoked a thin, white pipe whose stem he held as if it were a flute with which he would entertain his visitors. But from it issued not sweet music but a smell which, if it belonged anywhere on God's earth, belonged in a farmyard when the sun had fermented what the rain should have washed away.

At the other end of the table sat Master Tubbs, well named as it happened, since his body was so well rounded that if it could be preserved after his death it might serve to set beneath a gutter and collect the rain. Indeed it seemed to Pearl that she had seen few associated with the Swan who would not benefit from a month or two on bread and water and few not so associated who would not benefit from the roast beef and fowl which was to be set before them this night. But, justice being what justice is, it was unlikely that such an exchange would be effected this side of St Peter's gate.

Master Tubbs was a happy man, at least as judged by the laughter with which he felt obliged to accompany each contribution to the conversation.

'Finest ale in the country, Deptford's,' he offered to the table at large, then followed the remark with a barking laugh, something, Pearl thought, between the sound of a New England ketch scraping down the slipway, all squeals and rasps, and a cloud of rooks roosting above one's head. It was a sound which contained so many contrary elements overlaid that it was not clear at first whether it indicated pleasure or pain. She was distracted from it, however, by his eye. He had, it should be said, two, which must have been some consolation to his wife, whose expression was of someone who wishes to indicate at once her deep love and still deeper

59

loathing for her bedmate. But one of his eyes had evidently decided long since to have no commerce with the other and as a result they had mutually decided to go their separate ways. The problem was to know which one to address or to whom his admittedly somewhat random remarks might be directed. Nor was this eye inert. It wandered in its socket as our mind will sometimes wander away from those we engage in conversation. So, while he lifted his tankard and toasted her cousin, the eye, which seemed to grow in the course of the evening, looked Pearl up and down with such cool effrontery that she blushed deep red and turned to her companion of the afternoon.

In the light of day Mistress Tubbs had seemed plain. By some illogic, the firelight, which left all their shadows disporting drunkenly on the wall behind them, made her seem less plain than grotesque. Where a flickering light may bring a softness to the skin of some, and there is many a lover who cherishes a memory of his love seen in the warm glow of a dying fire, this particular fire, which would explode from time to time in showers of sparks, some of which fell unnoticed on her uncle's foot, seemed to exaggerate every flaw and imperfection on the poor woman's face. The shifting shadows revealed great rift valleys filled with a chalk-white powder and a whole terrain of hills and mountains. And Pearl saw now, what unaccountably she had failed to see before, a kind of mole with pretensions one day to become a tufted hillock. Certainly it already sprouted the beginnings of a luxuriant foliage in the form of two thick black hairs.

The inn was full of smells, from the smouldering leather of her cousin's shoe to the stinging smoke from the pipes of both men and that of damp clothes steaming by the fire. But above these was the rich, greasy, thick and satisfying aroma of roast beef, whose entry those at the table all anticipated.

Young Sam came through the door bearing a wooden tray on which were placed four large tankards, each with a foaming head standing up like a Frenchman's soufflé. Being small, he staggered under the weight. Beside him, smiling and ducking her head as she advanced, and shaking, as it seemed to Pearl, quite like a blancmange fresh out of its mould, came the hostess of the Swan.

'Aha!' shouted her cousin, with the same joy as Penelope might have greeted the first signs of Odysseus's tattered sails.

'Behold!' cried Master Tubbs, before relapsing into rasping giggles. 'My dear,' he said, between gasps, indicating the advancing couple with a sideways nod of his head and a roll of his eye, the other remaining obdurately stationary.

'Indeed!' replied his wife, dutifully.

Pearl felt some pressure to join this strange ceremony but try as she might she could not shape her mouth to form a sound.

'Our ale, I think,' shouted Master Tubbs.

On this there seemed general agreement as young Sam completed his passage across the uneven floor and with some difficulty slid the heavy tray onto the table. If he intended to offer each guest his or her drink he was relieved of the necessity by the hands which slid like eels across the greasy surface before closing around the stout handles of the still stouter tankards. Pearl, who could no more drink beer than swallow a frog, looked at the single unclaimed vessel and was about to make some polite demur when the great ship which was the proprietress of the inn arrived safely at the harbour of the fireside and herself reached down for the remaining ale. With her left hand she gave a clip to the back of Sam's head. He had begun to duck, apparently in anticipation of this familiarity, but clearly practice had provided what quickness of eye and hand may have lacked. Meanwhile, with her right hand, she raised the dull metalled cup into the air.

'Your health, masters and mistresses, and may God be with you. You still make the finest ale in London, Master Tubbs.'

'In London?' roared Pearl's cousin. 'Why, in the world.'

None seemed to notice that Pearl herself had nothing in her hand, for which she was truly thankful.

'And is this your ale, then, sir?' she asked.

'Master Tubbs,' announced Mistress Tubbs, as though

addressing a Tyburn crowd about to witness the ecstasy of human immolation, '*is* Deptford Ale. There is some claims to brew ale, my dear. There is some who wishes it to be known that they makes ale. But only Master Tubbs, and I know of, *is* Deptford Ale. He were born Deptford Ale and he will die Deptford Ale.'

Her husband looked a little uncertain at this last remark. No one, after all, would wish to be reminded of his mortality, especially when he is looking forward to fine roast beef and a roast potato or so.

'Tomorrow,' said her cousin expansively, 'we shall go to Deptford. There is much to see. And besides, there is a vessel I should like to inspect. To Deptford Ale,' he cried, with some conviction, raising his arm.

His companions echoed him, tilting back the tankards and not emerging again until these were upended and their noses flecked with white from the foam. Whereupon they looked with some amazement to see how they could have been so easily emptied but by the simple expedient of turning them upside down.

'Sit down, Mistress Nibbins, sit down,' invited cousin William, with great vigour and equal redundancy, for she was already in process of collapsing, by degrees, into a chair both large and stout.

'It is my tradition,' announced his hostess, 'to dine with such guests as I respects and who is worthy of the Swan. And such, as you know, sir, is how I choose to judge the present company.'

Across the room the darkness resolved into the form of Jack, who edged backwards towards them, carrying a huge platter on which a side of beef still crackled and spat in its own fat.

'Thou art not drinking,' observed cousin William of Pearl.

'Indeed, sir,' she said, indicating a small goblet, 'I have a glass of water.'

He paused, as though the idea were so novel as to require some effort of the intellect to understand. Water, to his mind, was what was to be found beneath the keel of a ship or falling inconveniently from the sky. It was what in other inns than this was used to adulterate the ale. His face lit up. 'Cider!' he shouted.

'Indeed, sir. I am quite content.'

'Content! With water? Mistress Tubbs?'

'Even so,' she replied somewhat vaguely, her eyes being fixed on the dish of meat which now rested on the table, a trifle black at the edges but evidencing a rich and satisfying smell.

A knife was passed ceremoniously along the table to Mistress Nibbins. She flexed her ample wrist (in the process nearly inflicting severe injuries on Mistress Tubbs whose nose seemed to have extended since the roasted meat had been placed before them) and approached her ritual task. With a fork like a devil's trident she impaled the waiting beef to the accompaniment of exhaled breath from those gathered about her, a collective sigh not so much of satisfaction as relief. Then, with an extravagant gesture, she began to saw away as though she were felling a great oak to become the mainmast of a frigate.

'Beef,' she observed, 'does get the juice flowing, I dare say, better nor anything you would care to name.'

'Indeed it do,' agreed her neighbour, who had judiciously removed her nose out of range, 'saving perhaps your goose.'

'Your goose!' screamed their hostess, 'your goose do have juices of its own, I dare agree, but it do prompt little from those as eats it.'

At this point Pearl began to feel a little faint and was reduced to taking in several gulps of air, an article in scarce supply so that mostly what she inhaled was that atmosphere unique to the Swan, a blend of smoke and sweat and ale and sawdust and cooked beef on which its inhabitants seemed to survive and prosper. A jug of cider was placed in front of her, serving to break the trance into which she had fallen.

'Drink up, my dear. It is not ale but it will serve its turn.'

So hot was it by now, what with the fire, the still spluttering meat and the glow from her companions who themselves seemed to have been basted with lard and fresh emerged from the oven, and so tepid and foul-tasting the water which had nothing of the freshness of Boston well water, that she did his bidding. And indeed it was refreshing. Straight from the cool, dank, cellar of the Swan, it tasted of autumn, and somehow, in the midst of the noise, as Jack sidled backwards towards his lair and all about her beamed with anticipation, she was transported for a moment across the ocean to another place and time. For she had tasted cider once before and now it served as a key to unlock memories and open wide the door to emotions she had thought safely stored like winter wheat in a barn. Thus, in this company of souls at an inn in London's Cheapside, where plenty drove out thoughts of the want beyond the door, there was one who travelled her own path to a moment when she had crept into the cool of a larder, lifted a muslin cloth fringed with beads, and dipped her finger into a golden liquid. And from that one cool drop of memory came another, linked not by logic but association, of a lifetime when she had watched her mother vilified by those who passed. Then, faster now, like a young girl skipping across stepping stones, other scenes tumbled into her mind to be replaced by still others. She saw a white face, cruel and determined, lips pulled back, eyes like burnt raisins, and shuddered quite as though there were no fire in the grate. And she remembered, too, a forest clearing and two figures who seemed to meld in the dappled light, form and re-form, now two, now one, and herself a witness to such a mystery. The face was that of Chillingworth; the figures, those of her mother and the man whom passion had drawn to her side.

And as these wayward figures formed subtle patterns in her mind, so she felt both sadness and determination. Her life had a direction and a purpose and though its resolution lay ahead, its meaning, she suspected, lay behind. She had, she felt, a task and a destiny. And though she could know nothing of what they might be, yet she had a quiet certainty that she would prove equal to both, a conviction as cool and as real as the sharp cider which stung her throat and which in the merest fraction of a second had recalled her to herself and unpacked memories like so many treasures placed carefully away for a future she could only imagine. Pearl may have stumbled into a farce – though there was something about the bizarre performance which appealed to her rebellious spirit – but beneath it all there was a story in which this was but an interlude.

'Thy health, my dear,' cried her cousin, lifting his tankard above his head so that drips of ale anointed him. 'Thou art welcome to old England and thou may have my beard if this is not a jollier place than that which thou hast come from, as I hear.' The wager was hardly worth the winning, not least because he forgot that he had worn no beard for more than a twelvemonth, but she acknowledged the truth of what he said. She had seen more smiles that day than in a month in New England and if they were mad, as in her heart she half suspected they might be, it was a madness which did no harm and which eased her arrival at this place.

The carriage, promised by an expansive Master Tubbs the previous evening, duly arrived outside the Swan. If Pearl had expected something grand, then she was disappointed. For this was a kind of cart with unwarranted ambitions, though, as if by way of compensation, it was drawn by two great dray horses whose flesh shivered with muscles and whose eyes revealed spirits not yet broken by labour. It was behind their twitching shanks that the company was to ride, on a raised bench so high that lifting cousin William to such an elevated seat posed a considerable problem, solved with casual good-will by neighbours who, after standing in a huddle to work out the various angles, weights and forces which might be involved, managed the task with a series of boxes, some almost co-ordinated pushes, and a profanity or two. The object of their efforts permitted himself to be thus raised like the final section of a bridge, nudged first this way, then that, until he stared uncertainly down at the rounded rear quarters of the chestnut-coloured horses which steamed quite as had the beef the night before.

Pearl, taking the proffered hand of the drayman, put a foot lightly on the hub of the wheel, rounded like the squat nipple of some exotic animal, and pulled herself up beside the relative who was now looking, somewhat alarmed, towards her, as though he might jump ship before she should pull away from shore.

The journey to Deptford took them along the river, eastwards towards the sun so that at times Pearl was all but blinded, while her cousin closed his eyes and emitted what could only have been a snore. But, then, London was no mystery to him. For her, all was a novelty and she longed to see everything she might, including the Royal Dock. She knew, too, that from Deptford had sailed the ships that defeated the Armada and that Sir Francis Drake had knelt on board his ship in Deptford Creek for his untrustworthy monarch to rest her sword on his shoulders.

Today, London stretches in all directions as though it would reach out and fill the world with its noise. What once were separate villages are now no more than names on a signpost as street gives way to street and buildings multiply. For Pearl, though, grassland and field opened up and the houses fell away from the river like a dark coat opening to reveal a lithe body.

The shipyard itself was a sprawling mass of masts, like a forest stripped of its leaves. There were vessels in every stage of construction, so many corpses, as it seemed, laid out for dissection. Here, there was but the suggestion of a keel, a spine laid bare of flesh by the knife; there, two decks were open to the world as men hammered and sawed and measured and climbed ladders lashed to the side of a ship whose ribs shone white in the sun. On near-completed ships, men spun spider's webs of rope, hanging by a single hand or sliding gracefully down towards the stationary deck. At half a mile she could hear the noise of mallet and saw and the distant cry of men who called to companions far below them. It all seemed part of a pattern, a grand design. Seen from close to, the pattern vanished and each man became the centre of his own drama, running a finger along the face of a plank, greasing a rope, sighting along a straight edge, reaching into a leather apron for awl or spike, hammer or plane. From a distance the ships themselves were so many broken toys disassembled from perfection; from close to, a symbol of what men might do as those same ships towered above their industrious creators.

Her cousin had spoken of inspecting a ship but, as she half suspected, this had evidently been no more than a ruse, for the drayman nudged his horses away from the river, skirting the edge of the dockyard, and doubled back in the general direction he had first come. Fields of tangled grass reached into the distance, green with a shadow of blue, flowing with currents and eddies in the wind. Men clung to the river, here. Beyond was what passed for wilderness. Then, as the shadows shortened, the nodding horses, their bridles ringing silver clear, were turned again towards a cloud of steam which seemed to hang about a tumble of dock buildings, a private mist or a meeting of spirits. And this last, it seemed, might have some literal truth, for this was the home of Deptford Ale. The air turned sweet, then heavy with the smell of Kent hops, the open secrets of the brewer's art thus betrayed by the smell of barley and yeast which rolled towards London.

Something of all this evidently penetrated the slumbering mind of cousin William for, having slept since leaving the Swan, swaying perilously from side to side, by some instinct never falling into street or mud, he opened his eyes, looked about him, stretched his arms, took a deep breath and uttered his other name.

'Ale!'

'Is it even so?' asked Pearl, with a smile, as the metalled wheels of the wagon ground grittily on the cobbles and the horses' hooves struck sparks and brought a sharp echo from the dark buildings.

Men with leather at their shoulders and on their heads bent forward under the weight of sacks. Piles of barrels stood in precarious mountains which threatened to collapse and, everywhere, ale. It swilled brown amidst the cobbles and the dung. It seemed to drip from the brickwork and rain down like drizzle.

Master Tubbs hallooed from the steps of a nearby building and called out to two men to abandon their sacks and assist. They drew a heavy box across the stones and helped down first Pearl and then her cousin. She smelled the sharp sweat of the men even through the cloying aroma of beer. Together they walked with some care across the yard and up the steps.

Inside, another fire blazed. These people, she thought, seem to feel the cold when in New England we should be giving thanks that spring had brought a return of summer heat. Indeed, though memories of her youth seemed to contain more summers than winters, yet she remembered the bone ache of cold drawn from stone floors and the numbness which came with a wind which sifted the snow through the trees like a white sand to cut the face and sting the eyes. Yet she huddled towards this fire herself, for it seemed to drive out the smells which she had begun to think might make her sick.

To her surprise, it was a day not without interest and something more perhaps. For Master Tubbs, who had been but a fool, as it seemed to her, as he played out his role at the Swan, was here as earnest and concerned, as committed to his task and as courteous, as any she had met. His work was more than labour and he conducted her around with such pride that it could not but infect her, too. Her cousin contented himself with staying by the fire with some of Deptford's best in his hand, having, as he explained, visited its birthplace many times before, but she allowed his comical friend to take her hand and lead her through a hell which he so clearly felt a kind of heaven. Little of what Pearl learned of brewing could she have repeated a week hence but something she learned of people would perhaps remain with her in her future life.

In her room that night, Pearl looked at a single star refracted through the thick bottle glass of her window, its leaded panes shadowed in silver. As she moved her head from side to side, the star fattened and shrank, grew tall or compacted into a tight point. She had the power to expand or contract the heavens by the simple expedient of moving herself. Yet if she

68

had the arrogant faith of youth that the universe turned about the axis of her life, she was not so young as to mistake this feeling for truth. Nonetheless, she had willed this journey. She had wrenched at the roots of her being and torn them from the soil. But in truth those roots were shallow. She did not belong in New England. She had known that from the first. Her mother's isolation, her banishment from the company of men, only slowly revoked, was one which daughter and mother alike had embraced without shame but which had kept Pearl from making a commitment to the site of her birth. She did not belong, either, in this time or place. Like a salmon drawn back to its spawning ground, she longed, without knowing why, to return, not, in her case, to the location of her conception but to where her story had had its beginning. She wished to turn back the pages to see how it had all begun.

Had you asked her why she had journeyed so far, no answer would have come except an open smile and a closed mouth. The truth was that she followed necessity and necessity may not be interrogated. She was, if you like, a constable who, knowing a crime to have been committed, goes in search of the cause in order to locate the perpetrator.

Then again, she was travelling against history, and there were those aplenty in New England who thought the country of her destination Satan's pit. To be sure, there had been moments on that day when she could have believed it true: huge vats of hops, boiling on great oak fires, men glistening with sweat like the damned caught in eternity's vortex. Was it without significance that she seemed to have come to a land of fires?

The moonlight bleached all colour from the room. The scarlet design of needlepoint which she wore at her heart turned to black, and yes, she too wore a design, though, unlike her mother's, it was shaped not as a letter but as a device which seemed as yet not to have found clear shape. In common with the solitary star which cut across the window like a diamond, she was quite alone. Yet she had never felt closer to her mother. She had only to reach out her hand, as it seemed, to touch her, to feel the warmth of her love. And who would not

69

do as now she did, sobbing into her pillow and yet not knowing why, for she had long since braced herself against the pain of separation. Such was the limbo in which she resided, such the way-station on the road to truth. Because truth, no less, was what she sought, though she was unsure whether she would recognise it were she ever to encounter it.

The noise had quieted somewhat. No longer did horse and cart pass by her window nor late-night revellers shout goodbye or wrestle in the street below. If this city ever slept it slept now, though she could hear the distant clanging of a river buoy and further still the striking of a clock. For once, rich and poor, unhappy souls and brides on wedding eves, lived together in a place where hopes become realities and sorrows fade to black.

Then, sleep would be denied no more and with the silver windows reflecting on her bed she slipped into a dream – even as the lead which framed the glass threw the dark shadow of a cross on her pale face as though she were an emblem of divinity.

It was with some surprise, the following morning, that Pearl found a tear start to her eye as she embraced in farewell the cousin she had known a bare three days. For in that time she had learned to see beyond the clown. There was a ballast to this man more significant than the weight which he carried every day. To be sure, a pig's bladder in his hand would not have seemed out of place, were it possible occasionally to remove the tankard which otherwise seemed a part of his very body. But on her return journey from Deptford he had begun to talk. He spoke of his wife, dead these thirty years, and with such simplicity and love that you would think it were but yesterday. It was, he told her, the anniversary of her death and he found it insupportable still. She had died in the fullness of her life, a fullness which he recounted with such quiet dignity that Pearl no longer saw the passing scene but instead only this great whale of a man who leaned forward in the cart with his hand to his brow in a vain attempt to conceal his tears. But they soon found echoes in those of his companion as he recalled a woman whose hand he had not felt these three decades.

She had died of fever, a fever born of morning's light which had betrayed its presence by no more than a scarlet flush upon her cheek, a flush, indeed, which mimicked health. Within the hour, though, she had collapsed, walking across the kitchen with a jug of milk. He had turned to see it strike the stone floor in an explosion of whiteness, with her at its centre falling among the shards of pottery. Through the morning and past noon he sat beside her until one called who claimed the skills of life and death. He set leeches on her arms, black, shining scars which mocked the paleness of her skin. And though she burned with fever he had placed about her head a poultice of hot clay in linen so that when it was removed a transparent wafer of skin hung down.

All this he recounted, as the lights of London began to appear and the river darkened to a ribbon of black crepe. She had died in the evening, before the last light had faded from the window, nor, as he explained, did she speak the whole day long. And this last seemed to haunt him. There were words which should have passed, he explained, in a voice she could hardly hear above the rumble and crunch of the wheels as they passed along the river path. There were truths which should have been spoken before she commenced her journey into infinity. And there came a moment, as the last glow of red in the western sky disappeared, on this day thirty years beyond that which had seen her consigned to her grave, when cousin clung to cousin as though together they might breathe life back into the past and restore one whose loss had caused such pain. How long they thus embraced she could not tell for though he no longer spoke his shoulders shook and his breath came in quiet gasps.

As they entered the jagged buildings of the city and the stars were seeded in the sky he loosed his grip and sat back in his seat, brushing a last tear away with his hand. They rode together side by side before, some five minutes later, he turned

to her in the gathering dusk, the lines of his face smoothed flat
by the light of moon and stars, and said, with quiet intensity:

'I loved her, my dear. And I have not loved beyond that day.
What thou seest is not what I was nor yet what I might have
been. It is what was left when the heart was taken out of me.'

Then he turned his face back towards the city and they rode
together in silence for a while, though, after a moment or two,
Pearl reached out her hand and grasped his own. It was a
familiarity he scarce seemed to notice, save that, as they neared
their destination, he squeezed her hand in return, though
whether in gratitude or some distant memory of a more
important touch she could not say.

There must come a moment for us all when we realise the
fallibility of our judgements. The lives of others are a mystery
we may not know. She had been content to laugh behind her
hand at this man who had so simplified his life as to become no
more than an object for her amusement. But, in a second,
another had stood before her who felt true pain, who had a
history and a life he concealed from himself no less than from
her. For a bare hour or two the veil had lifted and she had seen
what she should have known, that there is none who is not
acquainted with despair, none who has not known love, none
who does not demand of us the respect which is born of our
attempt to make our way through a life which may leave us, in
the still of night, with nothing but an emptiness the world
cannot fill and memories which time alone can never hope to
redeem. Here, for the first time, was a man who had her
sympathy and, even, her love.

So, she parted from him, as one does from a lifetime's friend,
with sadness and yet with a quiet calm; and all this for a moment
of remembered pain on a riverside track. And more had fallen
from her than the false image of a solitary man, for we
discover truths where we least expect to find them. The comic
figure was comic no more, though that same night he had
assumed the familiar disguise. But something in the way his
eyes met her own told her that he knew such pretence must be
in vain. For she had stared through those eyes and seen, like

him, the soft bruise on a cheek, watched the beads of sweat gather round a brow suddenly furrowed with pain. And she had heard the hollow sound of dry earth on oak coffin.

It is true that pain never crosses the barrier between two separate selves but something communicates, riding the imagination as a gull rides the wind. She had felt his pain and though the mask was back in place it was not entirely as before. Every voyage a lesson: every life a truth.

The day of her departure dawned clear. At London Bridge a fire had tumbled a house into the waters, partly blocking one of the dozen or more rough brick arches and leaving a hole in the next like a mousebite in stale cheese. A thin calligraphy of smoke hung in the still air. At Chelsea an explosion of starlings rose from their roost into a whitened sky already edging towards the colour of thrush eggs. There was no suggestion of wind. Sails hung limp at the mast. On the Tower the flag had surrendered its form, like a cloth hung out by washerwomen and, indeed, between the battlements, someone had pegged out the household wash. Beyond the city, in the fields and woods of Hampstead and Highgate, fawns paused in the dew, ears turning for the sound of threat. The city held its breath. At the mouth of the Fleet, where its brown waters spilled into the Thames, a body floated, snagged on an old oak beam. It was hardly more than a tangle of rags except where some sharp object had ripped these aside, and the flesh beneath, so that the grey wound seemed to pulse with the mockery of life as the water passed in gentle folds.

Pearl rose early. She had set her clothes out the night before and though the voyage which faced her could hardly match the rigours of her previous one, yet she had lain awake and felt her pulse race at the thought of another page about to turn. On the window ledge a pigeon grumbled and fluttered before rising in a throbbing flurry of feathers. Early though she was, there were those who were earlier still, for far below she heard the clatter of pans and the unmistakable sound of a hand impacting on a young man's head. As she buckled her shoes, so the smell of cooking bacon seeped under her door and she realised with a shock that she was indeed hungry, more hungry than she could remember feeling. But what she longed for was not bacon swimming in fat and the deep yellow duck eggs of the Swan; it was fresh-baked Boston bread and a glass of milk and perhaps a pancake with syrup tapped from the tree.

The goodbyes at the door of the Swan were more emotional than would be warranted by an acquaintance of only a few days. The inn's owner, flanked by her assistants summoned from the depths of the cellar, advanced segment by segment, as was her way. So overcome did she seem that she almost failed to cuff young Sam who jumped aside, as always a moment too late to avoid the blow. Pearl's cousin embraced her, pulling her to him with a vigour which surprised her. Pearl herself was now lifted bodily into the carriage and, as the tip of a whip was flicked at the dun-coloured rump of the horse, it jerked forwards making her put out a hand, lest she should fall back into the arms of those who had just relinquished her. She turned in her seat and waved to the receding group. Her cousin, whom business delayed further in the city, pulled a cloth from an inside pocket of his equally dun-coloured jacket and alternately waved it in the air and drew it across his eyes and nose.

Chapter Three

The *Nancy Jane* moved easily away from the dock and out into the current which simmered in the centre of the river, a breeze having been summoned from nowhere as the sun climbed in the sky. Only a few days before, this place had throbbed with novelty to Pearl. Each new vista had excited and been compared, favourably, with her distant home. Now it seemed merely familiar, and as the ship cleared the dark buildings and the low blue haze of smoke, so she recognised the track down which she had travelled to Deptford and Greenwich. With the passing of an hour or so the river itself slowly broadened, relaxing something of its nervous drive. More canvas was pulled squeaking to the mastheads as the dockyards came into view, with what seemed their nursery of toy boats. She felt the urge to wave as though they were friends but contented herself instead with standing on tiptoe the better to see those who laboured from the tip of the foremast to the curve of the new-laid keel. Then they were past as was the brewery where she had dined.

Only then did she note a fellow passenger who stood further aft and looked with no less attention than herself at the passing scene. It was the selfsame man she had noticed at a distance on her first sight of the *Nancy Jane* and she felt the same strange flutter in her heart. Suddenly, the river bank, with its cows, stationary in flying fields, and its fishermen, perhaps the same she had seen on her arrival, had lost all interest. Only this imperious figure, dressed in black, with one hand on the rigging and the other in his coat, commanded her attention, and when, after a minute or so, he turned and faced her, she felt a shock as physical as though she had been struck in the face. For a second he seemed to stare beyond her to where the river had begun to broaden towards the still distant sea, but then their eyes met and for a moment all movement seemed to still.

She cannot have known how precisely she repeated what had been before. For thus had Hester stood some twenty years before and stared into the eyes of another. Indeed, had she not done so there would have been no Pearl to act as echo to that moment. So are the defences we prepare with such care broken through in a second when we had thought them strong enough to withstand even the most determined of assaults.

Crossing the Atlantic, Pearl had once seen St Elmo's fire, a strange flickering of yellow and indigo, red and orange and blue, around the masts. There was a wonder in it which afflicted even the most experienced sailor aboard so that all heads tilted, all eyes were focused above. Something in the playfulness, the flowing waves of light, entered the mind and stirred the spirit. She felt it now. No lights spilled around the shrouds. The sky, indeed, was the deepest blue and the sun a burning halo punched in it as a blacksmith's awl will burn its way through hide and emerge glowing and fiery red. But she felt again the thrill of discovery. They stood quite motionless and might have continued to do so had the helmsman not chosen then to spin his wheel to avoid a waterlogged skiff. He reached for the rigging, she for the ship's smooth side. They smiled with equal embarrassment before he strode towards her, his face open and amused.

'You have quite knocked me off my feet, I am afeared.'

'Sir?' She was not used to being addressed so directly by a

stranger but added, with some amusement, 'I had thought it was the ship.'

His hair was as dark as his clothes. A thin scar on his forehead gave him the appearance of one permanently surprised but there was in his green eyes something more of recognition and warmth rather than mere astonishment. Pearl inclined her head in greeting, which substituted for the words which had fled quite away. He reached out a hand to steady himself.

'I am nothing of a sailor. We have not left the Thames and it seems I have forgot my legs. You, though, seem quite assured.'

'I have had time to learn. It is only a few days since I completed a voyage from Massachusetts.'

'Massachusetts! So you are one of those who regard such as I as a mere enthusiast.'

'You? Enthusiast?'

'I am a preacher of the Lord.'

He could hardly know that nothing could have pleased her less, for she had come to believe such either bullies or cowards.

'Indeed.'

'Indeed. I am. But there are those in Massachusetts who would have me sing a simpler song than I would wish to sing.'

A wind blew up from nowhere, fretting the surface of the water. The sails shook and snapped and the temperature seemed to plummet even as they spoke. A cloud passed over the sun, its shadow flowing darkly towards them across the open fields and grey sands. Only a moment before the sky had been clear. It was as if the river itself had given birth to this chill gloom. A ragged line of gulls rose into the sky, only to be snatched away by the wind. Pearl clutched her cape about her and looked around with some alarm. The squall had come from nowhere and the deck was suddenly alive with sailors going about their tasks. In an instant, too, the man before her was transformed. A yellow light which flooded the scene turned his pale complexion jaundiced. His hair, caught by the wind, blew in a disordered tangle before a sudden splatter of rain, which advanced greyly across the stippled Thames, pressed it flat and wet across his face.

The *Nancy Jane* shuddered in the face of the squall and the helmsman began to look across the river as though afraid to approach his destination directly. And then, a second later, or so it seemed, the gale abated. The sun shone through a break in the rapidly thinning cloud and a rainbow arched high above them, stretching from bank to bank. The wind dropped away and the water's surface smoothed quite as though a heavy iron had been drawn across it. But the tide now ran strong and the first real waves they had seen soon lifted then dropped the ship as it angled towards the open sea. A lone seagull, which had fallen unnoticed to the deck only a minute before, now fluttered to life and, like a sailor drunk on board, staggered from side to side before lifting heavily once more into the air.

And in those moments, when the world went from fair to foul, she had seen him quite altered. The very colour of his eyes had seemed to change and for a moment there was a wildness she would have sworn was not there before. A brief alteration in the light had made him seem almost diabolic. But the devil has his fascination.

Far off to the east the clouds seemed to be gathering for another assault while above them the sunlight slanted down in great shafts of light such as one sees in paintings but never expects or believes to encounter in life. Off the starboard bow a man struggled with a small dinghy, a dog in its bows putting two huge paws on his shoulders as he endeavoured to pull in a net which flashed silver with fish. The deck, a moment before slick with rain, had already dried. Pearl, like her mother before her, was used to the strangeness of the sea. She had seen the blurred blue line of an advancing storm before, and heard the great rush of air from leviathan, but never such a swift change as this from bright to dark to bright again in a trice, no, nor seen a man pass through the same sequence as though he had a secret self conjured only by storm and fury.

They parted thus, with the weather undecided as to its mood, bright sun and deep chill taking turn about. And much the same could be said of Pearl's spirit. She had cared for no man nor believed she ever should, and in particular distrusted the pious, doubted even the word of God. What was the Bible to her but a man's book full of men's names: Matthew, Mark, Luke and John? Yet here was a man, whose profession she disliked, but who nonetheless quickened her pulse and compelled her eye. The heart, it seems, is no more consistent than an April day.

The *Nancy Jane* dealt in cargo rather than people, as the *Hope* had done those years before, and Pearl found herself sleeping in a space no larger than a coffin. Indeed, its shape was curiously akin to one. Nor was there a goosedown pillow. A small jug and bowl sufficed for washing and when she splashed a little water from the one into the other she watched with amusement the phenomenon which had so fascinated her on her first days out of Boston. For though the ship rolled ponderously from side to side and the bowl tilted with it – stopped from sliding by two thin wooden stays – yet the water remained level, refusing to mimic the greater water beyond as though placed there with the purpose to recall a true horizontal. Indeed it was quite as though this were a piece of the horizon itself which merely played the same trick on a larger scale. So, she might have thought, it is with us who must seek the meridian when all about us is movement and unease.

Only now did she remember her diary, kept with the regularity of religious devotion until the day of her arrival in London. She took the book from her linen bag and placed it before her on her lap, there being no tables in coffins. She took out, too, a small wooden box, inside which, when she pressed a catch, were two glass containers with silver tops. And, inside one, a liquid which shone a deep crimson save round the rim where were black encrusted crystals with a hint of green. Green for her first sea voyage, she had told herself, and now red for this.

The diary was bound in cloth and on its front, in her mother's needlepoint, a letter P, almost lost in the elaborations of the seamstress's work and glowing with a virgin blue as though lit by some inner light. There was a lock on this book of her life to which she alone carried the key, it being the essence of diaries that they be conversations with oneself and that one may write what one does not choose to speak aloud. It was in that spirit that she now chose to write of him she had encountered and of the feelings, contradictory and yet strong, which her encounter had engendered.

But as she opened the diary and stared where the flow of tight-packed writing ended, she saw, with a shock, one word, separated from the rest and written with a boldness and a size which stood out clearly. Of course it was written with the coast in sight and the sea so calm that for once the words did not fly off nor the ink spill like an unstaunched wound, but it was a word which surprised her nonetheless and which the last days' activities had quite blotted from her mind. It was HOME.

It is true that the excitement of imminent landfall had driven sleep away and she had felt a kind of fever, but why she should claim as home a place unknown she could neither recall nor imagine.

She dipped her pen in the ink and, though she wiped it on the edge of the glass jar, as she paused for thought so a red tear formed at the end of her quill and fell like a drop of blood upon the page. She had no sand to pour on it and sought to blot it with her kerchief. Placing the corner in her mouth she wet it with her lips and then touched the meniscus of ink, already clotting with a skin which dented gently to the touch. Slowly the red seeped into the woven linen and stained the fingers which held it. The blot was thus removed, leaving a white centre with scarlet surround.

She did not begin her account with the story of her cousin nor with the cast of characters who had performed their comedy for her, though she had the wit to do them full justice. She wrote instead a simple sentence: '*I met a man today.*' Her pen ceased. She dipped it once again into the ink and watched it swell towards the tip of the quill as she lifted it free of the bottle. Then, touching it to the edge to prevent a second tear falling on the page, she thought to continue her account. But the thought had flown away. What was there to tell of him? That he was tall? That his face was earnest yet with a smile that seemed to come from within? That his eyes held hers a little longer than they should and that they had changed from green to black? Or should it be that other fact which struck an echo in her mind: that he was a minister, like he who had denied her mother and herself, that a path had opened up before her down which her life's experience had taught her she should not walk? But we have an infinite capacity to deny what we would not know and who can be sure that such thoughts even entered her mind? Certainly, when, after a few seconds' pause, she once again put pen to paper, it was to write a simple truth: *'He travels to Yarmouth and then on to Norwich and shall thus be my travelling companion.'*

John Standish, for as such he revealed himself the next day, as they ate a lunch of bread and coarse goat cheese at the captain's table, was on his way to the great cathedral of Norwich. From Cambridge, he explained, he had travelled to London where he had an appointment secured for him by his cousin, himself a churchman in Epping. Now he went with his books and worldly goods towards a city as new to him as to Pearl.

'Books is very well, and churches, too,' said the captain, himself tearing a piece of bread, 'but they keep a man in one place. I'm not a lover of walls of stone, nor yet sitting for a day to read what others have writ, even had I the skills, which I have not, being at sea since I were eight. I like to write myself in the world.'

To Pearl this was eloquence indeed, for she felt much the same.

'And are you not surrounded by walls, captain,' asked Standish, 'except that they be walls of wood?'

'You are trained in argument and I can see how it might seem to be so to such as might spend their time below deck. But I stand in the wind and can change my course as I please. Those on shore cannot say as much.'

'I am with you, captain,' said Pearl, eating as hungrily as her companions, the wind and salt air stimulating her appetite. 'Except you need not be at sea for that. I have run in the forest and am my own person, I believe.'

Standish seemed taken aback at this and certainly such sentiments from a woman were strange indeed. England did not breed wild spirits, nor were women free to see themselves as anything but stitches in the weave of God's cloth, fixed in their place.

'Ah, but you are from a distant land,' he said, almost with relief, as though he were thus relieved of a perplexing paradox.

'That I am, though I think it is my soul that is free and not my body.'

'Your soul is in God's hands. We are His to dispose of, I think.' Then, as though aware of his pomposity, he smiled. 'But I have learned that there may be many ways to serve the Lord.'

'That there are,' replied the captain, spearing a piece of cheese with a knife and himself, for a moment, as portentous as the cleric.

'When shall we be in Yarmouth, captain?' asked Pearl, looking at the lowering skies.

'Tomorrow e'en, unless the storm chooses otherwise.'

'So you are not quite free, then,' said Standish with a smile.

'Who can say as much in the face of a storm? But out here we make our fate within God's good grace.'

The storm did indeed delay them and Pearl learned what many a sailor before her could have told, that the North Sea when pressed can enter the ring with any Atlantic bruiser. At first she had braved the open air but then was ordered below and was not unwilling to comply.

It was dawn on the third day before the Norfolk coast appeared through a thinning mist. The sea was scalloped, the land low and dark. Both Pearl and the cleric stood uneasily on the deck.

Around them a cluster of boats was returning, fishing skiffs caught by the storm. Pearl looked to the sky, perhaps for some shaft of light to signify the return of another lost child, but nature seemed preoccupied with other concerns.

She had risen early to see what first Suffolk and then Norfolk might have to offer that should differ from her erstwhile home. Chiefly, it seemed, a sky filled with birds. To be sure, there were such aplenty which crowded the rocks of Shawmut whence she had come, but here they seemed to cover the heavens in great clouds of white turned pink by the dawn's light. They twisted such arabesques that she watched with wonder. How should they know at which moment they were to turn from east to west, to plunge downwards or soar into the sky? She sought to pick out a leader which might signal the moment, but could detect none. It was as if she looked on a single creature. Yet here and there was a solitary bird which chose not to join the general throng and wrote its own signature above the breaking waves, and it was difficult for her not to see something of herself in these few independent creatures, for had she not decided to break with her society to see what she might venture on her own? Yet she saw that there was a strength in that subtly shifting mass, in which each was connected with another, and recalled the bird beaten to the deck by wind and rain only three days since, and also a whale, in a swirl of red, in the midst of a desolate sea. But she, more than anyone, perhaps, knew the danger of metaphor. It was the sharp edge of a new reality she sought, not a life lived in subjection to a symbol, still less a crowd.

They docked with a powerful lurch, as the sea sent them a painful reminder of its power, should they still need it after such a night, and Pearl fell to one knee, grazing it on the deck and crying out as much from surprise as from pain. And so she returned whence her mother had left, not in fear and darkness but in the day's clear light and a tangle of embarrassment.

Standish, too, had fallen and their mutual accident brought them together in laughter as ropes were thrown ashore and secured around iron bollards.

He had thought to offer his assistance in travelling to

Norwich but her cousin had made arrangements for her and both watched as their belongings were loaded into carts. They stood side by side, meanwhile, each locked in thoughts of their own, each anxious to speak but unsure what to say.

'So, we are both strangers together,' he offered.

'Indeed, though no longer quite so as when we stepped on board.'

Their breath hung before them in the cold air.

'My mother has described this place.'

'And your father?'

Pearl drew her shawl against her, as though against the morning chill.

They were interrupted by a call from the deck where the captain raised a hand of farewell. Then they were both greeted in turn by those sent to carry them to Norwich.

They parted thus, for she was summoned by a man who called himself Widgery and who raised a crooked finger to his brow whenever he addressed her and seemed quite strong enough to lift both her and his horse and cart upon his shoulders and run with them should he have need. She sat beside him and watched the ship diminish in size as they swayed along the road which led away from the quay. Ahead of her the land fell away so flat it seemed to reach to the very edge of the world. Widgery flicked the reins. The horse paused for a second, and then, with a protesting groan of wood, stone and metalled wheel, moved the cart forwards and on towards the distant city.

Widgery was a man of few words. Though Pearl tumbled with questions they broke, wave after wave, on the impassive rock of a man whose energy seemed all to have been transmuted into muscle and bone, leaving very little for conversation. Would it take them long to reach Colney? Did their path take them by way of Norwich? Was the strong wind which had sprung up a feature of the area, as she supposed from the stunted trees which seemed to point their branches, like so many indicating hands, away from the sea and towards their distant objective? When should they see the distant spire

84

of the great cathedral? Did he work at the hall where she would live? Could the horse not perhaps travel a little faster? Were there no hills? Why so many windmills? Like a child, she built question upon question but in return there came a wall constructed brick by brick of monosyllables. And each time, as though instinctively, a brown finger would be raised to his forehead, a finger which, she could not but notice, was covered with enough black dirt to grow a mess of weeds. After a mile or so she was left to her own surmises.

Windmills did, indeed, grow like tall white flowers in the green fields, their sails throbbing, their machinery groaning and rattling so that she heard their sounds above the grinding of the cart on sharp flint and the thud of horse's hooves. They seemed like pieces on a board game, like stately kings surveying their small kingdoms. Dykes lined many a field and she saw the glint of water and realised that they must drain the land as she had heard was true of Holland which lay behind her on the other side of the sea.

The horse stumbled and pulled back a little with a sharp sound like air being drawn through a fireside bellows. Out of the corner of her eye she saw a flash of silver as something seemed to flow across the roadway. It was like a sudden pool of moving water, gone in a second. The horse was treated to a fierce pull on the reins and a sharp flick with a switch of willow.

'A snake?' she asked, falling easily into the mode of conversation of her companion.

'Eels.'

'Eels?'

'Mistress.'

'But eels are water creatures.'

'Ay.'

'Do they then travel on land?'

'Ay.'

'And is that usual?'

'Ay.'

'Why?'

This last seemed to perplex him. Certainly she received no immediate response, as they bumped and swayed along. It was a full mile before, staring intently at his black boot, encrusted with mud, he suddenly remarked, "Cos they can.'

For some reason this seemed answer enough. Though she kept an eye open for another silver stream of creatures she saw none, but there were other animals aplenty, small sharp-nosed things which ran so fast she wondered that their legs did not outstrip their bodies. Rabbits sat and watched their approach, as though unable to move, until they were upon them. Hedgehogs prickled along the way. And though they saw no other human soul, except in one field a man who laboured with a hoe and was as oblivious to them as the rabbits, the world seemed alive with animals which went about their busy lives with fierce determination.

'Is it far?'

'No'm.'

'Ten miles?'

'Could be.'

'Twelve?'

'P'raps.'

It was not abruptness nor yet sullenness, she realised, simply a wish to avoid conversation, together with a kind of stolid acceptance. And what was a mile? Travelled fast it was near, travelled slow it was far. Time can seem a sea with many eddies and distance a function of time.

They did not pass through Norwich . . . 'Market day,' said Widgery . . . but turned to the south by one of a dozen large churches she had seen, left abandoned, so it appeared, by the villages which had once combined in pride to construct them. Successive outbreaks of plague, followed by purging fire, had reshaped the countryside, as a tide undermines a cliff. The gravestones of this church leaned towards each other as though those conversations begun in life were continued after death. Some names were sharp-edged, cut cold and precise into the stones; others were all but wiped from time's memory by wind and rain and the green and yellow petrified flowers of lichen.

Widgery was silent again. They were hoarders of language here and, as she later found, spoke little, though to effect, and would often see if they might not press two words into one and thus save much time and effort, though it be at the cost of sense to an untrained ear. But, then, they spoke still less to strangers, of whom, God knows, there were few enough, unless you were to count those who frequented the city taverns and stood around the horse fairs, sallow-skinned travellers to whom nowhere was home.

Colney Hall – her promised inheritance – was as she expected. And yet not. She looked for it as they climbed a gentle hill but it was lost in a soft fold of the land. It was not until they pulled onto the narrow lane which led to Norwich, some three miles distant, that she glimpsed it through the trees. It caught the morning light but seemed to absorb it in its own darkness. She could see only the roof and the upper part whose windows stared across the land to the north. A track led into trees and seemed to be that which would take them thither, but they continued on their way, past another building set back from the road and surrounded by a low flint wall. This wall, a hundred and more years on, would be rebuilt of brick and rise a good ten feet to cut off inquisitive stares; but to Pearl's gaze Old Hall, as Widgery called it, was clear enough, turned sideways from the road amidst a deal of land quite overgrown. This, she realised suddenly, had been her mother's home before necessity had forced a move to the nearby farm, as nobility's birthright was exchanged for a yeoman's lot.

Somewhere out of sight a bell tolled; out of sight because the land rose at that point before falling away to the church whose flint tower was hidden by elder and beech. They had passed Old Hall now, as they had the house which was home to the clergyman of this parish and the next. Then, to the left, below the level of the road, she saw a farm and knew it for the one her mother had described. On one side it faced the road; on the other, the river. But though she saw chickens pecking at the ground there was no sign of life. Then, at the door of the farmhouse, she made out a shape, a length of black cloth. There were curtains at the window drawn close against the morning sun.

Still they did not stop but travelled on towards the church which now came into view beyond a barn. Suddenly they were not alone, for alongside the flint wall which fringed the churchyard, the very place where Hester had once met Chillingworth fresh from his encounter with the river, was a cluster of people, dark against a blaze of yellow flowers which fringed the graveyard. At their centre was a simple cart, no more than a few flat planks of wood laid side by side and held in place by two more which sloped up on either side. And on this oaken floor, beneath two fluttering black flags, was a coffin, also made of oak.

'And who is that?' she asked, already feeling the stirring of unease.

'That be kin of yours.'

'Of mine?'

'Even so. That be your uncle. Brother to your mother.'

'I were to seek him out.'

'You have no need to seek him further. There he be.'

'When did he . . .'

'Yesternight.'

'What was the cause?'

He looked at her askance. 'Why, mortality.' He spoke the word with due deference and pride, this being the longest word she had heard him utter in a score of miles. 'Mortality,' he repeated, as though delighted with his discovery.

'And did he have no other kin but me?'

'Certain he did.'

'And where are they?'

'Why, over hither,' he replied, with some cheerfulness, pointing ahead through the trees.

'Hither,' she echoed, looking in vain for a crowd of mourners.

'Churchyard, mistress. All in a row.'

＊

And so Pearl returned to Colney, to see an uncle buried she had never known.

For some moments no notice seemed to be taken of her. The coffin, it appeared, had only just been slid over the rough-edged planks, for a tall man, thin of face and still thinner of body, bent to adjust it. But then they turned, like some kind of corporate creature touched at one extremity. There seemed no life in their eyes but perhaps that was a function of the light, for a yellow-edged cloud had passed across the watery sun, making their faces pale. Then one stepped forward, a woman of her mother's age, looking at her as though Pearl should be a ghost, and, as the cloud passed and the sun shone weakly down, Pearl saw that she was more than simply her mother's age. There was something to her eyes and nose, something to the way she held her head that seemed familiar. And in that instant the same recognition passed across the face which looked up at hers. The woman opened her arms, the pinched and questioning look disappeared, and she said, with still the shadow of a question in her voice: 'Pearl?' And then again, before answer could come, 'Pearl?'

There was a stirring in the group, a kind of softening in the way they stood, for though the youngest among them still turned blank faces towards her, others nodded a confirmation and she heard not only her own name mentioned but that of her mother. Words stored away for years were now brought to light. So intently did she look at those about her that it came as a shock when hands closed on hers and Widgery lifted her to the ground. The woman who had spoken came forward and held her gently by the arm, looking intently into her face. Then she raised her right hand and, like a blind woman, traced a finger gently over the features of Pearl's face before embracing her with a grasp so fierce it threatened to drive the air from her lungs.

All her relatives, then, did not lie in the churchyard, merely those in the parish, which was, it seemed, a whole world and universe to Widgery. And in particular this woman, who had

89

waved her mother on her way those twenty and more years before, and who now stood before to welcome her, could be none other than sister to the cousin she had left in London but three days since. And so it proved to be, though she had thought to greet her relative some other place than here.

Pearl sat beside her cousin in St Andrew's church, a round-towered Saxon building of napped flint, with an aisle barely more than fifteen paces long. The service was as plain and simple as the church; the cool, dank smell appropriate to the business of laying one to rest.

As they emerged it began to rain with such heavy drops that Pearl could almost count them as they sent the leaves bobbing. The horses along the track flinched; the congregation hesitated at the porch. The drops became a cascade and then a grey blur turning to white as a shower swept across the fields and embraced the churchyard like so many cavorting spirits. The hail bounced on flat gravestones, a mocking jig of life. One man ran to his horse, his jerkin pulled over his head, as it slewed in terror away from the flint wall where the white ice danced. Then, the shower swept on into the valley and across the river, picking at its surface with invisible fingers, before ebbing up towards the forbidding Hall at the hill's crest.

The mourners moved slowly out from the darkened porch, their feet crunching on the fast-melting whiteness, as though they walked on pages discarded by some celestial scribe. And ahead of them, the coffin, which swayed on the shoulders of those who bore it in some dance of death where none could hear the music. The place to which they came was a dark rectangle with a pile of turned earth. Behind it was a holly tree and beyond that the forge, a red glow from whose fire could be seen through the sharp-edged leaves.

Two planks of wood were placed across the grave and beside that two lengths of rope. Pearl stood to the rear, for though joined by blood she was not a part of this ceremony. The rough coffin was placed on the planks by men who bent together over black soil and, as they straightened, took the strain on the ropes as others slid the wood away. Then, in a series of graceless spasms, they lowered the coffin unevenly into the grave. When at last the ropes became slack they were pulled up, rattling on the casket as though the sleet had begun again. The minister stepped forward, almost plunging after the dead as he lost his footing in the wet soil. He raised his hand and spoke of the dust from which we come and the dust to which we shall return. A flash of sunlight came to mock them. He lowered his hand and stepped aside to allow others to bend to the earth and send a handful of mud and stones onto the coffin. A hollow sound came from the open wound. Then, silence again, before they turned, almost as one, to the iron gate which squealed when it was opened and squealed when it was closed as each passed through.

Her cousin was once more at her side, seizing a cold hand and staring again into her eyes, perhaps for signs of her absent mother.

'Thou shalt come home with me, my dear. Colney Hall is empty now and there is nothing there for thee. And I have lost one dear to me this day.'

'Shall I not look inside? I had so fixed my mind on that place that I shall scarcely know what to do. It has been left to me and I must take possession of what is mine.'

'Well, let us do so. But first to the farm, for a bite to eat. Oh, Pearl, what a homecoming is here and how I wish thy mother were with us. Thou art not alone, my dear. By no means. Thou hast a home as long as I shall live.'

A young man sat on the low wall, swinging his feet, his broad face smiling vacantly. 'Come and go, come and go,' he chanted, of those who passed in and out the gate and one who passed in never to pass out again.

No one paid attention to him, except Pearl, who had never seen such a face before and who could not but be struck by his features as by a smile so inappropriate to the day. She smiled back.

'Hester come and go,' he called.

Pearl started, as did her cousin. 'He will have heard us talking, my dear. There's no harm in Charley, none that I have found. Don't be disturbed.'

Nor was Pearl disturbed. To hear her mother's name when she was so distant was a curious consolation.

The group of mourners walked back towards the farm she had passed and which lay beyond a sheltering wall. There were those who touched her hand in greeting but mostly they walked in silence.

'And how didst thou find London, Pearl? And how is William?'

'He is well. He was kindness itself to me.'

'Ay, and he can be when he does not have a tankard in his hands and a pipe in his mouth.'

'He introduced me to many there.'

'And so thou art acquainted with the Swan and its menagerie.'

'Menagerie, indeed! Thou know them, then.'

'That I do. I went with him some years since, thinking he lacked a woman's company having lost his own dear wife, as I lost my husband. The experience quite cured me of any desire to return. They all seemed to me quite mad. But, then, how could they be other in such a place which hath neither religion nor sense?'

'He was nothing but kindness and he showed me the city as I should never have known it otherwise.'

'Indeed,' she replied, nodding her head. 'I am sure that is so, for he knows London well. It is a London, though, whose river flows with ale, and but that his income – and therefore my comfort, since I live with him – depends upon the trade he follows, I should stamp my feet and insist he stay in Norfolk. Heaven knows there is ale aplenty here and companions, no doubt, as strange as any found in London's streets.'

But though her words said one thing her tone said another and Pearl contented herself with a smile and a shake of the head, a smile which only faltered a little as a figure ran beside her, his feet seemingly dislocated from his legs, shouting in a thick and toneless voice, 'Hester. Hester. Come and go.'

A room had been cleared for the funeral feast and a fire lit in the grate, despite the season, but it dispersed neither the cold nor the sadness of those who entered. None removed their shawls or jackets and all were drawn towards the fireplace where thick branches crackled and exploded in showers of sparks.

Funeral feasts have ever been the strangest of gatherings. The tears of the churchyard give way to laughter and joke. None come but that have foreboding as to how to conduct themselves in the face of death. Yet there are few, even among the grieving family, who do not grasp one another's hands with a smile and within the hour the room is full of talk and laughter. And so it was now, though the occasion was more subdued than many such. Nonetheless, they fell upon the food as though to blot out all thought of death. Roast fowl and thick dripping are perhaps an unsubtle antidote but they were consumed with a relish which suggested that few now gave a thought to the open grave into which they had stared.

And in the van of the assault was Charley, for this was a society which had not learned, or so it seemed, to treat any such of their own with fear or suspicion or dread. Charley was born in Colney. He was of Colney. And though strangeness was sometimes taken for sign of witchcraft or the mark of the devil, those who worked, as they did, on the land, and noted the accidents of birth among their animals, acknowledged without difficulty the random pain which left a mother's arm closing around a damaged child. He was neat in his appearance and even somewhat formal in his manner, as though he were old before his time. His face seemed smoothed flat, yet a smile was constantly on his lips.

On the table was bread – home-baked – along with cheese and cake and fruit. The fowl had been carved, its heavy dark meat cascading in slices from its side. Hard-boiled eggs, white with hidden blue, lay in a dish; pewter platters held radishes and onions. In a corner, on two intersecting pieces of wood, was a barrel which fitted neatly into the X so formed. It contained a cool, rough cider. Within half an hour the room began to fill with an animated chatter and Pearl quickly found herself the centre of attention. The coldness which she thought

93

she had detected in their manner now dissolved in that strange hospitality in which death is so quickly swallowed up by life and the grave driven out of language, if not of mind.

There were some who remembered her mother and questioned her about the land from which she came. Even at that time it had begun to perform something of the function it was to serve in later centuries. To these people, it was a place of promise and danger. It was a province of the mind, the grit which the imagination would turn to pearl and she, by name and fact, its embodiment. So she was asked not only of the animals and plants, whose simple description brought gasps of astonishment, but of the houses and churches as though some other geometry might determine their construction.

At first she spoke shyly, being among strangers. But, as she spoke, so all the feelings of regret and nostalgia, which until then had been subsumed in her own wonder at the world she had discovered, swept over her. And though no tears came to her eyes, yet she described her native Boston and its surrounding territory as few but a poet would have done. And she spoke of the lives of the Indians with a simplicity and truth which few travellers would have emulated, in truth in terms which few of her fellow Bostonians would have assayed.

Then, as though she had been recalled from a reverie, she realised that all eyes were upon her. She blushed and the blush permitted her listeners to smile and turn away or touch her hand with kindness.

It was only as the first of the villagers began to leave that she gave thought to her situation. She was alone and come to claim an inheritance in a place which, for all the friendly faces, was still strange to her. One relative, who was to have guided her, was here dead upon her arrival, nor, she thought suddenly, had she asked how or why, so taken was she with the unfamiliarity of her situation. And yet, of course, she had. 'Mortality.' The word echoed for a second in her mind. Like many a traveller who reaches her destination she felt both tired and confused.

'Come home to Caistor with me,' her cousin said, gripping her by the arm. 'Colney Hall can be no place for thee. The journey will take us no more than an hour or two.'

But it was precisely then that Pearl realised she could travel no further. A bone-deep weariness had come over her and though she saw kindness in the eyes of her new-discovered relative, she sought only a nearby bed and sleep.

'Tomorrow, perhaps, for to tell the truth, cousin, I have not the strength to stir a further step than to my home.'

'Not cousin, my dear. Nancy. And a strange home it be. It were partly burned some twenty years ago and since its repair there has been none did live there but a man paid to keep it in good order. I've had it heated with fires these past days, as my brother wished, but it be a cheerless place to spend thy first night among us.'

The truth was, though, that tiredness aside, she felt she must step this short way further and complete her journey. And so Widgery and cousin Nancy together accompanied her on the cart, her sea chest by her side, towards the hall which looked down on this hamlet in its gentle valley.

When, years before, Chillingworth, her mother's suitor, had looked across the river to see a light in the farmhouse window, drawn by powers he knew nothing of, there was a barrier he could not cross, save when the river should be low. But now, and for some ten years since, a rough bridge led from the eastern to the western bank and it was across this that they swayed.

'And how did my relative come to die?' she asked Nancy, feeling the chill of the evening air and pulling her shawl tight about her.

'Thou had best not know. It were a painful end.'

'Even so.'

'He cut his finger while working in the soil.'

'And is that all?'

'It was enough. There is that hereabouts which will enter the blood and enter his, it did. He died of lockjaw.'

'Lockjaw?'

'And is there none of that where thou come from?'

'Perhaps there is, but I know nothing of it.'

'It is as terrible as any death.'

'And is not all death the same?'

'No, my dear. 'Tis not. And thou must be careful thyself, for the poison is all about.'

'And what is it that makes it so particular?'

'The body works against itself. All the muscles pull at once until the head is drawn towards the toes as though that body were a willow bow.'

Pearl shuddered, as well she might, for though at twenty years she felt invulnerable there are still moments when we are made, by fortune, to acknowledge the slender hold we have on life.

'In the end it were a release that he should go to meet his maker. I should have been a poor cousin who wished him linger when life was no more than pain.'

Pearl looked at Nancy and saw that pain may take more forms than one.

The light was fading fast and when they arrived before Colney Hall, gaunt, its windows dark and blank, she insisted that Nancy should leave her there. Though her cousin pressed her to change her mind and spend the night under a friendlier roof, Pearl was determined, agreeing only that on the morrow Widgery should return to carry her to Norwich to spend the day. So tired was she that she declined, too, an offer to accompany her around her new possession.

It was only as she closed the door, and listened to the cart draw away, that she realised she knew nothing of the geography of her new home. Beyond the window the sky was darkening so that the dim world within was matched by that without.

She lit the candles which stood upon a table by the door. A steady drip from the roof into a barrel below the window told her that the rain had returned. And that dripping sound itself seemed to alternate with the heavy ticking of a clock above the mantel, like the slow clip clop of an exhausted horse. So, the house had indeed been kept ready for someone's return, if not her own. She was in a room, she saw in the flickering light, which reflected her own state. It was quite worn out.

Lifting a candle above her, and in doing so sending shadows swooping downwards, she went upon a swift tour of the ground floor. The house was turned around so that it presented its side to the approaching path. A narrow corridor ran from front to back and along this she passed. Behind the room in which the clock still ticked, was another, dank and with a fireless grate. She shuddered, and not only with the cold. Death in a foreign land is death indeed. It seems to unstitch the very fabric of existence. She thought again of him into whose grave she had looked and who was to have been a link between this place and the one she had left.

Trembling still, she opened another door. This one revealed a kitchen. The floor was made of irregular stone slabs and, as she stood a second and looked at the blackened pots which hung in a row along the far wall, she felt the cold being drawn up into her feet and legs, quite as though death were reaching out to her, too. This did not seem a place where contented souls had lived a busy life nor where well-ordered servants had toiled. Whatever money the mysterious Chillingworth had possessed had clearly not been lavished on this house by the agents in whose hands he had placed it during his absence.

The wooden table had been scrubbed clean and bore fresh bread and a pail of milk in preparation for her arrival. But otherwise what she chiefly noticed was a musty smell, like rusted nails or mildewed apples left a winter in the barn. In the grate were ashes piled high and the charcoal stumps of logs.

Then, out of the very corner of her eye, she saw one dark shadow seem to grow, expanding along a dresser which held a row of plates, themselves so many white eyes in the gloom. This time a cry did escape her lips, to be answered by an echoing sound like a soul in torment. For a moment she could neither move nor speak. Then the shadow began to shrink again until, with a graceful flowing movement, it fell to the floor with a rasping sound which transformed Pearl's terror into relief as a heavy black cat turned a figure of eight around her ankles. She dropped gratefully to her knees, and, setting the candle on the floor, gathered the warm creature in her arms, pressing its fur against her face. It purred its pleasure. So, there was life here, after all, she thought, the simple presence of the animal transforming the threatening house into a home.

Once again, tiredness replaced excitement and fear and she opened her arms to let the cat return to the floor. Whether in playfulness or surprise, however, it reached out a paw, stretched its claws wide and laid a red ribbon on her face. It was no more than the slightest cut but the blood shone brightly in the candlelight as she retreated along the corridor to the stairs which led to the bedrooms and the sleep which she desired.

As she walked up the stairs to the upper rooms her hand trailed along the waxy wood of the bannister. Each step creaked and sang with its own note while the cat flowed beside her, a moving shadow. On the narrow landing the smell of dampness was even stronger. It was tangible, like a cold November mist.

Though she held a candle in her hand, the sky was not yet fully dark and an open door and its windows beyond offered a rectangle of grey light. She walked towards it, feeling tiredness and despair in equal portions. Was it for this that she had forsaken her home? Indeed, question her now and she could have offered no answer. In truth, a tear began to trace its way down her cheek, pausing only when it encountered the line of blood on her face.

A pleasant surprise awaited her, for after the decay of the house at large, and the marks where fire had blistered and burned the wood, here was a room which was both neat and comfortable. It had all the small adornments and objects of a woman of gentle sensibility. A miniature had been placed beside the bed, itself spread with a quilt whose many colours shone through even in the uncertain light of the dusk and the flickering yellow glow of the candle. A hoop of needlepoint lay abandoned on the dresser, the needle still pinned in it. She held the candle above it and could make out the outline of a design which seemed to show a man and woman divided by a red and orange flame. In one corner was the steeple of a church. It had perhaps been but recently abandoned. Neither figure yet had a face, though their clothes were picked out with great skill, the man in black, the woman in white. So this was her cousin's work! It suggested a ready skill and fanciful disposition.

Pearl drew a heavy brown curtain across the window and then turned back the counterpane. With a faint rustle the cat leapt past her onto the bed. For a few seconds longer Pearl stared at this scene of domesticity in the heart of a house whose chief characteristic was darkness. Then, scooping the cat to the floor, she undressed slowly, laying her clothes over a plain chair. She snuffed the candle and was about to climb beneath the sheets, surprisingly clean and crisp, when she glanced towards the window. It occurred to her that she no longer knew where she was. Turning about the house she had lost her sense of direction. Accordingly she moved forwards carefully, her feet cold on the smooth wood floor. She pulled the heavy curtains aside and peered through the lace covering behind. She looked out over the tangled garden, through which she had entered, and the track beyond. The light was all but gone. She tried to feel some connection to this place, a place which her mother had known, though she spoke little about it, a place which she seemed to dread. Then, as she stared at this unfamiliar scene, she thought she made out a figure staring back at her from the edge of the trees which fringed the track. It was a man, dressed in black clothing. He took a step or two, then turned. Pearl could make out nothing of his features but it seemed to her that he was distorted in some manner. Then he was gone and, as she fell upon her bed, it was no longer clear what might be a dream and what reality.

Chapter Four

A new day is a new life. If one had ended darkly, the next opened with the sky a cerulean blue and Pearl a focus of pure energy. The vision of the night before was no more than a smudge on her mind. Indeed, though she had woken with a start, as though disturbed by some night-time phantom, all memory had faded.

The house, so dark a few hours since, now shone with a golden light which spilled through the windows and was diffused by the dust into a gentle glow. Certainly the Hall was dirty but it was the dirt of neglect. There was a neatness and simplicity which appealed to her. Drawing ice-cold water from the black depths of the well, she set the pail on the flagstones of the kitchen and set about the business of lighting a fire in the broad grate.

Starting with the kitchen, she scrubbed and brushed and dusted. The pans and ladles and spoons were plunged in boiling water and replaced in the drawer, their dull sheen buffed to brightness. She worked along the inner corridor, having stripped back the curtains to allow light to come where it had not penetrated for many a year. She worked with no thought in her mind, exulting, indeed, in a labour which drove all thoughts away. Here was action with a purpose; here an objective easily realised. At mid-morning she paused to make herself a cup of camomile and watched out of the kitchen window as a kingfisher flashed blue above the river before splashing twice into the water, smashing the mirror of its surface. Steam from the boiling water on the fire made it necessary for her to squeak a swathe of clear glass with the flat of her palm, a bright silver rainbow bordered by a beaded mist. And still her mind was blank, as that same steam made her eyes mist like the windows and as she looked out on an unfamiliar scene yet one which could have been her native New England.

The morning wore on. She moved into the front room and tugged at the yellow lace of the curtain, pulling it sharply back. Made brittle by time, it tore from its horizontal pole in a series of silent explosions of dust. Sighing, she pulled again. These were curtains which had served their time. They fell slowly, with no more substance than a dying butterfly.

With the curtains down, the room was filled with a bright light which almost seemed to make it recoil. This was a room long since dedicated to gloom. The chairs were pulled together and covered with a funeral shroud. No decoration adorned the stained walls. A lifetime of flickering candles had left dark haloes on the ceiling. This was a place which wished to keep its secrets, but Pearl now swept them all away. She wished no secrets, save her own. The light was to flood every crevice. All was to be made known; everything was to be revealed.

By lunchtime the room was transformed. One chair, too grim for her taste and worn smooth by the weight of a person who must have sat in the gloom for many a year, she dragged backwards down the corridor and through the kitchen. It stood, now, naked, beyond the kitchen door where a large crow soon fluttered blackly down. It lifted its feet one by one, testing this new offering of nature. The other chair remained stranded in a room whose floor gently steamed with lye.

The cat stood in the doorway, a front paw raised gingerly, as though unsure that the ground would any more support its weight. Its black muzzle was flecked with white from a saucer of milk which Pearl had placed on the freshly polished kitchen tiles. As her new mistress knelt on a wad of cloth and scrubbed, slowly edging backwards, so the cat watched disinterestedly until the moment she regained her feet and dropped the wet rag into a bowl. 'Finished,' she exulted. At which the cat touched the floor once with her paw, flinched, and turned around, tail in the air, retreating with dignity down a corridor now so bright with spring sun that a dark shadow strode beside her on the painted wall.

Pearl sat a moment, surveying her accomplishment and something more. For in a cupboard, hidden from sight by a roll of cloth, she had found strange objects which meant little to her. There was a glass retort, stained yellow at its bottom with a kind of crystal glaze, some smaller vessels, also streaked with colour, and a crucible, whose scooped interior was encrusted with black and indigo. Had she but known it, she had come upon the very implements of Chillingworth's experiments. When the house had been raided, and partly burned, in that time of turmoil when king and parliament were in contention, the equipment with which he had laboured was for the most part smashed. To the superstitious eye it was proof of witchcraft and hence to be destroyed. Some few objects, though, were stored away and the frenzy of the night quite passed them by. Placed on a newly scrubbed table, they seemed less sinister implements, more simple curiosities.

It was past noon now and some of the sudden energy began to leave Pearl. She was beginning to feel the need for food when a sharp knock rang out. Through the window she could see a cart. Widgery sat and watched as the horse which drew it lowered its head to the wayside grass and last year's blackened apples which had fallen there. Cousin Nancy approached the door.

After a brief meal of bread and cheese Pearl rode beside her cousin. If her sudden attack of cleanliness had been a ceremony to mark her rebirth, then this was another, for they rode towards Norwich, which her mother had spoken of with affection and some awe. And so she might. Norwich was a city with a weight of history far greater than Boston's. There were many in Boston who had seen the beginning of their settlement in New England; and though the Indians reached toward more distant times, they took pleasure in wiping clean their tracks. They raised no churches to the skies, constructed no castles, left no marks to signify their passing. Norwich built itself on time, quite as though that were a solid foundation, each generation accepting a gift from those who went before.

'And what shalt thou do, Pearl, now that thou art alone?'

'I do not know, cousin. I had not begun to think.'

'Thou art welcome to abide with us.'

Pearl shook her head.

'If it be my brother who bothers thee, he grows on one like ivy.'

'Indeed, cousin, I had no such thought. It is . . . I must make my life, I think. There is a lawyer here who I must see who will explain the details of my inheritance. Then I shall begin to plan. For the moment I am content to see all and know all I can.'

'Nonetheless, spend a short time with us.'

'It would be a pleasure. But what should I do?'

'Do, child, do? Why, thou should do nothing, unless it pleased thee to take a hot cup of something of an afternoon or stroll in the fields with me when we should need a little air. Do? Thou shalt do nothing.'

'But I am used to earning my living. I paint a little and my mother and I sew. Her talents are far greater than mine but even I can make some pieces which will sell.'

'Sell? Do thou and Hester sell thy wares?'

'Why, yes. How else should we have lived who had no support?'

'Thou had no support?' Then, flustered, as though recalling a forbidden truth, 'I had thought . . .'

'There is a sum left as an inheritance by him who called himself my mother's husband, but she will not draw upon it. I have no such scruple or else I should not be here. And when shall we see this city of which I have heard so much?'

Even her cousin, not the most sensitive of creatures, recognising that no further questioning along that path would lead to anything, turned back in her seat and pointed ahead to a slight rise in the land.

'In a moment or two. Be patient a little while longer.'

Almost without her noticing, other carts had joined theirs, as had men and women on foot. There, a man carried a cage with chickens fluffing through its bars, there a woman with a basket of loaves swayed heavily from side to side as though the rhythm alone might carry her along. Then the road narrowed and all were required to pass a deep hole in the track where the earth had fallen away.

'What might that be, cousin?'

'Ah,' she replied, with a mysterious shake of the head, 'that be the entry to hell.'

'To hell? The ministers in Boston said as much of the forest where I played. It seemed no hell to me.'

'That may well be but this one was opened up by man. It is said that, many centuries since, men worked underground and that it were possible to walk hither and yon through tunnels great and small. They dug for chalk, the chalk which now holds together the buildings thou wilt see. And when they ceased they left behind great spaces for those same buildings to fall into. Such is man's intelligence. From time to time, after rain, the earth takes it into its mind to fill those spaces and then it is greatly worth thy while not to be standing on that spot or thou may meet Beelzebub before thy time.'

The horse skittered somewhat as it passed the edge but, after some hundred paces more, the land began to drop away, not into a cavern but a valley's sloping side, and across the fields, rising into the pale blue sky, she saw the white arrow of the cathedral spire tight on the bow of the earth and ready to be loosed into the heavens.

'Norwich,' said Nancy, who at times had a talent for the redundant observation.

'Indeed, cousin, I had thought as much,' replied Pearl, and then regretted it, but irony is a tongue not spoken by all and no offence had been taken.

They swayed and jostled down the hill and then turned towards the great wall which surrounded the inner city, passing through an arched gateway which took them along a street called St Giles. The street seemed to Pearl surprisingly clean but then here lived many who had prospered on wool – merchants, members of the guilds – and money can buy much, including cleanliness. Indeed, it was only a minute more before the Guild Hall, faced with flint, came into view, as the land dipped towards the market place, itself as much a turmoil of man and beast as any she had seen in London. Each seller had an allotted space where vegetables were piled and buyers and sellers mixed together.

'Shall we not stop, cousin?'

'Later,' she replied, waving a hand vaguely towards a tangle of horses, handcarts and men with sacks and boxes, the whole a swirl of colour and movement. 'The cathedral, my dear. The jewel of the city.'

They continued past Blackfriars, itself more imposing than any building Pearl had seen in Boston, tall, grey and massive in the morning light, and then on, down Elm Hill, cobbled, stately, with more of the city's wealth on display in houses whose leaded windows concealed men of business and power.

'Hester loved this place, my dear,' said her cousin, as they pulled past an inn which was at the meeting point of two roads, and the cathedral came into view again.

Those who built the great cathedrals did so out of a strange combination of humility and pride. They humbled themselves before God, devoting themselves to His worship, but did so by reaching up towards the sky. Each outdid the other. Every added foot brought them closer to God but closer, too, to the vanity which every architect and artist has in equal measure with those who urge them work. The fluted beauty and flying elegance of limestone buttress and gracious column were compacted of civic pride, of ambition and arrogance as well as of pious fear. For there are few quite so arrogant as not to fear the consequences of their action when some final accounting should be made. The wonder is that high art can be born of low motive. Yet there was humility here, the skills of men who revered their duty, who planted trees whose fruit would be gathered by others. The Church was power and its cathedrals so many exclamation marks written in the sky. To Cromwell, though, they had been tainted places of idolatry and, as Pearl looked up in wonder, it was no more than a handful of years since metalled heels had struck sparks in its cool interior and put to the sword the images of those who had died once already and now once more were violated by hilt and blade. The nave sang with steel, the transept with brittle laughter and contempt.

When Pearl pushed open the great west door, however, she felt almost driven to her knees by the size and astonished by a splash of colour spread before her on the ground as the early afternoon light was filtered through such fragments of stained glass as the Puritans had spared. Yellow and green and blue flowed before her like spring flowers on a river. Yet it would be untrue to suggest that this was all she felt. For there was one part of Pearl's mind which made her look down the receding central aisle and off into the shadows in search of a form not made of stone. Was this not the destination of John Standish, and had they not promised to meet again, and were they to do so would it not be here? Thought piled on thought and it was as well her cousin knew nothing of this as she gripped her wrist and guided her through a gloom lit only poorly by candles and the slanting light of the windows high above.

'The ceiling, my dear. I have always loved the ceiling.'

Pearl looked up and her heart did indeed respond to the sheer wonder of what man can do. The fluted fans had both a grandeur and a delicacy, like the base of some vast trees curving outwards, a fossilised forest.

'Oh, indeed.'

'Even William has stood here some ten minutes and more. Wilt thou kneel with me a while?'

'In a moment. Let me look a little further. Thou art used to this place. To me it is a wonder.'

Her cousin pressed her hand in answer and joined some dozen others kneeling in the murmuring gloom.

Pearl, who had formerly been stirred only by the beauty of the forest, for the first time found herself in awe of the works of man. If those who had raised this building had done so in order to humble those who walked within, they had performed their business well. Those who strolled around the grey stone floors were dwarfed by its size, their voices lowered in respect. But even then there were those drawn to it not only out of conviction but as a place of quietness, of beauty and sometimes also of assignation. A flash of light and the rattle of a scabbard drew her eye to a soldier who bent towards a young woman in the dark at the base of a rising column. If it was love which brought them here it was not love of God alone.

She slowly walked the length of the outer aisle looking at the stone figures of noblemen and prelates resting for ever, their calcined hands clutched together, their stone chests pressed down by stone bibles. Under her feet were the graves of many, recalled in chiselled letters, while in an alcove was an effigy in which the face was half skeleton, a reminder of death beneath the skin. The Church, it seemed, was ever intent to remind of mortality, as though it wished to rush humankind towards the grave. She shivered in the cool, half drawn to these images, half repelled. Then, in a small side chapel, she saw the warm glow of a painting in the wavering light of a ragged line of candles placed there by worshippers. She entered through a small wooden door. The walls were subtly coloured, a remnant of a brighter church where worship of God had called for blue and orange and green to be dusted in pastel shades throughout its length. Most had faded a hundred years since, but here was a reminder of another form of piety in which it was felt no crime to bring within the building the colours of the natural world. Here was an echo of another time and another kind of truth when Christianity still compromised with other, perhaps deeper, faiths born out of the seasons, of trees and plants and animals, a world in which resurrection was a yearly fact and not a distant narrative, faiths which also knew of sacrifice and births which seemed engendered only by the wind and a sweetening of the air.

The painting, illuminated by the nervous flames of candles, was of a mother and child. Its glow, however, came not from reflection but from deep within. The colours seemed as fresh as ever they had been and the gentle smile on the face of the Virgin was so serene that it drew the eye away from the Child, the very object of her veneration.

Pearl moved to the wooden rail before a low altar, a rail made smooth by centuries of hands, and stared into the face. Something within her seemed to move. This was surely a face she knew. There were no likenesses of her mother, no portraits hanging in great halls, no remembrances of that familiar form, yet here, before her, stood the woman into whose face she had looked all her life. The same eyes, same hair, same soft look of love, same solitary pride of mother-hood. Whether it was the light, which dimmed and brightened with invisible draughts of air, or simply her own need which looked for comfort, this appeared to Pearl a perfect rendering of the mother she had left behind. Almost without realising it, she slowly knelt on the cold stone, itself worn into a soft depression by others who had bent the knee before the simple beauty of the portrait, who knows, perhaps themselves seeing there the image of another that they loved as though this were some universal picture of a mother's care.

It was thus that she was discovered by Standish. He stood, prayer book in hand, and watched this scene of apparent piety, his eyes moving from woman to painting and back; but, whatever it was that held him, he stood in his black robe, like an elm tree seared by lightning and hollowed out by time.

How long each stayed thus neither could have sworn, but eventually Pearl rose slowly to her feet, tears in her eyes, and turned to resume her walk; and though he had watched her rise, nonetheless he gave the same start as she, as they were woken from their separate reveries.

'Why, Reverend Standish, you shocked me.'

'And you me. I had not thought we should meet so soon.'

'Fate, perhaps.'

'God's will, I think.'

'And then again,' she said, recovering something of her poise, 'it was likely, was it not, that I should come to see so great a monument as soon as I might.'

'And how are things with you, Mistress Prynne?'

'Something strange.'

'Even so?'

'Even so. Fate, or God's will if you prefer, seems to have prepared a cold welcome. There was a deal of black awaiting me at Colney. A colour I see is your preference, too.'

He glanced at his robes and returned her smile. 'Indeed, sombre is the colour of my calling. But what blackness was this?'

'The uncle who was to greet me when I arrived in Colney died even while we were at sea.'

'What will you do? Return?'

'Return? Why should I do such? There is a roof above my head while I have room enough and more, since I am at present quite alone in a building large enough for ten. Nor do I lack for friends. My cousin, indeed, is with me even now and is doubtless searching for me as we speak.'

'And shall our paths continue to cross?' he asked, with a sudden urgency impelled, perhaps, by the news that she was not alone.

It was an urgency she could not but have noted, and, indeed, her heart seemed to race within her, yet when she spoke it was with cool assurance. 'How could it be otherwise? There can be no such place as this in England.'

Certainly it seemed that at this moment John Standish could think of no other place in England that could be as beautiful as this and no other place he would rather be. 'Indeed, it . . .' Words seemed to have become sudden strangers. 'There is not.'

'Pearl, I thought I had lost thee.' Nancy busied herself

towards them. 'I am quite frozen to the bone.' She seemed not to notice the man who stood beside her cousin. 'Shall we go or is there more that thou wouldst see?'

Pearl had seen all that she would wish except that, had she the power, she might also have wished her cousin away.

'This is the Reverend Standish, cousin,' said Pearl, stepping away from the man who was no more than half an arm's length from her. 'We met on the ship from London.'

'Didst thou so.' She bobbed her head, but scarcely seemed to notice him, which was perhaps as well since he scarcely looked at her, unable, as it seemed, to look anywhere but at Pearl.

They might have continued thus for some time were it not for the fact that a group of children from the cathedral's school burst suddenly around them like a cloud of tumbling butterflies, dutifully silent but unruly nonetheless and pursued by a tutor who lacked the net of a butterfly catcher but swooped from side to side to gather up an errant form or two. Nor did Standish net his butterfly on this first visit. But, as its night-time sister will flutter more than once around the flame so may a cabbage white, a painted lady or a nymphalid, approach again if you but wait awhile.

The following day, Pearl sought out her lawyer in the narrow streets below the castle walls. She carried within her cloak the letter of authority which would endorse her ownership of Colney Hall and confirm her in her rights. There were deeds to be secured, as there were monies to be disclosed and conveyed. But first a lawyer by the name of Simple must be found. Nor was this a simple exercise, for though she quickly found his offices in Opie Street the man himself was more difficult to locate. A clerk in the outer office, perched on a high stool and blinking like an owl in the sudden light from the door, appeared not to understand her enquiry. Indeed, he seemed so surprised that anyone should venture within that she supposed herself the first visitor to these chambers in many a month. He had dark brown hair, pressed down on a forehead whose pale colour was doubtless a consequence of the gloom which surrounded him. His clothes were dark, as though he were in mourning for his life and, as it seemed to Pearl, this might be an apt place for the dead to lie for there was nothing to disturb them beyond the scratching of a quill and the ticking of a clock.

Her papers evidently meant nothing to the clerk. He hardly seemed to see them, glancing nervously around as though looking for some escape. At last Pearl tired of the game and rapped her knuckles on his desk in annoyance. She who had never shown undue concern for authority was hardly likely to be defeated by such as he. He jumped and a trail of black ink spilled across the document before him. He looked appalled, as well he might who had spent many hours copying in a tidy hand the words of tidy men who filed experience away from the air, having reduced every human transaction to copper-plate and every human desire to memoranda and deposition.

He nodded to himself, to Pearl, and, so it appeared, to the four corners of the dark room, before slipping silently to his feet. Behind him was a door which seemed so solid that it might have been designed to resist the assault of barbarians.

'You will not wish to see him.'

'But I do.'

'You may think so.'

'I do so.'

'I have spoken and speaking plainly does no good. Shall I knock?'

'And it please you.'

'Oh, it do not please me. Nor you neither. But you will have nothing of that, I see. My advice, being free, carries no value. Very good. See what paying may accomplish.'

He knocked, but so gently that Pearl, who stood impatiently behind him, scarcely heard a sound. He bowed towards the wood, as a Catholic towards the confessional grille, and, hearing something she could not, turned the ornate brass handle and opened the door into a gloom deeper than that in which they stood.

'Well?' said a voice, querulous and high-pitched. 'Well?'

That the first words of Lawyer Simple should have been a repeated question proved an apt introduction to a man who had apparently foresworn direct statement in favour of an everlasting interrogative. He sat behind a desk half hidden in the shadows, his face framed by two piles of papers stacked so high it seemed they must fall at any moment. At first Pearl could hardly make him out but, as her eyes accustomed themselves to the light, she saw a man whose sharp nose and sudden movements of the head resembled those of a bird. His eyes were set deep and seemed to stare out at her from two pits. If she had thought his clerk pale, this lawyer, who leaned forwards, his head to one side, was as white as the underside of a fish. But, fish or fowl, man or spectre, he held the key to her fortune and must needs be faced.

'What have we here?'

'A Mistress Prynne, if you please.'

'Please? Please? And why should it please me who have never set eyes on such a personage before and who am not to be disturbed until noon?'

'Mistress Prynne would have business with you, or so she says, though I know nothing of it, being left to copy documents and no more these twenty years. As to it not being noon . . .'

'And what kind of business might such a personage have within this office, if you please?'

Pearl, who objected to being spoken of as though she were not there, decided to speak on her own behalf.

'I have been left some property.'

'Property? Left? And am I supposed to know anything of this? Hawkins? Am I?'

'And if you were, what then? But were you inclined to listen, as you are not, experience having taught me otherwise, enlightenment might perhaps follow.'

At this the lawyer shook a fist at his clerk who responded with a scowl which was half crazed smile and half grimace.

Pearl watched this performance with some bewilderment but, being a young woman of some determination, would not be delayed at the very threshold of her future. Accordingly, she entered and settled herself, uninvited, in a leather chair before the desk on whose other side Lawyer Simple sat much as a cat will rest contentedly before a mouse hole.

'Sitting down, are we?' he observed, quite as though otherwise her actions might have been misunderstood.

'My name is Prynne and I am here on the subject of my inheritance, about which I believe you have been informed by lawyers Jackson and Rey of Boston.'

'Jackson and Rey?'

'Those are the names, sir. Of Boston.'

'Boston in, ah . . .'

'Not Lincolnshire, I'd wager,' smiled the clerk, who perhaps had seen the correspondence or heard in Pearl's accent the trace of a place further abroad than the next county.

'So. And what have I to do with you, mistress, other than to furnish you with a place to rest yourself in my office, as it seems?'

'I have letters and instructions which I would have you read and act upon.'

'Have you? Well, mistress, I would beg you sit had you not already taken the liberty of doing such. Where are your letters?'

Pearl reached within a bag, the very one, as it happens, which her mother had carried two and twenty years before as she hurried towards Yarmouth on a cold November night. She placed two documents, one sealed with red wax, on the table in front of him, though there was little enough room between the twin mountains of paper. He looked at her doubtfully.

'These are they?'

'In each particular.'

'In each particular?' He turned the words over in his mouth, apparently pleased with the taste. He looked across at his clerk, who nodded towards him. After this dumb show he reached forward and took a letter between thumb and finger, as though uncertain as to its cleanliness.

'You will find it is addressed in your name and to these offices in this street.'

He looked at her for a second, as though considering whether the time had now come to summon an officer of the law. 'Indeed?'

'It but requires action.'

'There is little of that here,' commented the clerk, half to himself.

'If it is action you require there is copying to be done, is there not? There are documents to be read, I think,' hissed his employer.

'I may go, then?' replied the clerk.

'Go?' echoed Lawyer Simple, before returning to his work, reading slowly through spectacles which gradually slipped further down his nose.

'Ah. So you are Mistress Pynne?'

Pearl let out a snort of exasperation. 'Indeed. But I was introduced as such ten minutes ago.'

'But now it is verified, is it not? I am required, it seems, to surrender certain deeds and to place in your hands certain funds which are described here within. Is it not so?'

'It is,' replied Pearl, tiring of so many interrogatives in a row.

'And assuredly I should do so had I such to hand, would you not say?'

'I am beginning to doubt.'

'Doubt is the beginning and end of law. It is its very foundation, its lifeblood, its reason for being. Let me never hear a word against doubt. The definite is the enemy of law since that which is certain can never be the cause of dispute and without dispute is no rhetoric and rhetoric is the noblest gift of man, that which raises us above the animals of the field. Are we dumb creatures?'

Not, it was evident to Pearl, in his case. She made no reply, rightly judging that none was required of her, but instead endeavoured to return the conversation, if such it was, to the subject in hand. 'Do you not have the deeds and the . . .' she hesitated, '. . . funds to hand?'

'Have I said such?' he asked in astonishment. 'Did you hear

me make such an incautious admission?'

'You do not have them?' Pearl, it seemed, had fallen into his habit of speech.

'Certainly if I had I should be obliged to deliver them, should I not?'

'You should, indeed,' observed the clerk from the safety of the doorway, receiving a Gorgon stare from his employer for his pains.

'May we complete our business, sir? I have but one life and can ill afford to squander it in question and answer.'

'Can you not?'

Pearl let out a cry of exasperation and was about to rap her knuckles on the desk, as she had done on another, when Lawyer Simple himself seemed to tire of his game.

'Fetch the papers, will you?' he asked his clerk, who leaned casually against the door jamb, his legs stuck out like the wayward limbs of a leaning tree.

'Am I a dog, then, now?'

'I hardly know. Do me the pleasure of sniffing them out nonetheless would you kindly?'

The clerk collected his limbs together and with a last look back over his shoulder and a kind of sardonic smile on his lips, walked with studious nonchalance into the outer office.

Lawyer Simple plaited his fingers together and leaned back in his seat. He showed no sign of further awareness of Pearl, who felt inclined to turn mimic and plunge into her own privacy, but hers was not a spirit to be thus easily subdued.

'You seem little troubled with clients,' she observed, peering through the gloom at a man who himself seemed intent on inspecting the ceiling.

At first he affected not to hear and then with a sudden start looked down. 'I? Clients?'

'Indeed.'

The very thought seemed to trouble him, though the piles of papers on his desk suggested that there were those aplenty who trusted him with their affairs. 'I am, I think, kept busy enough, do you not think?' he replied, indicating the papers.

'It seems to me, sir, that you must be exceeding thorough, or is it that paper, like wine, matures with delay?'

'Delay? What can you know of delay? Delay is but another word for consideration, for a turning over in the mind, for a wish to pursue truth wherever she may choose to hide. I am a seeker after trifles, for who may know but that trifles may contain the essence of what I seek. The law is not to be hurried, I think.'

'Not here, certainly, it would seem, but the fact is that I merely come to claim what is mine.'

'Fact? Claim? Mine? These are familiar words, to be sure, and I have certainly heard them many a time both here and in the court, but this is a profession in which we know those for the snares they be. What is a fact?' He settled back, as though to begin a lecture and begin a lecture he did. 'A fact is a field of war, our Agincourt. It is where we do battle. We carry the favours of our clients on this field. Words are our swords and our shields, are they not?'

'It is a fact, sir,' said Pearl impatiently, 'that I came hither only to receive some documents which are mine by right. It is a fact that I have not received them. It is a fact that I shall die of fatigue if I am not satisfied soon.'

'Right? There is another word, I think, that could detain us for many an hour. What are rights to some are presumptions to another and downright theft to still others, are they not?'

'May I ask your clerk if he has found the documents?'

'You may ask what you will. But in my experience questions directed to that source are likely to go unanswered. Is that not so?'

The clerk ignored him and instead addressed himself to Pearl. 'He has them,' he said, nodding casually at his employer. 'He always had them. He had them before he sent me on the errand and he has them still. There was a counter claim.'

'A counter claim?'

'Ah. What is your fact worth now? What are your rights worth? What is this "mine"? Where your claim?'

'A counter claim? Surely this cannot be. Chillingworth was
. . .' She stopped, suddenly unsure how she should describe
her relationship to Chillingworth. 'I have letters. I have
documents.'

'Do I not have letters? Do I not have documents?' he asked,
indicating the piles on his desk.

'And who is this claimant?'

'Ah, that, of course, you may not know.'

'Am I to understand that you will not give me what is
mine?'

'Mine? We have heard that word before, have we not?'

'Pay no heed, mistress. I have seen the papers.'

'Have you indeed?' asked his employer, pinching his face up
so that it seemed he sucked on a dozen lemons.

'And if I did not, who should? We both have our functions.
You put the dust on. I brush it away.'

'Away is where you shall go if there is more of this, do you
not think?'

The clerk resumed his position in the doorway, leaning
back with nonchalance.

'There was a man. And behind him other men. They were
here.'

'I see you have decided that walking the streets and begging
have their attractions, is it not so?'

'There are Guilds here and groups there and those who meet
from time to time. And such may have long memories.'

'Take care!'

'What? No question? Just a statement. I may be a dog in a
kennel but this dog may bark.'

'This dog may howl, and it please me, may it not?'

'There are those with memories. Even twenty years on.'

'What am I to do, sir?' Pearl turned naturally to the slight
figure in the doorway, who seemed to offer her understanding
and information.

'Beware,' snapped Lawyer Simple.

'Still no questions? As you see, mistress, I may not speak
save to say that the papers of your case lie near the top of

yonder pile. Nor do I think you have need to fear.'

'Turned lawyer, are we?'

'Turned, at least. Turned at last.'

'I have a client and must needs prepare. Mistress?'

'And what am I to make of this?'

'You are to make of this that I shall give my time and attention to this matter and that we shall meet again, by which time . . .'

'All will be resolved,' added the clerk.

'By which time I shall have examined the claims with a view to . . .'

'With a view, I think, to reinserting them somewhat lower in the pile before you,' said Pearl, with some acerbity. 'I am not without friends here, I think, and there are other lawyers, I presume, who will secure my rights. My letters, if you please.'

She held out her hand. Lawyer Simple shrugged his shoulders and nodded to his clerk who placed them in Pearl's hands.

'There is no need for this. We are aware of the rights of this case, I believe.'

'We?' echoed the clerk, smiling to himself, as though appreciating a particularly fine piece of wit. 'Rights?'

'We,' repeated Lawyer Simple. 'Should you return in three weeks' time . . .'

'A fortnight,' corrected his clerk.

'At your convenience,' said Lawyer Simple, staring deliberately at his clerk as though daring him to continue their game of verbal tennis. 'I am sure we shall be able to resolve this problem.'

'I know of no problem,' observed Pearl acidly.

'And what might be your relationship with the deceased?'

It was the question she wished to avoid. 'I shall return in two weeks' time.'

Lawyer Simple seemed on the verge of disputing the time once again but caught the eye of his clerk and instead plaited his fingers together and renewed his contemplation of the ceiling. The interview was clearly at an end and Pearl stood up and followed the clerk into the outer office. Even its gloom seemed summer brightness by comparison with the darkness of Simple's domain. She was about to leave when he placed an ink-blackened finger on her arm.

'Have no fear, mistress. You have a friend in me.'

'Am I in need of a friend who come here only to complete a simple piece of business?'

'We are all in need of friends, I think.'

'Besides, why do you offer help?'

'Though this be a lawyer's chambers yet I have retained a sense of justice, as I think. There comes a time . . .' He seemed to abandon the thought and looked around in some confusion.

'Who might be this claimant?'

'Who, indeed! I should not speak.'

'I know you not, sir, but I am in your debt already, as it seems, if you should help me. I will understand if you tell me nothing, but I am alone in a country which is not my own.'

''Tis true,' he replied, looking for a second into the eyes of a young woman whose beauty had brought a sudden brightness into his world. 'The past is powerful here, mistress. Yesterday is not yesterday nor are the dead ever buried for eternity. I know nothing of your story but there were in this city, twenty years or so ago, those who met together, for what cause I know not. They were scattered and some paid a price for what they did commit. But not all were called to speak their truth, to name their lives. There were others who hid what they might be as a squirrel stores food for another day. That day may perhaps have come. I think, perchance, that squirrel's hoard may be your own. Nor am I sure but that yonder lawyer, with the imperious tone and naught but questions, may not be of their number. For certain, there are secrets he would that we should not seek out. It is, perhaps, the only power that I possess. I, too, have claws. Take care, mistress. Such men are not about justice nor do they serve your interests.'

'I thank you.'

'I thank you, mistress, for I see in you what is not in me, a courage which may yet carry the day. The law were never about justice. In certain hands it is as far from justice as we be from Yarmouth, and perhaps a mile or two further.'

Pearl counted her coins. What had seemed wealth when it was merely a part of her inheritance now seemed less so when it might prove her entire resource. There was enough, to be sure, that she should have no immediate need. Indeed, should she live frugally, and why should she do other, there was sufficient to secure her for a year or so to come. But if the Hall were not hers where should she stay and, besides, who were those who conspired against her?

Lawyer Simple's words echoed in her mind. How could it be that there should be others who could lay claim to this place? She and her mother had nothing to do with Chillingworth, to be sure. From the moment that the man she came to know as her father had died that other, who had dedicated himself to his destruction, had himself begun to fade away. It was as though he had accomplished his life's work by taking life from another. Never again did he walk down Boston's streets but kept himself aloof. For Pearl he was no more than a memory, an image to frighten her on a winter's night. He had once been a doctor to their community, visiting homes when illness struck, but, by degrees, he was treated as a kind of pariah. It was believed that ill-luck would accompany his visits. Now he walked only in the forest or by the water's edge, another piece of flotsam among broken spars and torn skeins of fishing net. His body had been found there, gently washed by waves at the water's edge, waves that know nothing of time or of person or of cruelty or love. None had come to his funeral save those driven there by duty. But he had sought redemption beyond the grave, offered restitution for his crimes, or so she had thought, by delivering to the daughter what was owed to the mother.

Now, in Colney, she had perhaps learned otherwise. Had she only sprung a trap set many years before? But who was there who could have waited her arrival, kept a flame alive across the years?

She walked the tangled undergrowth which surrounded Colney Hall. Where once there had been order now all was overgrown, and amongst the wilderness of weeds which sent out tendrils in all directions, turning about rotted gate posts and climbing trees until the living sap was sucked dry, were crimson, purple and black berries shrivelled by winter frosts. Green shoots suggested they would soon swell and fill again with bitter liquid. Each path she followed ended in a mass of brambles which halted her steps. Her skirts were adorned with green and brown burs which tore at her fingers when she tried to free them. The air was full of thistledown. The wilderness was a reflection of her mind, for whatever path her imagination might take she ended in uncertainty and confusion.

At last she ceased trying to find a way through the wild garden and retraced her steps. Sometimes, she told herself, it is necessary to retreat in order to go forward. Not all backward steps are a regression. She found herself at last free of the bindweed and the ivy, blackberry and wild rose, in the paved stableyard. It was years since any horse had sheltered here, years since the sound of hooves had reached a young woman who waited in fear for the return of one she had grown to distrust. Time and wind and rain had done their worst. Three of the four stout doors now hung at an angle, like the shoulders of the old man who had once opened and closed them each day no matter the weather. There was a melancholy to the place, drained as it was of function. Moss had grown between the brickwork and a barrel full of green water leaned forward as though at any moment it would discharge its load across the yard. The stables themselves had long since been cleared of straw and aside from a broken shoe or two there was little to suggest that life had ever been sheltered in the dark stalls.

There was too much here of the past for Pearl, whose eyes were fixed in another direction. The house she could scrub and polish until its memories were brushed and scoured away. The stables had to be left for another day, though there was evidence that others had found another use for this place since the shutters had been nailed shut these many years. There were names carved in the planks which formed the stalls and in one place a heart with initials inscribed. There is no place so dead that life may not be breathed into it by those careless of any history but their own. Was there a lesson here for her, too? She shook her head and lifted her skirts as she walked through the mud and around splintered wood.

She had had enough of enclosure. After a misty start the sun had begun to make its presence felt and she yearned to put some distance between herself and this sepulchre of discarded hopes. Pausing only to change her shoes she set off down the hill to find out the limits of her possessions, Lawyer Simple permitting. She cut across a field towards the river and then followed its bank as best she could, though her path was impeded by nettle and reed which grew in great abundance. A kind of path had been trodden down, no doubt by fishermen, and at one point, indeed, where the river broadened and ran shallow, she made out a shining tunnel made of net and within it the writhing black and silver form of an eel. And as though to prove that what the water concealed so, too, might the land, there was a sudden movement in the grass and into view there slithered a snake. Coming from New England this was no surprise to Pearl, nor did she fear for she had heard that there were no dangerous snakes in this country, or none that New Englanders would count as such. Nonetheless she was enough of a Puritan to feel that there must be some meaning in this encounter for there is no chance in the Puritan world, no, nor much gaiety neither since such signs seldom signified great happiness. The snake stopped its sideways advance and slowly raised its head, black diamond markings glistening in the sun. Pearl stood still, as she had long since been trained to do, and watched the black eyes which seemed to fix upon her own. Then, with a sudden lunge which made her stumble backwards and fall, it plunged forward as a whip will snap at the haunches of a horse, and the next second the rear legs of a frog twitched from its mouth as the doomed creature seemed intent to swim down towards its own extinction. It was a shock to one who had looked for no danger in this place, who had thought herself safe in a country where spiders had no venom for other than their insect victims, where poison ivy was unknown and where you could wade in a stream without snapping turtles destroying peace of mind. She scrambled to her feet and stood still once more as the adder twitched itself about and the thrashing legs disappeared, the frog now no more than a smooth lump passing slowly down the length of the snake, magnifying the black diamonds as it passed. At last it lowered its head and sailed, this way and that, through the tall grass, like a ship tacking through emerald water.

Pearl was too accustomed to nature in all its guises to allow herself to be disturbed by what she had seen, though she walked now with more careful step and looked not just at the summer sky but at her feet. The river ran slowly here, the reeds having all but stopped its flow. Nor could she any longer see down to the bottom, as she had done before. A dead swan, no more than a sodden grey shape, drifted gently, its neck out of sight as though eternally rooting for weed on the river bed. Across the stream, meanwhile, she glimpsed the buildings which she had first seen from the other side as Widgery had conducted her towards her sad welcome at the church. From the road they had seemed forbidding. That was their public face, closed, suspicious. From here she saw their domestic face. Not so, though, Old Hall, where her mother had been born. That was dark and its garden no less overgrown than that of Colney Hall on the hillside above. But the rectory beside it offered another sight. There was washing hung out to dry and a bonfire sent a thin pillar of smoke into the windless sky. Someone was at work with a hoe in that part of the garden given over to vegetables. It was a live house. Further along was her mother's childhood home, the farm now afflicted by death. At the front, where prying eyes might look from a passing cart, curtains were drawn, blank eyes closed to the world. Seen from behind, life continued. A pig rooted amidst the mud at the river's edge while chickens jerked and scratched their way beneath a walnut tree.

The land rose here in a small hillock formed by mud dug from the river's bed where shallows gave way to a broad sweep of water which bent back on itself, once, twice, forming an elongated S. She climbed this incline, treading down nettles, and sat on the top on a small area of rough grass. From here she could see into the farmyard and, to the left, up to the flint tower of St Andrew's. Here, had she but known it, was the very spot where Chillingworth had struggled with the freezing waters one winter afternoon and set a story moving which still moved this summer twenty and more years later. We live in the present, blind to the world that made us, unable to reach back to that moment before our birth which made that birth as sure as the morning sunrise. Now, though, Pearl tried to do no less. More aware than most that she was indeed the result of a tangle of emotions, of hopes and errors, no easier to penetrate than the paths of the wild garden back at Colney Hall, she stared at the scene before her. But stare as she would it revealed no more than it was, a low farmhouse, a tall barn, a scattering of animals in the spring sun.

After a while she reached in her pocket and pulled out a sheet of paper and a piece of broken charcoal wrapped in a twist of cloth. With the sun casting her shadow onto the green translucent water, she began to sketch the scene before her. Line followed line, at first disconnected as though she did no more than note a plane or an angle, delineate the slope of a roof, the curve of a tree. What she saw was not what you or I would see were we to sit beside her on that pretty hill. She saw, it seemed, the inside of the real, the very structure of its being. With time the tree emerged and then the cottage, though not quite as they were, or not quite as they seemed, as how could they when reduced to a matter of lines, marks on the paper? But it is the essence of art to transform, to tell lies like truth, to tell lies which become the truth. Some chickens disappeared, to be replaced by a cow which seemed to her more fitting to her composition; the church, half concealed by laurel and holly, stood out more boldly. And could it be that there was a figure lurking there in the churchyard, in the shade

124

of a beech? Certainly Pearl looked up sharply, as though expecting what she had drawn to come into existence by the merest action of her hand. There was no one there, or at least none to be seen, so that anxiety alone, perhaps, had made present what was indeed only in her mind. Whatever the truth, she reworked that portion of her sketch, shading in what might have appeared to be a man. Then she tossed her paper down, wrapped the charcoal back in the square of black cloth, and lay back in the sun. There was nothing of Boston's humid heat about this English spring, turning towards summer, though there were those who had only to look to the hedgerows and watch the gathering birds to predict that soon there would be heat aplenty. The snake was forgotten as she stretched out her arms and let the warmth seep into her.

Further upstream, boys were splashing in the weir and after a minute or two it was thither that she directed her steps, stripping a willow branch from a tree to beat down the nettles which threatened to block her path. The field, though part of the estate, was clearly treated as common land for a number of cows and horses wandered about it while the village boys jumped into the river and allowed themselves to be swept down a small cascade as the water plunged downwards by the loke. They wore no clothes but felt neither the chill of the water nor any embarrassment when a lady came along the bank, swinging a stick from side to side. Neither did she feel disturbed but smiled and waved as they were swept, arms and legs in the air like upturned turtles, amidst a swirl of bubbles, down a gently surging sweep of green water.

She turned her face now towards Earlham where she could reclaim the further bank. And as she walked she saw a cow, which had slithered down a muddy bank, swimming white-eyed in the middle of the stream, in front of it a swan, for once not in command of its domain. At one moment it would rise up and spread its wings, then run along the surface as though to escape this monster of the river; the next it would cease its efforts and subside into the water. Pearl watched this comedy acted out, yet the terror of both creatures was real enough, unlike her own at a figure she had summoned into being with a burnt twig and a scrap of paper.

At Earlham Pearl crossed the rough wooden bridge and saw the solid bulk of Earlham Hall, set amidst parkland. There was money in Norfolk, it seemed, money and power. She had neither, nor craved them, to be sure, though if all went well she would find herself mistress of a hall of her own. But for what purpose, she now asked herself, and for the first time questioned what she would do who was on her own and who had never known anything but a cottage on a forest's edge. She had crossed the Atlantic with only the most uncertain idea of what she might be seeking. To leave Boston and to have the means of doing so had seemed all that mattered. Now she was no longer so certain. What would she do high on a hill when in her heart she would rather be in the village or, in truth, in the woods beyond?

She turned towards the south and followed the road back to Colney, past the church, down to the river and, forsaking the bridge, stepped lightly across a line of stones, dry with the river so low. And so back up the hill to Colney Hall, having drawn a circle with her walk, a shape which contained much of the land which would go to any who established their right to the inheritance.

There was a man who watched. She had seen him before. He stood in the shadow, a shadow himself. She would never have noticed had not a passing cloud been followed by a sudden flash of sunlight. He lifted a hand to shield his face. Then, another cloud, and he was gone again. Truth dissolves so easily. Had he been there? The doubt was born with the darkness. Perhaps it was Charley, he who called her Hester and smiled and who had a face which seemed flattened, inward, blank. Yet she had been told there were others: people with a past. But what could that past be to her? She completed her walk in a state of puzzlement and perhaps, too, the beginnings of alarm.

That night, as she retired to bed in the empty house, she reached for the curtain to pull it against the night but as she did so she saw again the figure she had seen before, this time not indistinct, but standing in the moonlight. He wore a cloak and hat but what struck her most was the crooked shadow he cast on the grass. She stepped back with a gasp and stood a second, her heart racing. Then she retreated into the room, reached out a hand and snuffed the candle at her bed's side. The room was cast into deep shadow as the moonlight shone through the leaded windows. But she was not one to cower beneath the sheets. She advanced towards the window again and looked out to see the man. He was gone, as she had half suspected he would be. But he was no phantom. This man had cast a shadow, and, besides, she had seen Chillingworth's grave in the corner of a Boston churchyard. Yet his shape recalled the man. And if not Chillingworth, then who? And what did he do here unless to terrify her? She had no sooner thought this than she saw the plausibility of her idea. There were those who wished her gone, who, for reasons of their own, sought what had passed into her hands. She was a woman. They perhaps thought to terrify her so that she would do their will without further effort, whoever they might be. Well, she would not take fear at a man who did no more than stand in the moonlight. It was proof of something, though. They meant her ill and perhaps they might do more than offer her a night-time scare. She thought of the doors bolted tight at her cousin's insistence, who feared she knew not what. Nancy had lived through dangerous times and knew the value of oak and iron bolts, though should anyone mean Pearl harm there was little she could do here, alone, and far from friends.

She had said no prayers until the day her true father had climbed a scaffold and acknowledged his paternity. Since then she had done so but infrequently and with no true faith, merely sufficient fear to impel her observance. Everything she had seen of the church had taught her that salvation could be a cruel affair. She prayed now, though, for her mother, first, then for herself as she faced she knew not what. And as she lay awake she even saw herself taking ship and returning whence she had come. Mistakes may be rectified, nor was she bound to keep her feet on a path which indeed might prove a false one. And yet. In the cathedral she had found a man who had, in the merest moment, as it seemed, become a kind of lodestone to her soul and if she struggled against the forces which drew her to him yet those forces were strong and true enough to make her feel that she had been led here to this small village, on an island far from her home, by destiny.

Scarcely a week passed before Pearl and Nancy were back at the cathedral, the one drawn by faith and a touch of local pride, the other by something which had yet to find its way into words. Again they admired the ceiling and the paintings and the cool marble effigies. Again a figure emerged from the shadow.

'Ladies,' said Standish, 'this place is as new to me as you, or rather as to my fellow voyager, Mistress Prynne. But I have discovered a singular beauty here.' He blushed at what he perceived might appear an ambiguity. 'Could I take you to the upper gallery? It is not a place that many go but the view both within and without is astounding to the eye.'

Pearl's cousin gave an involuntary shriek, then clapped her hand to her mouth with shame. 'Gracious, no. I thank you, but to climb upon a chair to reach an upper shelf is terror enough for me. And besides, we must be upon our way.'

'Oh, cousin. We have time enough to spare. If thou wouldst take a turn about the cloisters I will attempt the heights. I have climbed a little up the rigging of a ship at sea. At least this place is rooted to the ground, and I would see the place where I shall live.'

'Art thou to go alone, my child?'

'Alone? Why of course not, cousin. I have the Reverend Standish as my guide.'

Far from reassurance, this seemed the source of further alarm to Nancy, who felt that she had perforce become the protector of one who knew nothing of their ways.

'I am not sure this could be . . .' She could no more finish her sentence than climb the stairs which lay beyond the locked door ahead of them.

As for Pearl, she was determined to proceed but could hardly be unaware of what her new-found relative found impossible to utter. Indeed, but for the cool darkness of the cathedral, which drained colour from everything not lit by candlelight, her companions would have seen a flush spread upwards from her neck to her cheeks.

'I must go,' she announced, setting her chin with determination, quite as though she were a five-year-old, sick with fever, yet determined to attend a fair. 'I shall go.' It was the tone of a child but it was also a statement which invited no further debate and her cousin was conscious that she had neither power nor authority.

'Very well, my dear. As thou say, I shall take a turn about the cloisters, though I suspect they will be disagreeably cold just now. We shall meet by the altar. My cousin, sir, be in your charge. See that all is well.'

So taken with the prospect was Pearl that the child within her almost clapped her hands with delight. Her upbringing, isolated in her early years from the company of others, with none but her mother for friend and playmate, had given her a sense of independence rare among women of the time, but had left her, too, without the constraints which required that she should curb her free spirit. She may no longer run freely through the wild wood, her hair floating behind as though she swam in a clear New England pond, but in her heart she ran still and felt the freedom of a youth in which her actions were determined by none save herself.

Standish nodded to the elder woman, who hesitated a moment, as though, even now, she might pull her charge behind her like the tutor with his pupils on their previous visit. Then she turned away. 'I shall be but a few minutes. Let thou be likewise.'

'That we shall,' called Pearl, instantly shocked as her voice echoed in the emptiness. 'That we shall,' she whispered as though this would cancel out her indiscretion.

Standish reached within his robe and produced a key which looked as though it would balance a pound of flour in the scales. He bent to the lock and the key turned easily enough.

'I shall go first. It is dark, I'm afraid, but there is only one direction to go. You will not get lost.'

'I am quite used to the dark, and I thank you. I was raised in it.'

'There is light ahead, though.'

'There is always light ahead. It is a rule of life.'

'So it is.'

She stepped into the darkness and stumbled immediately, not used to the height of the tread. Her hand brushed the back of his robe and she felt another hot flush on her neck. The dark was thus not without its benefits. The stairs were made to fit a man's gait but Pearl climbed with ease, adjusting herself to the pace of the figure before her as he adjusted his speed, as he thought, to match hers. They were alone together, as seldom man and woman were alone who knew each other as little as did they, and if Pearl's heart beat fast, as it assuredly did, it had little to do with the physical effort of climbing the stairs, she who was more accustomed to such effort and indeed found a kind of exultation in it.

They stepped not simply onto the great wooden balcony, which clung to the wall of the cathedral on one side and overlooked vertiginous depths on the other, but into a new level of existence. A sparrow fluttered against the stone as it squeezed into a frayed nest above the head of a bulging-eyed gargoyle. But that was the only sound. What was quiet below was utter silence here above, except that an occasional voice touched on a note which resonated like a musical instrument heard in the far distance. It was not a place which encouraged speech, but, then, neither felt the need of words. Above them, the graceful sweep of the fluted roof seemed almost within reach. The bosses, vague shapes from the ground, now formed into sharp-edged roundels, limestone roses, lugubrious faces.

Pearl and the minister stood side by side in a kind of awe, not alone of the work of man offered here to God but of the situation itself. There are times when feelings so overwhelm the self that it seems impossible that they should not communicate directly into the head of another. But such times seem to carry, too, the conviction that there could be no reciprocation. Exultation and despair thus occupy the same space and moment. Never can we be such mysteries to one another as at such a time. We long to speak and yet are afraid that speech might shatter the hope that somehow survives the silence. So, high above the stone floor of one of the wonders of Norman art and architecture, two people stood and gave only half their thoughts to their surroundings.

The sparrow fluttered from its nest and flew down to the ground between them. Here, where people seldom came, there was no fear, for this was a bird which never left the great cathedral but lived its life within its bounds. Yet it lived and died in a world quite as expansive as any of its kin who flew on the other side of the glass windows.

'Come,' he said, 'we can go a little higher yet.'

He held his hand out to her as he eased another door open. Warm hand closed on warm hand and courtesy came close to a caress. As the stairs turned round a central axis, a spiral of desire, lifting them upwards, so reason fell away; the mind's hard-won victories were surrendered and there was born a mutuality which required no comment. Doubt survived, of course, for what love is there that does not require reassurances and what certainty can there be in the pressure of a hand? But there was a kind of illicit pleasure in their being thus alone.

They stepped finally into a small wooden room whose single arch looked down to the floor of the cathedral far below. Pearl ventured to the edge, feeling her stomach seem to drop away within her.

'Take care,' urged Standish, who himself held back.

'It is beautiful.'

'It is, indeed, though you will forgive me if I do not join you there. I have no fear of climbing to these heights but there is something in me that keeps me from the edge.'

'There is no danger, surely,' said Pearl, leaning against the balustrade and seeing if she could pick out the figure of her cousin.

'Do you not feel that there is something within you that defies control? Some perversity that might urge you to your doom?'

Pearl looked round in surprise. 'There is no devil in me save that which I permit. It may lead me to the edge but never over, as I trust.'

'It is the nature of temptation that we may not recognise it. Look below. See the beauty. Would you not embrace it? Do you not feel it pull you down as in a faint?' He took a step towards her as she leaned further out to see what she might spy.

She looked at him again. There was something in his words that made her head spin, as she stood thus high above the stone-flagged floor.

Then she looked away from him again and down into the void. There was a giddiness in such a vantage point and though she could not admit as much she recognised the truth of what he said, for she felt a kind of fear that some part of her mind might countermand another and instruct her body to do what her will would refuse. Had she not delighted as a child to cross one leg over another and then strike below the knee with the edge of her hand, trying to force her leg not to fly up in response? And was there not something in his voice which urged her towards the very thing he warned against as though he infiltrated her will? She was aware of danger but uncertain what the danger might be. She held to the oak balustrade and felt a surge of energy as the sparrow below clung to the wall before swooping down in some final flight.

It was at this moment that she turned and saw the minister but a step or two from her, his arms extended, his face looking as it had on the ship, brow furrowed, eyes wild. For a second she felt a thrill of fear but even as she stepped back, coming to the very edge of the narrow balcony, his expression changed and she realised it must have been concern she had seen written on his face.

'Come away, Pearl,' he said urgently, and then, gently, 'is this not different from your Boston home?' But the second thought could not neutralise the first. He had spoken her name and a spell was broken. Here, in a world of their own, rules, codes, formalities, had begun to dissolve.

'Yes, quite different. We do not rise so far above the ground, unless we be witches.'

'Do not speak of witches.'

She looked at him for a second with a hint of contempt, then turned aside. 'What is that door behind you?'

He looked round at a small doorway in the wall, almost hidden in the gloom. 'I have only been here once before, to tell the truth, and I never noticed it. I have no keys other than the one to the door below and so I doubt we will solve this mystery.'

Pearl walked slowly towards him, as to her destiny, though who is there can recognise such? Something, she felt, must happen now. She was light-headed not from the height but from something else beside. This, too, was a territory strange to her. She was disappointed, though, for he did not speak the words she half expected him to say, but stepped aside.

'I have a little magic,' she said, with a wry smile, 'perhaps it will yield to me.'

'Do not speak of magic. There are those still who burn for less.'

'What, here in England? So, you have the same civilities as we. These be but women, of course. I never saw a man hanged for striking another or plotting his harm, but let a silver needle be found in a doll and heaven is invited to close its eyes to charity and love. Come, let me try your door and see what secrets it has to reveal.'

He half turned back but she reached it before him and twisted the circle of plaited metal which was its handle. To her surprise it swung quickly open as if someone had been pulling on the other side and, despite its weight, it was snatched from her hand and crashed against the outer stonework with a sound which seemed to set the whole building shaking. With the sound came light, a sudden and intense shaft of pure white. The very contrast with the soft-edged gloom intensified the beam which seemed to isolate them both, actors on an empty stage when the curtain has been accidentally raised. They froze like children in a game when the music ceases. And with the light came a wind whose clawing fingers reached towards them, tugging at clothes and hair. Dust spiralled upwards from the floor, only to align itself in the straight-edged rectangle of light. For a second both were struck with a kind of terror. It passed, as did the wind, whose sudden force had been in part a product of the contrast between a suspended stillness, the quiet poise of an interior world, and the rush and vigour of that beyond.

The door opened onto a small balcony which in turn gave access to the cathedral's exterior walls, for the convenience of those who saw no adventure in scaling them with rope and pulley to effect repairs. For those less practical it offered a view downwards, past the soaring buttresses, to the low cottages and the fields beyond. When she had sufficiently recovered herself, Pearl stepped through the doorway.

'I suspect you thought I had opened the door to hell. But, look, it is heaven after all.'

'Take care. It may not be safe with such a wind.'

'Why should I look for safety?' she asked, with a genuine puzzlement, for indeed safety had never been what she sought. 'Oh, do look. It is so . . . I have never seen such a sight.'

He moved to the doorway, his hand involuntarily reaching for a secure hold on the rough stone. 'Indeed, it is magnificent.'

'It is more than magnificent. You have laid the whole world before me. If you should but offer it to me as my own then I would suspect you as the devil. Look at the sheep on the hillside. They are no bigger than stars at midnight. And the river is like a silver thread. And see where two people walk together in yonder field. Your church has miracles to offer, John Standish.'

'Do step back inside, Mistress Prynne,' said Standish urgently, feeling, perhaps, no less ensnared than did the woman who now stood before him framed in the doorway, though, like her, he feared to speak of it.

Yet when she turned towards him there was a second when some kind of recognition seemed to join them: he just inside the doorway, his pale face illuminated by a sky which had suddenly turned the colour of verdigris as a storm swept down from the hills so clear yet a moment before; she a Medusa, a Raphael drawing, her face in the shadow but her outline picked out suddenly by a flash of lightning. What was this country where sun must always make way for rain? April showers, they had told her, but if these were showers what might lie ahead when a true storm must come?

He reached out a hand to guide her back into the darkness but the heavy door was caught by a sudden gust and, as rain began to dance and spatter along the stonework, swung closed with the sound of cannon fire reverberating round the building. Pearl was barely inside. Another moment and the door must have struck her. As it was she fell forwards so that she was in his arms who could have wished for nothing more. He clasped her to him, partly, indeed, in response to the shock. They stood thus not for one second or two. Not for half a minute, either. But no clock was running on this embrace. Indeed, only we can call it an embrace for they were not so certain of one another's feelings, or perhaps their own, even now, that they could call it anything but a response to the slam of a door.

Chapter Five

Pearl kept her appointment at Opie Street and on this occasion, knowing what to expect, she came prepared to accept nothing but her due. She was determined to be obdurate and not let them treat her as a helpless girl. After only a few weeks on shore she had located her latitude and longitude and was alert to those sandbanks not shown on any map.

She knocked on the great door. The knocker was a little like a lion, or perhaps a griffin, its teeth and claws bared as though it only awaited a signal to tear at the hand that touched it. The door was opened by the clerk, a blue flower pinned to his lapel and a quill pen behind his ear, an arrangement not altogether sensible since the black ink with which he worked had dripped a little on his cheek until it formed a kind of question mark, an apt symbol of the place.

'Mistress Prynne,' he said, with a wide smile.

'Sir,' she replied. 'And is he within?'

'He is. And another with him.'

'And who might he be?'

'He might be anyone at all, feeling no need to offer me a name. I would say by his looks that he might be the public hangman but looks may be deceptive so perhaps he is an angel in disguise. But if it came to a wager I would prefer my money on the hangman.'

'And will he be long? I am here by agreement.'

'That you are, and he knows it well enough. And perhaps this man may be on that selfsame business, or so I believe.'

'What can he have to do with me? I will go in.'

'Mistress Prynne.'

'Sir?'

'Have care.' He rested his hand on her arm and then looked at it as though it might have landed there of its own accord. He withdrew it slowly, as if it might not be noticed.

'It is he who must take care. I shall not leave until these matters be resolved.'

The clerk nodded, though half to himself, as it seemed to Pearl, then knocked sharply on the door and thrust it open before a reply should come. In the gloom within, Pearl made out two figures, one seated, the other leaning over him, like a bird with wings outstretched.

'Mistress Prynne?' enquired Simple.

'Indeed. I am come that we should settle our business.'

'Settle?'

'This was the hour appointed, was it not?'

Pearl was not unaffected by the smell of dust and decay, the darkness and the two figures who seemed at times to merge into one, but she was determined not to be deflected. She walked to the chair which perched before the desk, a chair set low so that whoever sat in it would be forced to look up over the mountain of papers to the man who commanded the room as a general would an army, from a height where none should come at him. She sat.

'Would you take a seat, Mistress Prynne?' he said, looking not at her but at his companion.

'I have done so.'

'Have you so?'

'And who is this gentleman, pray?'

'He might be called an interested party, might he not?'

'There is only one interested party here and it is I.'

137

It seemed to Pearl that he greeted her statement with a laugh, or was it a clearing of the throat?

'So,' hissed the person beside Lawyer Simple, turning now to face her. He did indeed have the look of a hangman, if only people did but look as they are.

'I have not your acquaintance, sir.'

'No,' acknowledged the man, whose face was a splash of white and whose head was devoid of all hair except for a black shading around the temples, 'nor shall do.'

'Sir?'

'Do not concern yourself, Mistress Prynne,' said Simple in a not at all reassuring voice. 'A man may keep himself to himself, may he not?'

'By all means, provided he has no designs on other people or their rights.'

'Damnable!' exclaimed the mysterious stranger, and seemed about to climb over the table to reach her. Even in the flickering candlelight Pearl could see the veins on his head stand out like so many flexing worms.

'Sir,' said Simple, extending a languorous arm to bar such an eccentric manoeuvre, 'trust the law. Have it ever failed you?'

'What is this you speak of?' asked Pearl, her anger growing with her fright. 'There is only one law and you have but one function: to render to me what is spoken of in the documents I bring.'

'Documents!' The man showed every sign of exploding, as a Norwich gunpowder store had done but two score years before when a naked flame and naked ambition had come together in one place, stripping the hair from he who stood close by.

'The problem, mistress, is that there are documents aplenty. You have your own but there are others who hold papers perhaps more plausible than these. And there is the problem, is it not?'

'And why should mine seem implausible?'

'They were writ in a distant place by those unknown here in

Norfolk. What do we know of them? They are at a convenient remove. Who is to verify, who attest, who assure, who confirm?'

'The papers speak for themselves.'

'Do they so? Let us listen.' He lifted a thin, pale hand to his ear. A ruby glistened on his finger, blood red, like the eye of a devil and contained within a strange design. There was no sound but the deep and steady tick of the clock.

Pearl got to her feet with such alacrity that her chair tilted over and struck the floor. Immediately the door flew open and the clerk, with his forget-me-not motto at his breast, stood before them, a hand raised as though to strike, though whom or why was scarcely clear.

'Yes?' asked Simple. 'Did I summon you?'

He lowered his hand, seeing Pearl standing before him, unharmed.

'I heard a sound.'

'Ah, that would be Mistress Prynne adjusting the furniture. That will be all.'

The clerk looked to Pearl, who, in spite of herself, was shaking, though with anger rather than fear.

'Perhaps you would be good enough to restore the chair to its position before retreating. Mistress Prynne has yet to conclude her business. Is that not so?'

'I think I had best seek out another lawyer whose hearing is more acute.'

'Ah, that is your prerogative, of course, though the documents in which you place such faith did specify these chambers, as I believe.'

'But you reject them.'

'Reject? Was I so unwary to make such a declaration? I merely asked such questions as would be prudent for any man to ask, knowing there to be others with claims which might yet prove of equal force.'

'Impossible!'

The clerk set the chair once more in place. Pearl glanced at him and then abruptly sat down.

'Impossible? It is impossible that I should fly. It is impossible that the sun should fail to rise. But when it comes to the law what is possible and what is not is a matter to be determined. This gentleman has papers.'

'May papers not be counterfeit?' enquired Pearl, looking at the unsavoury figure who stood beside this lawyer whose name was itself a warning that words may be a deceit.

There was another silence, interrupted by a kind of strangled sound from the hangman. Simple, meanwhile, stared at his clerk who, far from leaving the room, stood with one hand on the back of Pearl's chair and the other on his waist.

'And what would you know of such?' asked the lawyer.

'Is it not so?'

After a second or so Simple smiled such a smile as would chill the heart of a bride on her wedding day.

'Why else, mistress, would I query the papers in which you place so much faith? But have no fear, the law has an answer for the counterfeiter. The gallows are a great corrector of faulty texts.'

'Indeed,' said the clerk, in a voice which seemed to tremble somewhat. 'And those that pressed them to it.'

'I have no time for this,' said the ominous stranger, thumping his ample fist on the table. 'Settle the matter now.' Several sheets of paper, dislodged by this violence, floated gently to the ground.

'Sir, I will none of that,' replied Simple, sharply. 'We are here to make an accommodation, as I believe.'

The man was silent and turned his back on the scene, as though he would have nothing further to do with it.

'And you, sir, will return to your work.'

Clerk and employer stared at one another.

'You do her case no good,' he added, picking up a sheet of paper between thumb and finger. 'Come now, sir. I tire of this. Change your attire if you wish. Pin whole hedgerows on yourself if it pleases you. But in all else I expect obedience and constancy. Am I understood?'

The clerk stood a second longer, glancing from employer to

the young woman who had now resumed her seat, then, with a shrug of his shoulders, turned about, and left the room, closing the door behind him.

'He is a little touched in the head, I am afraid. I keep him by me out of charity. As to this case, I should warn you that the law has a way of stretching time until it should become a kind of eternity. For myself I regret this tardiness but it is the nature of my profession and of the law itself which requires that every particle of doubt should be expunged. The papers you have may be true or counterfeit. I have no skill to know. But what I do know is that it may take some years to tell fair from false. And I would judge that time may cost you dearer than others. Whereas this gentleman is patience itself. Is that not so?'

'Damnable!' shouted the aforementioned, failing, as is so often the way with lawyers and their clients, to evidence the quality so generously ascribed to him by the man who endeavoured to work on his behalf.

'Ay, well, he is at least a gentleman who has wealth enough to make patience its own reward. But a solution is at hand. He has, out of sympathy for your plight, offered one hundred sovereigns and passage on a ship whence you came, if but you accept that his claim takes precedence. Or if not that, then time's delay may serve you unkindly and this compromise is therefore worthy of your acceptance.'

Pearl let out a gasp of exasperation, though Simple seemed pleased with his speech, looking round, as it seemed to her, for an audience suitable to recognise his talent.

'You are impudent, sir. I shall to another lawyer.'

'It seems you know little of the law. There are but a handful of us in the whole of Norwich and we see the world much alike, I believe.'

'Then perhaps those in London have a clearer vision.'

There was a silence. The hangman swung round and glared not at Pearl but Simple. The clock ticked.

'I told you we would be better . . .'

Simple held up his hand: a peremptory command.

'We are a united band,' he said quietly, though with less assurance, as it seemed to Pearl.

Now, at last, the dark presence turned to Pearl. The candle caught his eyes, which seemed rimmed with red. His fist opened and closed as though he wished her neck might be within it. He seemed for a moment a kind of implacable force, the more powerful and threatening because deprived of speech. In spite of herself, she recoiled, feeling the shock of his brute presence, almost as though he were an extension of Lawyer Simple, all that dark man's evil become incarnate. Once again she got to her feet, this time ensuring that her chair remained in place.

'I shall trouble you no further. As to returning whence I came, I travelled with a purpose. That purpose is not yet achieved. I will not be bribed nor yet coerced. If you be the law then the law hath great need of mending. As for you, sir,' she said, turning to the man who stared across the table. 'The devil seems to have got your tongue. I trust he do not have your soul as well. May God be with you, Lawyer Simple, for I think you have need of Him.'

'Wait!' said Simple, making to get to his feet.

'I shall not. And you, sir, who are you?' She spoke in a clear and penetrating voice, surprising herself with the directness of her address.

'I am your nightmare, mistress. Look for me in your dreams.'

'I am not frightened of phantoms nor yet of children's threats.'

'That is as well, for phantoms you will see. Sign the parchment and you shall be free of me.'

'There are simpler ways of ridding myself of villains, unless Norwich lack the constables that pursue good and bad alike where I was born.'

The man laughed, if such a word could be said to describe a noise which was more like the choke of the dying. 'The constables?' he echoed, pinching out one of the wandering flames on the candles before him.

'Ay, and the magistrates.'

'The magistrates?' He extinguished another, leaving only

one light to penetrate the dark. 'We have no need to fear such here. You are the stranger. You the usurper.'

'I am not afraid of the dark, sir.'

'No? Then you had best be. Light is so easily put out.'

'I shall leave now.'

'Leave, then. But you had best write your name on this parchment while you may.'

'I shall not.'

'I had a brother.'

'A brother?'

'Ay. They grow in these parts. I am owed part of his goods.'

'He had no brother.'

'Who is this whose life you know so well?'

'He had no brother.'

'You have proof of this?' asked Lawyer Simple, leaning forward in the uncertain light.

'Do you not see something of him in me?' asked the man, thrusting his face towards her across the desk until Pearl thought she must smell the stench of hell.

'I see nothing that I care to look on any more. As for you, sir,' she added, turning to Simple, 'I came to you as I was bidden. I have discharged that responsibility and will now learn to put my trust in others.'

'Bravely spoken, but foolishly too. That there is more than one who claims this property and this money signifies nothing but that a certain enquiry must be made and a dispute argued where all disputes come eventually. You are too hot. Have confidence, mistress. Do I not have your interests at heart?'

'Good day, sir. And as for you, burn your fingers with the last candle if you will. I will accept no interference in my affairs.'

'Mistress, what can you know of life? Look about. Do you see any woman challenge men for power?'

Pearl turned, threw open the door, and strode through the hallway out into Opie Street, watched by the clerk who held in his hand a forget-me-not which he half extended towards her as she rushed by. 'I shall not step inside again,' she said aloud.

The days passed. No news came from Opie Street nor did she return to the cathedral immediately, except in her mind. For a while she resisted herself and her instincts, as though putting off a decision she was not yet ready to acknowledge confronted her. Her heart was touched. She admitted such. But she was not so free of her history as to be unaware of the danger she would both shun and hurry towards. She spent her time with her sketch book and walking the spring meadows. She spent time, too, exploring further the house which was not yet her home. And there were mysteries still to be explored.

She passed the cellar door, as she had passed it so many times before, but now she halted, drawn by something more than curiosity. Its blackened surface seemed to hint at an opacity. And if this was, indeed, her home, then how could such a blankness be permitted there? She passed her fingers gently over the black-crusted bubbles of tar which made it seem that wood, too, can suffer from the plague. She pressed her thumb hard into the centre of one swollen scab of carbon and watched as a shower of black powder fell like a dark cascade to the floor. The door must be opened, and if there was no key, as certainly she had failed to find such, then there are other ways of forcing access to the unknown.

She found an axe embedded in a heavy elm log in the woodshed. No King Arthur, it took her some effort to release and no little strength to drag to the house. A blow full on the lock seemed to spring the mechanism and the door swung back towards her, revealing a sudden darkness.

There is something about a cellar which stirs unease, some reminder, perhaps, of caves or graves which makes us unwilling to step into the cold unknown. Even so, Pearl moved boldly down the uneven stone staircase, holding above her head a candelabra whose three candles set dancing a trinity of overlapping shadows.

She had thought it would be damp, but if anything there was an arid atmosphere which seemed to draw the moisture from her lips and eyes. Nor could she see much of this netherworld at first, as the space was greater than she had imagined so that the candles only lit a wavering circle as she moved forwards. Then a glint of colour drew her eye, a spark of red, like the bloodshot eye of some creature walled up these past two decades. Other colours shone dully in the flickering light while rows of miniature candles reflected the yellow flames of her own. She was looking, she now realised, at row upon row of glass retorts and beakers, slender tubes with black coagulates and splattered colours. By their side were books, in irregular piles, with here and there one held open by a weight placed there many years before. And Pearl remembered what her mother had told her of tainted knowledge, of bitter smells which presaged still more bitter acts, of coloured smoke and flowing liquid and powder which rimed tall beakers and which had rimed the lips of one who spoke a kind of poison candied over as love. She sank into a chair where he had sat who filled her dreams as he had filled the dreams of her mother. He might have turned aside from his experiments and left the room only a moment before. She even fancied she could detect something of the acrid smell of sweat, though the ashes of a fire, over which an iron stand containing three crucibles had been placed, were as cold as a dead man's touch. It was as though a surgeon, dissecting a corpse, had come at last to the brain, there to discover secrets which death alone could expose.

At length she got to her feet, placed the candelabra on the dark-stained bench, and looked more closely at what she had discovered. She picked a clear glass container from its wooden stand and removed its cork. At its bottom there was a yellow powder. She held it up against the pallid light and, as she did, so it began to transmute. A greenish tinge seemed to spread from the bottom and the sides. Whether it was the warmth of her hand or the dampness of the air after such a long period of dryness, the change continued until, within a minute or two, she held not powdered yellow but liquid blue. It was as though she had breathed life into this darkness and it now sought its primal state.

Pearl had a strong nerve but not so strong that this transmutation did not affect her, the more especially when she saw that similar changes were working their way through several of the containers set before her. Accordingly she resolved to leave this dark and subtle world and regain the relative security of the domestic rooms above; but in doing so, perhaps to reassure herself that she was not driven there by panic, she carried with her a book and the crucible which had been placed upon it to keep the page.

She closed the door with a sense of relief and surprised herself by going to the kitchen for a weight from the scales which she could put against it lest it open and something from the depths emerge blinking in the light of day.

Yet, that evening, she chose to open the book which she had rescued from its burial place and to read from its pages. It was nothing more, it seemed, than a record of plants and berries, together with the properties they possessed to heal the sick or send the mind on journeys requiring no horse and cart nor even a pair of sturdy shoes. It was decorated with drawings so precisely done that though they but pictured aspects of the world which she saw around her every day they made seem strange what she had thought familiar. Was this, then, the bible of one who had turned his face from goodness to seek the night? Had he been an angel corrupted by a knowledge which otherwise might have redeemed?

There were recipes here for breaking fevers and for drawing poison from a wound. There were admixtures of herbs which, it was claimed, would take pain from the body and ease the breathing of those whose lungs seemed closed to air. There were also, though, other formulae which addressed pain which came not from the body but the soul, solutions for unrequited love or failing powers, which smacked of witch-craft. But these were times when such distinctions seemed less real. Sickness was perhaps all of a piece and love not returned as much a sickness as any other.

She turned the pages slowly and was not unconvinced by

what she read. She wet a finger in her mouth and placed it against the crystals which sparkled along the ege of a crucible whose underside was burned by fire. Then she returned the finger to her tongue and felt a gentle warmth spread through her mouth and flow throughout her being. For a second the world seemed to tremble as a disturbance passed through her. A sudden confusion made her reach out a hand to steady herself. The moment passed; but she was not the same.

Pearl woke slowly from a dismaying sleep and stared at the ceiling, trying to recall dreams which had faded with her wakening. But all had slipped away except a face which smiled at her and a voice with a gentle tone. She could feel herself begin to fall and knew she had only to reach out a hand to be secure. She recognised the fire for what it was and the blade's edge for the cause of pain. Yet she longed for warmth and the sharpness of the moment. She was now less than a year of one and twenty and in her life it was full summer. Time enough for austere regret and the long winter of the soul. She longed to run, to find the very edge, to see what she could chance, to give what she might receive, to refuse, to accept, to demand, to be.

But she did not forget. We may choose to gather up our history, as a child a snowball, and throw it to the sun, but she had made herself a promise and there was that in her which was implacable. She had watched and learned. When a father's hand should have held hers there was nothing but shadow to grasp. In one man, a cold will, like a winter mist, seemed to turn brittle all it touched. In another, the heart's inconstancy led him down tangled paths until he was quite lost who should himself have been a guide. There would be no such companion for her, she had sworn. She would be solitary, not abandoned. She would wear no letter at her breast nor would she ever place herself where she might be in another's power.

She was not yet lost. She was a separate person. A moment was merely that, and what if her eyes had met those of another, was that so much more than mere courtesy? Yes, it was more, but could still be less. In the world from which she came her defences had been secure. Her very history had turned her from girl to symbol, while she took pride in denying dependency. There had been those who sought her out, dared by others, no doubt, to speak with the daughter of sin, but she had looked in their eyes until they blushed and turned away. She had been left alone and found, as she had always known, that she was content with her own company, as with that of her mother. Her pleasure had come from the world about her and from her growing skill in rendering it with pencil and paint. But something had happened. Too many things had happened. She felt her new vulnerability. Her future was clouded. Perhaps he might yet prove the light to show the way forward.

'I shall not see him again,' she announced, hearing herself speak as though a stranger had just come upon her. 'I may do very well without him.'

So she could, but did she wish to do so? Resolutions are proud and courageous decisions until the time comes when they must be tested and then pride may be humbled and courage find its limits. Pearl would not name her feelings towards Standish, indeed was still in that delightful territory where nothing was yet certain. She was on the brow of a hill and could see down into the valley. Everything there seemed bright and clear and gentle to the eye. Yet she could still determine whether she should descend. There was that about him, though, which made it difficult to resist and when no other face and no other form has pleased so much, why not take the path which offers? But no sooner did such a step seem imminent than a cloud passed over some inner sun and a shadow ran along the valley floor. Had she travelled so far only to submit to another's will? But what reason questions the heart may answer, especially if we should feel our whole world turned about.

If time had slowed for Pearl and the minister, high above the cathedral floor, in the thin and dusty air, it began to flow again with a reckless speed in the weeks which followed. Despite her cousin's entreaties Pearl continued to stay alone in the Hall. She stayed because it was where she had first laid down her head upon her return, because it was her own, and because she revelled in her independence, newly won. It was, too, a bare three miles from Norwich, whither she went as often as she might. The intelligence she had been offered had left her vulnerable. Knowing that there might be those who meant her ill, she turned, as where else might she, but to him who had stirred her heart, if also her suspicion. What should she do but reach out her hand and trust that he who grasped it might yet prove true?

She grew quickly familiar with the cobbled space of Tombland. She strolled through the stone archway beside it into the Cathedral Close and down to the river where a ferryboat crossed to the far side for a farthing. Here you could think of time as no longer a sequenced order, a journey with one step following another. It seemed to collapse to a point. Certainly, as she strolled around, willing herself not to enter the cathedral itself, deferring a pleasure, delaying a problem, she seemed to move in a kind of parallel world. Then, as now, this place seemed quite set apart, as though a space had been provided where normal laws should not prevail. To step inside the cool, candle-smelling, echoing vastness of the church itself was to abandon time. Here was eternity made literal, as every object was offered as a symbol of something beyond. Pearl was herself held in another timeless void. There were moments, indeed, when she seemed to stand beside herself and recognise as folly what she had no choice but to feel and do. But she was joined in this folly by another so that it seemed no folly at all. She would kneel in the pew, feeling the waxed wood with her hand and waiting for the moment when he should appear. And he must be presumed to await the moment when he should glimpse her, like a start of light in the darkness. She told him of her problems with Lawyer Simple and he promised his help. Advising against resort to other lawyers who might prove as suspect as the Prince of Opie

Street, he undertook to enquire where true assistance might be had. Meanwhile, they had other matters to consider, other paths to walk down side by side, and if time was passing and her advancing birthday a warning that the hourglass empties no matter that we place it out of sight, new urgencies were born, new rhythms were beaten by a quickening pulse.

Beyond the cool of the cathedral floor, the soft echo of footsteps on cold stone, was the furnace of a spring turning summer, a summer which, as weeks passed into months, would lack all gentleness. Ponds would dry, rivers shrink, the very water in the well seek the depths of the earth. There would be those who collapsed in the street and others who found the air too thin and insubstantial for life. At such a time a certain madness enters the world. Dogs froth at the mouth and snap at the air. Quarrels flare up like bracken set to the torch. This lay ahead that summer. But there was madness already in Pearl's life. A certain balance was now thrown off. The heat made mirages shimmer above the fields and rendered clear thought a hostage to the noon sun. It was in this sudden heat, which seemed to swell up from the soil itself, that she found herself at a destination she felt she had been travelling towards for all of her life. The Reverend John Standish had come to call in horse and trap and together they had journeyed into the countryside. They rode together openly and yet kept to the quieter lanes, such was their relationship, innocent and yet not so, she being an unmarried woman and he set apart by his position. They rode with the sun at their backs, not touching yet together, looking at the passing fields and yet not seeing them.

Whether what now transpired would have occurred were she not in a certain fear for her safety and confusion as to her future, who can say? Whether it would have happened did she not find herself beneath quite different stars, rejoicing in her freedom and yet afraid that it might be denied her, there is none now and there was none then who could know. The fact is that she trod a path which her mother had once trod and broke an edict which was no less clear on a Norfolk day than it had been on a Boston night. So, we risk in a moment what we thought secure, do that which we believed we should never do.

Time passed. The horse grazed along the base of a hedge where bluebells bloomed and white-coned toadstools grew beneath trembling May blossom. There was no one in sight and anyone passing that way would have wondered at a cart thus abandoned. Certainly they would not have seen the two figures who stood silently in the shadows of a nearby wood and who then slowly seemed to fold into the ground, pressing down onto the fresh grass, crushing the bluebells so that a cloud of scent gathered like a mist about them.

The wildness in Pearl now softened to gentleness; the apparent softness in Standish was now transformed to an urgent violence. They drew a circle round themselves and within that circle was no church but their own, no society but the two of them, no law but that which governed all things. Manners change, proprieties are revised, even the moral law which we are told is inviolable and absolute is subject to revision. Without the heat of passion this would be a cold planet indeed, circling a dying star, a cosmic cemetery. Nor did the circle which enclosed them exclude anything but the artificial rules of the tribe for they were at one with all else, or so they might have told themselves had passion permitted thought and reckless abandon sought justification. For what is feared as anarchy by those who forget that they are its product is, perhaps, the deepest of harmonies, while the taboos and imperatives which would resist licence are themselves an artifice.

There is a country saying: the apple does not fall far from the tree. Was Pearl, then, no more than her mother's daughter, seeking consolation in the midst of distress? Was this moment pre-ordained and she required merely to re-enact the past as the seasons themselves return? She thought herself free and independent in her ways but who is there who does not believe as much? Was it, then, pride which brought pride's humbling?

Had she weighed in the balance her mother's natural truth and warm humanity and found them of greater worth than the cold injunctions of a society which sought to regulate the lives of those whose obedience it required, not for salvation's sake but to maintain the order of the state?

Whatever the truth, for one brief moment Pearl relented in her own resolution and so forgot both past and future as to believe the present were the only time. That she was wrong in part she knew, even then, but, as ever, knowing is but one part of truth and that the lesser when action may not follow on behind. Knowing what she knew, seeing what she had seen, nonetheless, intoxicated with the perfume of bluebells and adrift on an unknown sea, she mistook for safety what was, in truth, a threat to security itself.

High above, rooks circled in the sky, splinters in a blue eye. Rabbits nuzzled at the soft green moss. In the distance a curl of smoke spoke of a cottage beyond the fold in a low hill. Creation, in other words, went about its business as two people discovered in one another a harmony in the dissonance of the day. But passion, too, has its ending, though sooner, perhaps, for the one than for the other, for the very differences which pull together are also the differences which pull apart. Time, suspended for a while, now began again. The shadows had shortened. The horse had grazed some thirty feet of grass, only skirting a tangled bank of soft-leaved nettles. The bruised bluebells bled transparent liquid gently into the earth while, unseen and unknown, a biological clock had begun to tick towards the hour.

And what of John Standish, who entered this tale as no more than a reflection in the eyes of our heroine and whose existence until now was only an aspect of her emotions? This man of Cambridge had within him a spirit of rebellion, or perhaps of perversity. It was a rebellion which extended to his faith, for within him was a secular seed which took sustenance from the cruelties of a Church turned State. He, who gave the appearance of such assurance, in fact harboured doubts which could start him awake in the night. And though such doubts are the stuff of faith, had he but known it, yet he had other loyalties, loyalties to his father, and through him to another creed of which none knew and which would yet prove his undoing.

The day remembered by Pearl, that day on the dockside in London with the smell of spice in the air and a tangle of masts and rigging against the sky, was remembered by him no less acutely. There are times when the sight of another comes as a physical shock, and so it had been for him; during their brief voyage together she had entered his soul. He carried in his mind an image of her framed in that windy doorway high above the ground. In his small monastic room, close by the cathedral, he could summon her to his mind as there were those who believed a witch can summon the devil. He followed a path laid down for him by others but faltered in the face of a woman who had disturbed his design. But this he had never imagined. The height to which passion had lured him left him weak from desire, yet there was another imperative. He knew there was no retracing his steps from the cliff edge which he walked but who would wish for safety who had seen and felt and heard what rewards danger can offer? Yet was this the first such moment he had known or had he stood on this edge before? Pearl never thought such but Pearl was from another country.

When she met Lawyer Simple's clerk again she did not at first recognise him. The man who had seemed to tremble like a butterfly but whose black clothes and spindly legs had recalled rather a spider, stood upright and wore such clothes as betokened not a clerk but a gentleman. He wore a hat of beaver, perhaps fashioned from the very skins carried on the *Revenge*, and smiled with a boldness she would never have suspected him capable of affecting. And where once she would have supposed he were fifty or so, aged by the gloom of Opie Street, now she saw that he could be no more than in his late thirties, such the effect of daylight and a change of manner and costume alike.

'Sir? Master Hawkins?' she called tentatively as she

approached him outside the Adam and Eve tavern whither he had summoned her by note.

'Mistress Prynne.'

Pearl could think of nothing to say. Her mouth opened and closed but no sound came forth.

'You were not so silent last time we met.'

'I was . . . is it really . . .?'

'Could it be that I surprise you somewhat by my appearance?'

'Well . . .'

'For I certainly surprise myself.'

'You are . . . splendid.'

'Indeed. That is my opinion also. And since we are agreed upon this, shall we take a stroll by the river towards Cow Tower and see what else we may agree upon? The day is clear and bright and I have a lifetime of darkness to repent.'

They walked, accordingly, along lanes bright with late spring flowers until at last they reached the broad sweep of the Wensum flowing on towards Pulls Ferry and thence through the city to join with the Yare on its journey to the sea. The day was, as the lawyer's clerk observed, both clear and bright. There are such days, indeed, when the air seems to sparkle and there is a freshness which suggests that the world itself is reborn. This was such. The wherries which sailed to and fro seemed like so many brightly coloured birds gliding on the wind while the water itself shivered silver and gold in the noon sun.

Pearl's companion walked boldly. Indeed, every step he took seemed to fill him with energy as if he drew strength from the ground beneath his feet and the air he breathed. Neither spoke, each contained by their own thoughts, each responding to the simple beauty of grass and water and flint wall and green-sheened ducks. But at last they stood together by Cow Tower, which had been built to guard the entry to the city and which guarded it still, though against what none could say.

'Would it please you to sit awhile?'

'And it please you. You have summoned me and not I you.'

'That may be, though I beg leave to believe it may be otherwise, for I see in your arrival the hand of Providence.'

'How so?'

'What did you see in Opie Street? Was it not a humble clerk and an arrogant master?'

'A rebellious clerk, I think.'

'Ah. That may be. But rebellion was not before so public. You are the cause of that. You have been sent to rescue me.'

'I?'

'Indeed.'

'And what am I to rescue you from?'

'Why myself, first, and then that other, second.'

'Lawyer Simple?'

'As he calls himself, though I know him by another name and not just Beelzebub, neither.'

He paused and looked down at her, seated on a low bench.

'He means you harm.'

'How can he mean me harm who does not know me?'

'He can harm the unborn. Indeed he specialises in such.'

'How so?'

'Estates, my lady. Estates. Wills and covenants be the business of lawyers who are to be the servants of their clients' wishes. The dead, however, are ill placed to object to interpretations which do not match the text. Nor are the days of the week, the months of the year or the years themselves as fixed in their place as some did assume when they put down their quills and scattered sand over their names.'

'And you have known this?'

'I have.'

'And have done nothing?'

'Nothing.'

'And is this not . . . ' She could not utter the word, for this man, whom she had barely noticed when first she met him, now looked her straight in the eye.

'Wicked? Yes. It was. But it is over.'

He removed his hat and the wind caught his hair as he

looked away from her across the river to where a boy threw a stick for a dog to chase.

'He has a certain power over me as in a sense I do over him, though rather less, and as a result I persuaded myself that a piece of paper is no more than that. And what if one name replace that of another, well what of that? But you are so young and . . . There was once a young woman such as yourself and had he not had the power to cast spells I might have found with her what I know I will find with none else. And had she and I . . . well, perhaps we should have had a daughter and . . . you are both the mother and the daughter and have given me the chance to make amends.'

'But I am neither such.'

'No. Neither am I the man of twenty years who did not take the path I might. But today I am twenty again. Do you not see it?'

And he turned to her with such a smile that she could indeed. The pallor of the Opie Street chambers had dropped quite away. Translucent skin had given way to firm-textured health. At his lapel was a fresh bouquet of forget-me-nots, though twice as large as before. He carried the very spring itself at his breast.

'But, twenty or forty, I have news to tell. Not everything is known to me but enough to fear for you. First, though, I must ask what you know of your benefactor.'

A cloud passed across the sun, and a sudden wind lifted dust from around the base of the tower. Pearl pulled her cloak around her shoulder, in a movement which, had she but known, was the perfect mirror to a gesture of her mother's.

'Everything and nothing. He was a man who came into my life before I had knowledge or voice or ought else. He was my mother's past.'

'All answers lie in the past. That is half a lawyer's power. He owns the past, or at least he knows who might own it and knows how to read the traces left by time.'

'He was my mother's husband.'

Her companion seemed to jump as though stung. He put his

hat on his head and then he took it off again immediately.

'Then you . . .' He could not complete the thought. Indeed he looked around as if afraid some ghost might rise from the grave and Cow Tower prove powerless to protect him.

'No. I am not.'

He sighed, as though released of a lifetime's guilt. The cloud now obligingly moved away and once again they were in the golden light and warmth of the sun.

'But why then . . .'

'He would atone for the evil that he did.'

'The evil? In marrying?'

'In marrying one he did not love.'

'Ah,' replied the lawyer's clerk, and there was pain in the cry. 'He was older?'

'That were not evil. The evil was that he did not love and yet he would possess. And when another loved he sought his life and still more his soul.'

'It is the man, then. And did he not harm her directly? Your mother?'

'Is it no harm, do you think, to offer no love but to deny it to another? Is it no harm to destroy life? Is it no harm to cut into the spirit and to watch without blinking the death of a soul?'

With each question he cried out, as though cut by a sword, hearing an accusation directed at another as though it were a blow aimed at him. He nodded, though whether in assent to her bitter questions or to some more private enquiries of his own she could not say, for afterwards he remained silent and stared across the river to the fields which stretched away from the further bank.

Pearl looked at this stranger who nonetheless questioned her as none other had about that part of her life which had been a secret from all, indeed for many years even from herself. She fancied his hair had been trimmed and she saw, what she could never have seen in the Opie Street gloom, that his eyes were blue.

'You summoned me here,' she said, as gently as she might, for she saw that something troubled him. 'Yet I do not even know your name.'

For a second he continued to stare into the distance, then turned to her and stared equally intently into her eyes.

'I recall that a name was mentioned, but I have forgot.'

'A name was mentioned. Oh yes, a name was mentioned. Not mine but what he prefers me to be known by. My name is Daniel. The other will wait.'

'Very well, Daniel, and am I to know why I am summoned thus?'

'Not summoned. I have no power to compel. But we have something in common, you and I, and I have some small parts of a picture to place before you as you have just placed others before me. I know something of this man of whom you speak. I know, too, of others. There are companies of men who would wish not to be known as being party to one another's secrets.'

'And do you intend to speak thus generally or will you tell me what I must know?'

'I will tell you what I do know, and if not all it is because I have troubles of my own which I must resolve. The man of whom we speak was known as Chillingworth.'

'Known as?'

'It was no more than a name which he took. He had others. Some honourable, some not. Of his past I lack full detail.'

'But why should he take other names? Was this not already a sign of his villainy?'

Her companion smiled wryly. 'There are many reasons for choosing not to sail with one's true colours at the mast. You are a stranger among us and so may not recall or know the times through which we have passed. There were moments when to be asked one's name or religion or loyalty was but a presage to a knife across the throat. Names are nothing. The moral world depends not on appearance but on being. I make no judgement on him for that, nor yet for the fact that he delved into the secrets of nature, though there are those that did. But he fell in with a group, here in Norwich, who plotted against justice. It may be that he was not privy to all that they did nor all that they planned but his name appeared on the

158

indictment with those others. Not all the names were there, however. There were others not known then or since, not known, that is, except by a very few. And these confederates swore that their strengths would be joined together for the common cause. The cause is dead but some, it seems, still believe they retain rights over the property of their companions when it should come time for death to loose their grip on this world. They do not welcome your appearance.'

'Yet, if they are a secret confederacy, how could they venture into the light to challenge me?'

He shook his head at such naivety. 'There are documents. One document may be true. Another may be false. How do we tell the one from the other? With a coin a simple bite may tell the difference. With paper and ink we have a different case. Neither, I think, is in short supply.'

'There may be no certainty.'

He fell silent.

She repeated her assertion, which now sounded more a question. Still he was silent. Then he turned towards her and, as a father to his child, explained, 'Yes, mistress, it be certain. I have drawn the document.'

'You?'

'I have been ensnared. I am determined to escape the trap even should it mean I must chew off my foot to accomplish it.'

'Have I understood you? You have falsified the papers which determine my inheritance?'

He slowly nodded.

'And your name is not as I heard it pronounced.'

Again, a nod.

'And I am to place my trust and hope in you.'

'Do you have another?'

She looked at her feet, as the truth behind that question became apparent. Unless it should be that other. 'And could you not take this tale to the magistrate?'

'Ay. I could. If I should fancy a life in prison.'

'But you worked under coercion, did you not?'

'Coercion. Yes.'

'And has this happened before?'

'A time or two. I know what you think for I am thinking it, too. But there is another world at Opie Street. No sun, until you rapped upon my desk and woke me up.'

'And can you not place responsibility on Lawyer Simple?'

'Ay. I could.'

'And will not.'

'There are more mysteries and secrets than I can tell you now.'

'What may I do, then?'

'Take care. They mean you harm. For my part what was written may be unwritten, I suppose, or even new documents discovered.'

'But that would be to compound your offence.'

'You have never turned your head to arithmetic, I see. Two negatives may prove to have a value. This, at least, you must leave to me.'

'And do I have need to fear?'

'We all have need to fear. But consider, a few days since you were one against the world; now you may count it one and a half. A few weeks since I was but the shadow to a shadow. Now I cast a shadow of my own.'

He rose and dusted himself down a little. 'I must return.'

'Will Lawyer Simple not find your new appearance some- what . . . strange?'

'And he do? He is content for me to be as I will if only it will cause him no discomfort.'

'And will it?'

'I think there is discomfort for us all ahead but discomfort may have its advantages, too. I would wish you courage but know that you do not lack it else should I not have set my own foot upon this path.'

It may be imagined what thoughts assailed this woman of twenty years as she walked alone back to Colney. She who had travelled so far and with such high hopes now learned that there were those who planned her fall, people summoned from a past she knew nothing of. True, she had friends who would be her strength but what might they be against those who gathered in the shadows? But young women of twenty are not without a supply of strength of their own and Pearl had never yet found the limits of her courage. She and her mother had walked alone and were no strangers to conspiracy. Their whole lives had been lived in the eye of a storm and she understood well enough that there were some whose cruelties admitted no relenting. So there was a spring to her step nor did she look at the ground but held her head high. Some are made for battle while others are not and not all those made for battle are men.

As she walked, passing through the gates of St Giles and on towards Earlham, there was a great deal of bustle. It was market day and many a small flock of sheep nosed first this way and then that like so many ships sailing into the wind. At their heels were dogs who at one moment crouched low to the ground and the next moved in a rush to snap at the heels of a straying lamb. In between came carts, jolting sideways as a wheel sank in a hole, with fluttering chickens within rough-woven baskets. These were the animals which had made no sale, for the market had begun at dawn and now was done.

These were not good days in England. What wealth there was did not flow down to those who tilled the soil and tended the beasts. Money resided in land. There were great estates and great folk who owned such. Most of those who passed along the lane were tenants, owing labour and goods and money to those they seldom saw. Pearl was aware that the property which had been the subject of her discussion but half an hour or so since itself received payments from more than half the villagers of Colney. Life for most remained what it had ever been, a struggle from one day's end to another. Up with the dawn to serve the animals and crops upon which they relied, they were abed by nine to be ready for the next day's dawn.

They rode and walked for the most part in silence, save for the sound of the animals, for few had purchased and most had failed to make a sale. Besides, there was now a heaviness to the air as thunder threatened what until then had been a perfect day. By degrees, though, the farmers, labourers and serving girls took their leave, turning down lanes which led to farms and scattered hamlets. The gathering clouds had turned the pale greens of morning to olive and the grey trees to black. As she came to Earlham a first drop of rain set the leaves of oak and elm to nodding. It was then that, in glancing behind, for no better reason than that one has to look somewhere, she thought she saw a figure in the gloom. If there were someone, though, he must have stepped behind a tree or hid behind a bush for she had barely noticed him and he was gone. She was not afraid, not least because she could not be sure what she saw. So she waited a second to see if he – for it was a man, as she thought – would reappear, but the rain threatened and she still had a mile or more to go before she would be back at Colney and lacked protection against a storm. So, with one more glance behind, she went upon her way, descending the gentle slope from Earlham's oaks before the land rose again, equally gently, towards the beeches at Colney.

She had thought to pass across the stepping stones and hurry to her disputed home, but as she drew level with St Andrew's church the heavens decided to delay no longer and opened wide. Within a few seconds everything bent before the storm. Pearl, with a shawl about her head, ran, loose-limbed and almost exultant, to the church door, and swung it open with such force that it slipped from her wet fingers and crashed against the wall. The sound recalled another door which had evaded her grasp and one who had been at her side when it did.

She stepped within. There was little light. No candles were kept flickering here and the windows admitted only a green glow reflected from the rain-streaked leaves of the trees beyond. It was a plain church, with the smell of earth and damp stone. To her left was a rope which ascended through a planked ceiling to the bell beyond. To the right were the pews, upright, correct, unyielding, worn smooth with use. There was an order of precedence to those who sat within them, as she had seen, which perfectly mirrored that of the community it served. God's power, it seemed, endorsed that of those on earth. It had not been quite so in Boston. Though there was precedence, to be sure, there was nonetheless a crude democracy which prevailed amongst those who were elect. Neither was wealth alone to determine such, no, nor custom since that requires time to assert its true authority.

She sat down in the last row of the pews to wait out the storm and to think over what she had been told. She had sought adventure and such, it seemed, was to be her fate. She was grateful, nonetheless, that she had made a friend, nor had she ceased to be amazed at the transformation which had turned a grey, stooped clerk into a man of some up-rightness and distinction, though he confessed complicity in crimes.

Ahead, in the darkness, a pulpit leaned out into the nave from which, no doubt, a minister would call his flock to obey commandments as she had earlier seen the dogs snap at sheep who sought to leave the path. But what secrets of their own might such a congregation possess, what hidden sins marked by no gold embroidery might signify their fallen state? And how could she now be drawn by one who touched her heart when she had promised herself that she would never have to do with such? It is true that she had been reconciled to the man who was her father. She still remembered, and some nights would dream of it, too, that moment when she held the hand of a man she had once despised but finally had loved as he lay in death on a public scaffold. But she recalled, too, her mother's tears when she thought her daughter at last asleep.

She looked at the simple cross upon the altar, plain and unadorned, a symbol alike of salvation and salvation's pain. This was the bridge between the world she had left and the world to which she had come. It was a sign which she associated with betrayal, denial, abandonment.

The light had failed still further. She sat in a green glow as though she were under water and in truth she felt as though she might be sinking down into a world of mystery and alarm. The rain on the roof sounded brittle like wind in a field of wheat, while a distant rumble of thunder took her back to her ocean journey and the sound of barrels dragged across the deck. She who had set out with such excitement, if also with an aching regret, now sat alone, not a little bewildered by what had befallen her. These were days when few women would venture on their own what Pearl had done and here perhaps in part was the reason why that should be.

A flicker of lightning lit the church. Pulpit, pews and cross stood out, suddenly, in their stark simplicity, but something else made Pearl flinch and look up at one of the windows which faced the lane. She thought she saw the shadow of a man's head, framed by the diamond lattice, on the flagstones before her feet. The impression lasted only a second before it was gone again. She was fated, it seemed, to see such figures in every shadow. There came a second bright flash before the thunder from the first had swept across the valley but this time no such shadow was cast. The rain beat even harder until a thousand drummers seemed above her head. And in that instant the door flew open, though whether by wind or human hand she could not be sure for the darkness was now such that it might as well have been the dead of night.

Then another lightning flash flickered silver white and almost at once overhead a double clap of thunder shook the church. And in that sudden brightness she saw a figure standing with outstretched hand before the darkness returned, deeper than before.

'Hester go, Hester come,' said a voice. 'Charley see.'

It was the last rain of spring. From that moment all moisture left the air. The sun became king and ruled with a fierceness which never relented. It was a heat which engendered and a heat which destroyed.

Saturday was the day of the fair. By St Peter Mancroft, along Market Street and down all the lanes and alleys, was a bustle of people. Jugglers, fiddlers, performing dogs gathered small crowds while others spread cloth on the ground and laid out their wares for sale. By Guildhall a group of players, who only two years since would have chanced their lives, performed St George's encounter with the dragon, a dragon whose many legs suggested four young boys beneath the green cloth which swung from side to side.

Pearl, who had seen nothing of the like in Boston, wandered with her cousin from stall to stall, breathing the smells and listening to the sounds. At one place a suckling pig was turned above a fire and blackened slices offered to those who passed. By another, honeycomb from clover bees was held up, golden yellow, a miracle of design. Norwich had become London. There was no room to move.

'Hold close to thy purse,' advised her cousin.

'I have none. I had not thought to bring money.'

'That's as well. Not all those who thrive at fair-time do so by selling, thou may be sure.'

Music filled the air, that and the cry of sellers of pies and flowers and fruit and all that any could wish, as it seemed to Pearl.

'Some come from as far as Yarmouth and Cromer,' observed her cousin, 'and I have heard that there are others from Thetford and Newmarket, though why they should travel so far I do not know.'

There was indeed a tangle of wagons and horses and people of all kinds. Seeing her cousin look around in such bewilderment, she observed that this was but a once-a-year event.

'And I should think so, too,' said Pearl, who could hardly keep her feet in the crowd.

'I shall need to buy some muslin and a pipe, I'm told, though why William should require that I cannot think who has a dozen or more at home.'

Her cousin seized her hand, partly afraid for herself, partly for Pearl as the cobbles were already slippery from squashed fruit. The jostle of people and animals made progress all but impossible.

Ahead, a man walked upon stilts while another, beside him,

juggled apples. A child walked by with a pig's bladder on a stick but Norwich itself, it seemed, had decided that for a day all would play at being children for others, too, carried bladders and watched those who performed with no less eagerness and pleasure.

'Now, Pearl. Let's to Tombland. William will be there.'

'Why Tombland?'

'I could say because the horse fair be there and he has an eye for horseflesh, which it is and he has, to be sure, but there is also an inn that be his favourite and some companions of his who think much the same. But on our way we may buy the muslin on London Street and the pipe besides.'

So they set off, hand in hand, through the crowd of city and country folk for whom this was a holiday from labour and restraint. And muslin there was on London Street, that and worsted and wool and thread in colours which rivalled the rainbow. There were buttons, too, set out like armies marching to war across hillsides of cloth with silver lances thrust through, and thimbles made of bone and hoops of wood for drawing material tight for nimble fingers to create designs and children to mark their progress with a sampler, each word worked in a different stitch, each line a separate colour, their age, together with the date, a record to be held against a distant day.

Nancy stopped beside a woman who sat with her wares spread beside her, her face a deep and wrinkled brown. As her companion began to bargain, so Pearl looked about her. London Street climbed a little away from her so that she could see those who walked its length, a flowing river of humanity. Then she remembered where she was, for London Street led up towards Opie Street, the castle to her right, Blackfriars to her left. Even as this realisation reached her she saw, or thought she saw, some distance ahead, where the crowd had momentarily parted, two men in conversation. One, surely, was Lawyer Simple, a raven of a man, his black cloak folded around him. It was the other, though, who made her pause. For unless the light deceived her – and the sun was reflecting off the windows down the street, as though it had been shattered into a thousand shards of brightness – it was John Standish. The two seemed to lean towards each other like gaunt trees in a winter wood. Standish, too, if it were indeed he, was also dressed in black, Law and Church both preferring a dark disguise. Then the tableau was gone, dissolved of a sudden. The crowd closed in and once again the stream of people flowed. Her cousin's protesting voice rose.

'Such a price. Such a price. I have seen the selfsame cloth for . . .'

The argument continued but Pearl stood transfixed. Simple and Standish, John, who had . . . It could not be. Indeed, she realised that it might indeed not have been for she had glimpsed the two figures no more than a second. Her eye had been drawn to Simple. The other she had barely seen at all, for no sooner had she begun to consider who it might be than the two became invisible in the general tapestry. Indeed, the more she thought of the incident the less certain she became until she doubted even her identification of Simple who had appeared only as a dark figure at a distant point.

'Does this take thy fancy, Pearl? How dost thou like the pattern?'

Her cousin held out a length of cloth and in the instant all was lost without the thought of loss. Pearl stood back a pace, all notions of lawyers and ministers gone.

'I like it well, but is it not costly?'

'So I have said but we have agreed a price.'

The seller looked as though this were far from the truth, shaking her head and gesturing towards the other lengths of cloth spread before her.

'I will take it,' said Nancy, and began burrowing about her person for a purse which she had concealed with much care before leaving Caistor. At length it appeared, like an old stocking from the wash, and she paid out the price, placing each coin in the seller's hand and counting loudly as though expecting her to contest the amount. It was, though, Pearl could see, a ritual that was required, the woman's head nodding as each coin was placed in a hand which seemed grimed with the city's dirt.

'And now,' said Nancy, the ceremony complete, 'pipes.'

'Pipes?' echoed Pearl, quite forgetting their errand, so taken was she still with such a flow of humanity and such a variety of sellers and buyers.

A moment later they were at Opie Street. The revellers and those who went about their trade passed it by. It seemed closed off to all but its own solemnity. No one walked along its path and its windows were like the eyes of blind people, vacant, fixed and lifeless. Sawdust was spread along the ground, as was sometimes done when there was illness within doors, to deaden the sound of passing carriages and feet. Perhaps there was illness of a sort but no feet or carriage wheels disturbed what passed for its peace. If Pearl expected to see either of her apparitions she was disappointed and, in common with all about her, hurried on her way.

The pipe was soon purchased. Indeed, so many sellers of pipes were there that it seemed that Norwich must be one long conflagration.

'Careful, my dear,' said Nancy, handing her the purchase, 'thou hast but to breathe on it and it shatters. Such delicacy seems quite out of place.'

So, Pearl clutching the slender pipe and her cousin a fold of cloth, they made their way at last to Tombland where horses stamped and men leaned, at various angles, with tankards of ale in their hands, and where, had she but known it, many years before conspirators had met in a room at the top of a twisted staircase and among their number the man who had sought first her mother's hand and later her soul. And there, striding across the cobbles, came, not from London Street but the Close, one of the men she thought she had seen only minutes before. So she had been mistaken. We do indeed see what we look for, even if we do not know we search it out.

Some four nights later, as the shadows lengthened and evening drew in, she saw from her bedroom window a thin line of smoke. A few moments more and it darkened until, caught by the wind, it seemed to form a kind of letter in the sky. Ever curious and anxious to leave no mystery unsounded, she changed her shoes, drew a shawl about her shoulders lest the air should grow cool, and set out towards Earlham where the smoke had begun to broaden to a cloud. This was no bonfire of sticks and weeds and, besides, she required little excuse to leave her isolation.

She followed the path of the river which itself barely seemed to move. Despite the sudden squalls and showers there had otherwise been little rain for a month or more so that it was shallow and weed lay like a green cloak upon it. She passed the weir where three boys lingered after a day of swimming, their energy seemingly boundless. The land rose gently to the north but there were no cattle as there had been since her arrival, no smudges of brown against green grass. Walking in the valley she had lost the perspective which her Colney vantage point had given. The patterned strips in the fields, where the fresh shoots of wheat alternated with grass and turned earth, from here seemed little more than an improvised succession of textures, the product of no more than chance.

The breeze shifted and the smoke with it until, as she approached the ford at Earlham, and the wooden bridge beside it, she detected what seemed to her the smell of beef roasting on a spit. It was a smell which took her back in imagination to the Swan so that she could almost hear cousin William call for ale. Across the river to the east lay Earlham Hall, its windows catching the light of the sun as it slipped towards the western horizon, if horizon it could be called which was only the rising meadows of Bowthorpe. The smoke, however, came not from there but from the farm to her left and it was thither that she directed her steps.

Whatever she had expected, nothing prepared her for the vision which now confronted her for, as the sun disappeared at last, flooding the sky with a diffused light as though the whole were aflame, so another fire came into view. Where there had been smoke now there were flames. Where she had seen an idyllic rural dream, an English valley on a summer's eve, now she saw a rural nightmare. Figures moved in the gathering gloom, indistinct against the smoke and then sharply etched against the blaze. There was something about their movements, as though they laboured under heavy weights, which suggested more than the effort of their work, more than tiredness. There was, as it seemed to her, even before she understood the meaning of what she saw, a despair about them, too.

The flames reached up into the sky and every now and then a sudden shining of sparks, an upward, spiralling dazzle of lights, drew her eyes away from the dark and awkward shapes which seemed to breathe them out. Men came together in small groups, bowing for a moment towards the earth, as though in some grotesque parody of submission to an alien god, then moving or staggering towards the circle of fire. She could just make out a wide pit, its edges rimmed with evacuated earth. At various points a path had been trodden down and through these gaps in the earthworks of this diabolic rampart the men would pass, pulling objects which seemed too heavy for them to carry. At first she could no more make out what those objects might be than she could distinguish the features of those who pulled them. They were plainly heavy and sticks seemed to emerge from them, which aided in the carrying. Then, as they swung and pushed their burden between them, she realised, what her nose should long since have confirmed for truth, that they were cows, the very cows whose absence on the hillside she had remarked.

Another spiral of false stars rose into the air and the dark figures who stood out, like minor devils lit by the flames, turned to seek out further victims. The smell which had intrigued her now appalled. Why this slaughter, why this sudden death on a summer's evening? In the light of the conflagration she could see a sparrowhawk, hovering in the air, looking down on this false sunrise, to detect even the smallest life which might escape the searching heat.

The fire burned her face but a sudden chill made her draw in her cloak, though whether the cold came entirely from without, who can say. No one could watch such a sight and remain unmoved.

'Not pretty work, young mistress,' said a man who appeared suddenly beside her and might have spoken of himself, since his face was begrimed with the smoke as though he had himself risen from the flames.

Pearl started, more than a little afraid. 'But what . . .'

'They have a sickness. It is common enough. There is nothing to do but this.'

'But such a . . .'

'It is a terrible waste but where there is sickness it must be cut out or all will die of it. It is hard but hard things must be done.' He spoke like a minister addressing his flock. 'I pray God there is none other hereabouts that has taken it or we shall be without meat this winter.'

'Was there no other way?' asked Pearl, looking at the dark figures who pulled another animal towards the flames.

'No other way. It must be cut out. You had best turn away.'

'Yes,' replied Pearl, as the man returned to his toil, but she did not turn aside, watching this dark play performed against a scarlet cloth.

The men laboured, their faces glistening in the light of the flames, but to one side stood another, he whose cattle were thus sacrificed for the good of his neighbours. He had stood there since her arrival, watching impassively, as five and thirty cows were swung into the pit. From prosperity to poverty in a matter of moments, for how should he replace what was lost? So fragile the ground on which we stand, so temporary our state which seems so permanent. Then two men stepped from behind the barn so besmeared with blood that they seemed a kind of living extension of the fire. They were the executioners but even they, it seemed, required respite. Why, though, did they not slaughter at the pit's edge, she thought? Was there some propriety which made them conduct their trade in private? Was this a ritual which required the dark?

She had thought that England was a gentle place, that the

blood of violence and war was now past. Certainly her mother's stories told of a country which, sword and cruelty of soldiers aside, was enfolded in its own security. What should the ages have bequeathed if not contentment and a subtle rhythm of growth and decay? But there were no scenes such as this in her mother's tales, no blood spilled on the land nor flames reaching to the skies.

Two dogs ran back and forth along the edge of the pit, drawn by the smell of cooking flesh. They crouched low, from time to time creeping forward in the hope of seizing the meat which crackled and spat only a foot or two away. Then up again, restlessly crossing one another's paths, their eyes glowing golden in the dark. One rushed forwards, closed its jaws on the leg of one of the cooking animals, and tried to pull it back, bracing its own legs in the soil. The move served only to cloud it in a sudden wreath of sparks and it yelped its pain, running towards the darkness, its tail between its legs, its nose sliding along the ground, first one side then the other, as if it sought to plough the land. Its partner, learning nothing, continued to patrol, eyes ablaze, tongue hanging loosely from the corner of its mouth.

Pearl returned across the river, the flames behind casting her shadow before. It was night now and she trod with care but the river surprised her, glowing silver in the dark field, reflecting the light from a moon which had almost worn itself away and which the fire had rendered invisible until then. Across the valley she heard the hollow cry of an owl and, moments later, the scuffle of a badger, perhaps, or was it no more than the rattle and sigh of reeds shaken by a passing fox? Behind her in the fading glow was death. Here the air was alive with sound, though such sound as might mean death to some. There! Was that the slither of an otter, as that was assuredly the rasping croak of a frog? Night is never silent. Indeed, with the stilling of the self-important chatter of the day we begin to hear what other sounds accompany our lives should we but pause to listen.

As she approached the Hall she turned again to see the false sun in the sky, the glow from a fire whose cause she now knew. The night was clear, the smell of honeysuckle like a musk heavy in the air. Here she was again, alone. Around her teemed a life generated by something more than a solitary existence. This was no place for her: a dark building which crushed her spirits. Nor did she have any claim to it. The man who lived here had wronged her mother and her father. Could ownership wish that away? Was it compatible with her spirit? Bricks and mortar, wattle and daub, what were these to her? Whenever she dreamed it was not of such as these. She carried a key around her neck. The cord had rubbed her flesh and she would be free of it. Nor was she anxious to become her own gaoler, turning the lock on herself each night. She was not a solitary who could find her own company sufficient, though there were occasions, it is true, when that proved sufficient for her immediate needs. She was striving to possess what she no longer wanted for no better reason than that there were others who would deny it to her and the wilfulness of youth had yet to fade with the years. But even she recognised that to wish for something only that you may thereby deny it to others is no basis for a claim in law, still less for a life which must be led between the twin rocks of necessity and desire.

Chapter Six

May gave way to June. Pearl was still undecided as to how to act. A letter from Lawyer Simple had arrived in which he spoke of progress with her claim, urged patience on her and indicated the modest fee which his actions would command, itself evidence of his continued concern. This alone gave her the beginnings of confidence, for she was sure that the promise of payment and not her urgings would win the day. Simple made no further mention of Chillingworth's supposed brother but she could not forget his threats and had several more times seen one who resembled him in the woods. Well, she had told herself, if he should wish to live with the fox and the owl, then so be it. Nonetheless she barred her doors at night and did not always sleep as deeply as she might. Meanwhile, the Hall held one more secret for her to discover.

Above the fireplace in what had once been the study of the one-time owner, was a painting. In her enthusiasm for cleaning, for stripping out all that was old and broken and decayed, Pearl had scarcely noticed it, seeming, as it did, a part of the very fabric of the house, resting not upon the surface of the wall but set in a recess which matched exactly its dimensions. Another factor turned it all but invisible. Smoke and soot from the fire, which had seared the Hall those years before, had rendered its surface a sooty black. Indeed, when she sat one day, with a cup of tea, and noticed it for the first time, it appeared no more than a rectangle of darkness. Yet as she stared, so it seemed she could make out a shape and such gradations of black as suggested a hidden form. The curiosity was that every succeeding day she believed she could distinguish further details, a subtle shading of black within black, a hint of brown and then a kind of olive green.

As to the subject of this painting: at first it appeared no more than blackness itself, as though the artist had only a single colour, or absence of colour, in his palette. She felt sure the artist must be a man, for no woman, as it seemed to her, could have chosen to explore such a joylessness, such a revelling in sombre tones, and sought to see what variations might be wrought in paint by brush stroke alone. But by degrees she thought she saw something more, a kind of design, not openly expressed but held within the paint as the grain is captive in the wood; neither simple blackness nor a shifting pattern or hieroglyph, but a face. What had seemed mere imperfections in the resolute blackness, two whorls of paint, two implicit circles set a little above the centre of the design, now seemed none such but in fact a pair of eyes. No sooner had this passing thought occurred to her than suspicion became conviction and from that moment it was not she who stared at the painting but it which stared at her. She could feel the gaze even when she herself was not in the room. It was the gaze of a man. No woman could mistake it. It seemed to lure her back from wherever she might be. And once the eyes were set in place, as it were, then, by degrees, other features began to emerge. Was that thin line, that apparent attenuation of the pigment, that slight curve not, perhaps, a mouth? And if so, then might that other mark not indicate a chin? So slight were these suggestions, however, that it was possible to imagine any face which might match these hints of human form.

Pearl was not one to live with doubt, so one morning, following a night in which that face had appeared and dissolved in her dreams, she took water and soap in a bucket and set it in the hearth. In the light of the dawn the painting appeared opaque. All suggestion of a hidden portrait had disappeared in the pale light which shone whitely through the window. She took a cloth and wrung it out before wrapping it around her finger. She began to rub gently on the surface of the canvas and saw immediately that it was indeed no more than smoke and dust which obscured, for a small patch of brightness began to appear. She moved her hand in circles, shedding light by degrees, as though she were herself in darkness and held a candle in her hand.

It was a portrait. Soon she had revealed two hands, one resting on a pile of books, a ring on its finger shining a sullen red, the other holding, as it seemed, a flask. The whiteness of these hands, now exposed, gave them an almost spectral air, set, as they were, against the darkness which still surrounded them. Pearl stepped back and looked at what had thus far been exposed, at hands severed from a hidden body, and shuddered a little in the sharpness of the morning air.

One mystery resolved provoked another, for the ring itself had a strange design, a kind of serpentine flow which enclosed the red stone as a heart is enclosed by the body which it animates. The shock was that she had seen the ring before, yes, and those slender fingers, too. And yet it could not be. She plunged the cloth in the water, itself now grimed and grey, and splashed it on the surface of the painting with a sudden urgency. Within a few minutes she stared at the face of the man who had haunted her childhood dreams. And he stared back at her, his eyes as black as the soot which had shielded them from full view until a moment since. It was the pale flesh around them which she had detected before.

The soap and water gave a freshness to the surface of the painting so that it seemed to glow with life, itself a paradox since the figure thus animated with well water and lye was so pale that he seemed himself a corpse. His coat was black, which was why she had seen nothing but the pale outline of his face, while behind him were lace curtains, the very ones which she had torn from the windows opposite when she had first arrived.

She stepped back, oblivious to the soiled water which dripped on the ground. Here was a man she had never thought to meet again in this life or the next and she felt once more the physical revulsion which she had experienced before: yet this time, and unaccountably, a kind of pity too, which was why, though shocked, she felt no fear. He was part of a story which was complete.

At last she dropped the sodden cloth back into the bucket and turned towards the kitchen. His eyes followed her. She stopped and turned about. Once again his eyes met hers and she felt at once a kind of mute contempt and yet an appeal as well, as though he sought if not her forgiveness then some recognition that he was both more and less than she had supposed: more man and less devil at the least. She moved to one side. The eyes followed her, the mouth appearing to open as though he would speak.

For all her assurance as a child, for all the perversity, even, which had made her step into shadows which others dreaded, Pearl was not so secure in herself as to venture to cohabit with this painted ghost. Accordingly she went to the kitchen, opened the drawer and selected a knife which had doubtless carved many a joint of beef. She stood a second before the doleful picture and then stepped forward and stabbed that knife into the very corner of the painting. She drew it down and along, then up and across again until the persecutor of her father, and thereby mother too, lay limp across her arm. The frame was now like an eye socket when the eye itself has been plucked out.

She carried the canvas into the garden, along with a box and a low stool which she set in the shade of a willow, before returning to the house to fetch a large wooden board from the kitchen, a heavy spoon and some pins. A third trip brought a kitchen chair to place beside the stool. The painting lay staring up into the sky as she prepared herself. Lying, as it did, on the grass, it no longer seemed to threaten while the sun, in drying the soapy water, had removed the illusion of life in death or death in life. She took it up again and pressed it to the board which she swiftly turned so that the portrait was staring down at the earth into which the man himself had long since passed.

Nor were these actions quite as strange as they might seem for she was not intending to torture in effigy one whom she could not call to account in person. She was an artist with a piece of canvas to work, a fortuitous surface for her own designs. Yet there was more than this, for she was not content to reverse the canvas and paint where the surface was as yet unmarked. She pinned it to the board so that the face still stared at her as she set it on the chair and bent to her box of paints and brushes. The fact was that she had determined not to destroy what seemed to her a hateful image but to obliterate it with her own art. Accordingly she reached first for white so that she might purify the canvas of its image.

There, in the dappled shade of morning, shot through with shifting lights, she began the task of unmaking. First the eyes, the staring eyes of jet, then the mouth, thin and purposeful. What a soldier might do with a sword she accomplished with a brush and pigment. And when at last the work was completed and her white paint quite used up she began to create a summer scene. Determined to cover the image which confronted her and with no further white to soften, she worked in bold colours until what began to emerge was no pastel portrait of a gentle season but a bright and almost lurid other world such as she had never painted before, in Boston or in Norwich.

By evening it was finished. The hours had passed without her noticing. She sat back at last, her body aching and the beginnings of a headache narrowing her eyes. She nodded to herself, then rose and carried chair, stool, box and wooden board inside. Once in the kitchen she propped the day's work against the pantry door and stepped back. With a start she leaned forwards again, for could she not still see the face of the man she thought she had buried beneath blue and red and green? Certainly she thought she saw his eyes staring from a tree, quite as though he had hidden in a hollow stump and looked out at her. Was her art, then, not sufficient to challenge this man who chose to haunt her thus? But such are the fancies of one who has sat in the sun too long and whose head has begun to throb. She carried the canvas back into the study, now dark with evening, as though she might replace it in the niche over the fireplace. Certainly the vacant frame invited some repair, but she lacked the skill or inclination and laid the painting down instead by the brass-edged surround which guarded the fire. But as she stood once more in the uncertain light of a room whose shadows deepened, the space looked more sinister than before, a hollow socket staring blindly into her soul as the eyes of the portrait had done before. She looked at that blank vacancy until her head seemed to swim and her mind to cloud, but at that moment she felt the soft fur of the cat brushing against her legs and was recalled from the trance into which she had begun to slip. Then, lifting the candle above her head, she stuck out her tongue and, spinning upon her heel, strode out.

The heat of June edged towards the furnace breath of August. Everywhere life was in the balance. The parched soil gave refreshment to neither goose nor fox. Birds would tumble from the air for want of water. Yet life still bred.

Pearl was pregnant and it needed no folk wisdom to tell her such. She carried certainty within her as surely as she carried a child. And though for one such as she, unmarried in a strange land, far from the comfort of family, this spelled a kind of doom, she felt nothing but joy. The chemistry of her body had begun to shape her feelings to ensure a welcome for the child even now beginning its journey towards birth. Yet, though she knew for a certainty that she carried a new world within her, she must allow time before she could share that knowledge with another.

She and Standish had continued to meet, though a new discretion seemed to have infected him. The shock of their encounter in the wood, its fierce realities as well as its gentle fictions, had, it seemed, shaken them both. They were perhaps a little afraid of each other as they were of the certainty that they had trespassed together. She visited the cathedral and sat in the coolness of the nave as outside the temperature rose. He smiled at her as he passed and twice their hands touched, leaving her, and perhaps him, trembling for hours, but somehow that moment of intimacy had also driven them apart as though they sensed some danger. But, if danger there were, they were already its victims. They did not repeat their afternoon amidst the bluebells. They seldom met in public and even their private assignations were few. For her part, Pearl was bewildered, feeling sometimes that he burned with a true passion, at others that he withdrew in shame or guilt or some other preoccupation. He seemed a man torn, while she herself was in need of certainty. As to her problems in Opie Street, he assured her that he was at work on her behalf and she believed him as we believe all who tell us what we would hear.

Still she stayed on at the Hall. Still nothing had been resolved about its future or hers. She knew she must tell Standish about the child and yet something held her back, some doubt, some echo from a past not her own. But tell him she must. So, some three months after their encounter, she wandered one day in the transept of the cathedral and waited for his appearance. Shafts of light angled down from the great windows. She was aware of the space which had opened up between them and was uncertain how to proceed.

When he appeared it was with a woman who leaned towards him as he spoke to her in a low voice, another sinner, no doubt, seeking absolution. Pearl watched, waiting her moment with all the trepidation and excitement of one about to impart a secret which will transform her life. Standish and the woman parted. Did their hands meet for a second? Was she deceived or did their fingers touch and linger? But the moment was gone and she rose from the pew where she had knelt. He walked along the nave and then turned and passed through a door into the cloisters. She followed.

The air was warm and humid, almost soporific. The cloisters enclosed a square lawn, newly cut. Several sickles rested against grey columns and the smell of grass was intoxicating. As she followed she saw him sit himself at the base of a column where the sun spilled across the broken stonework. He took a document from his pocket and began to read. She looked at him as an artist will look at her subject. This, then, was the father of her child. In a moment or two they would share that knowledge. She was, she felt, staring at her future, and was suddenly unsure if this was a path she wished to take. It was a path which had narrowed without her noticing and for the first time she was aware of a sense of genuine alarm. He was a stranger. She knew nothing of him. Her own nature, she knew, was impetuous and she regretted nothing but now impetuosity presented its price.

'So, John, thou art turned student again.'

He started and thrust the letter he had been reading deep into the pocket of his black gown.

'Pearl.'

'Thou and I have become strangers this past month and more.'

A blush started at the base of his neck. In this, at least, they were as one. 'Not strangers, I trust. There has been much to do. And art thou well?'

'Ay. I am well. More than well.' She paused and looked into his eyes, her own clouding with a sudden doubt. 'And dost thou think of me at all, John Standish?'

'How could I not? Thou and I . . .' He hesitated, as though he could find no words to describe their relationship.

'What are we, John? Sinners?'

'No.' He spoke too quickly for assurance. And then, looking in her eyes, he said, in a voice at once gentle and intense, 'What thou and I did had a consecration of its own.'

If there is irony in heaven a kind of sad laughter must have sounded around the many mansions of God's kingdom at these words. For all he spoke so quietly there was a whispered echo which came back to them from the ancient stones. And beyond that was another echo which neither heard.

'That it had. And now more so.'

And so she laid her secret before him, calmly and with a

181

certain reverence. 'I am with child, John. Thou and I are wedded in our souls.'

He received the news as countless millions of other men have received such news, with a mixture of terror and despair.

'It cannot be. We did but . . . it was but the once.'

'Then once were enough.' She spoke slowly, watching his face for sign of the pleasure she had perhaps hoped to see, the strength for which she yearned. What she saw was turmoil. But for that, too, she had been prepared. He thrust his hand into his vestment and removed it clutching a paper before, realising what he had done, he thrust it back again. This was not the John Standish of a dappled woodland clearing. This was a young boy caught in an orchard with a russet apple in his hand. This was a man brought to confront a wayward truth and looking around for an open door.

'Dost regret it? What thou didst tell me? What we did signify?'

'No, Pearl. Only the result.'

'The result was implicit in the act, I think.'

With a suddenness which surprised her he got to his feet and strode a few paces away before turning and looking at her in a distracted way. The shadow of a moss-stained pillar fell across his face which was thus part in sunlight and part in shade. He seemed to struggle for speech. And curiously, as it seemed to Pearl later, sitting alone, quite alone, in an empty room, it was only at that moment that she felt a deep and profound sense of betrayal. And with that came guilt and a sense of solitariness. And though she stood in the bright sunlight, so bright she had to narrow her eyes to see him at all, a sudden coldness seemed to reach into her heart.

'Was there no love, then, John?'

She spoke in a whisper, as much to her own troubled soul as to the man whose form had stirred her heart by the river's edge in distant London. The space between them was only a few paces. At that moment it might as well have been the width of the Atlantic. Indeed, when he looked about to see if they might be overheard she realised that he was touched with fear, that he was considering his position in the public world and not the truth of their private feelings. For a second he swayed back into the shadow so that, blinded by the glare, she could barely see his face, save as a pale spectre. Then he moved towards her again, with a smile which suggested the John Standish she had known. He did not touch her, though she longed for his embrace, but there was something in his eyes which reassured her. Without speaking they sat on the low stone wall. A fine silt of soil nearby boiled with ants. Everything stood out in sharp relief as if nature had resolved to present herself only in detail, all pattern lost. Pearl noticed a wisp of his hair, a single strand, almost translucent. There was a blemish on his forehead, above the left eye, a crescent scar like an insignia.

'What are we to do, John?'

'We must meet.'

'We are meeting.'

'Alone.'

'And are we not alone?'

'Not here. Oh, Pearl. What have we done?'

'We have done what others have done before us.' Can one other not have been in her mind? Was that precedent not perhaps what had led her down this path? With a curious perversity she had set her feet in the prints left on the path of time by her mother before her. 'I will not be ashamed. Do not ask me to regret.'

'Thou would not wish it undone?'

'Only if thou did, for then its meaning would be halved and I alone.'

'Thou art not alone, Pearl.' He smiled at her and yet still his hand did not search out hers. How not alone, then? 'We must meet again.' He looked distractedly around, as though in search of something and indeed appeared to find such for in the distance was the green hillside of Mousehold where sheep grazed the gentle breast of land. Then, at last, he reached out a hand and touched hers. 'Do not be afraid.'

'I am not afraid, though I think thou may be.'

He smiled. 'Perhaps a little. Perhaps more than a little. Dost thou not feel it, too?'

'I feel so many things I scarcely know who I may be. I need assurance, John.'

His hand no longer held hers.

The following day found them on Mousehold. The air trembled in the heat. Weeks without rain had turned the gorse, bracken and grass brittle. Dust blew in thin spirals. Overhead the sky seemed almost white. Pearl had struggled up the hillside only to collapse at the top, her white dress soaked with perspiration, her face red and smarting. She was there ahead of the appointed time and watched as martins swooped low, adjusting the angle of their flight, looping up and plunging down before following the same invisible pathway once again. Far below was the cathedral in miniature and, round about, cultivated gardens tended by figures so small it was hard to grant them human status or form. It was, in short, a perfect English summer's day, if perfection were to include a sun which burned all moisture from the earth. But there perfection ceased for Pearl was caught in such a contradiction that she could scarcely think at all. Nor did the heat assist for, along with moisture, air seemed in scarce supply.

Then she saw him approach. He had ridden on horseback, still dressed in black, no matter that the sun must seek him out. He saw her at once but did not raise a hand. Instead, he reined in the horse and dismounted, tying it to a stunted tree. He, too, was red about the face and his clothes stained dark under the arms. He stood before her, his form seeming to waver in the heat.

'Pearl.'

She stared back, as though facing a stranger. A decision was forming in her mind, here, high above the city.

'We must marry,' he said, staring not at her but into space. 'We must marry, and soon.'

It was what she wished to hear, what she had thought she wished to hear and yet in that very moment it became what she could not do. She shook her head slowly. 'That may not be.'

'Not be?'

She could barely speak. He had said the very words she had imagined, offered what she had thought she must demand, but this was not a bargain she could accept and she amazed herself in responding as she did.

'Pearl, I know that ours was but a moment of foolishness.'

'Then I was the fool, it seems.'

'No. Together we were foolish. Thou art sure . . .'

'Sure?'

'Of thy condition?'

She turned aside a second, biting her lip. There was a deadness there, a coldness which chilled her heart. 'Ay, sure. There are certainties, even if thou art not to be one of them.'

'I? But it is thou who refuses the solution to thy plight.'

'I do not know, John. I do . . . thou art he who . . . If . . .' The words would not come. One part of her wished to hold him close, to tell him of her love, but another would not be bound, not to him or any man. And she had felt withdrawal, a retreat. Even as he offered marriage something warned her that she must walk another path. It was as though he spoke lines given to him by others. She heard two voices. The words spoke one thing, the tone quite another. And she remembered, suddenly, the moment of the squall which had swept towards them on the Thames and a face that had appeared for an instant almost diabolic. Here, in a heat which threatened to absorb the air itself until she could hardly breathe, she felt a sudden chill.

He looked away from her, across a city of churches where every street worshipped God in flint buildings of prayer. What he saw she could not know. For her part she turned and walked towards the edge of the hill where the land dropped away. She looked round at him. Still he stared ahead, floating, as it appeared, a mirage conjured up but by the occasion as passion and commitment evaporated in the thin atmosphere. They stood thus a moment more and then she took the path down towards the parched fields below, willing herself not to run and run until momentum should lift her above the shimmering city to fly towards her destiny.

Chapter Seven

One morning, after drawing water from the well and drinking the cold, clear liquid, Pearl felt a sudden nausea and dropped to her knees before she should fall. She felt struck down by the hand of God and indeed would scarcely have been surprised had this been so.

She took to her bed with a fever which sapped her strength. This was a period when illness was never without its threat and plague was a memory which lay in the common consciousness. She was from another place and, as it seemed to her, from another time, but, even so, as her limbs lost their strength and her face began to swell, she, too, felt a certain terror, mixed with despair.

Some illnesses creep up slowly so that we can prepare for what is to come. Others strike with a suddenness which crushes the spirit. This was one such, so that she half crawled, half staggered to the door and into the kitchen, her forehead already beaded with cold sweat in the heat of the summer sun.

Once on her bed she entered a world in which everything seemed to dissolve and flow, as it had before when she had tasted of strange crystals on a glass retort, a world of faces and events that seemed at once so strange and yet familiar. The room was cool but she burned with heat. She saw her mother's face, not as it was when she had left but as it had been when she was a child. Her hair was pure black and there were no wrinkles around eyes which seemed to look deep within her. She saw other faces, too. Her father, Dimmesdale, dressed in black and with a haunted face, strained, inward. He, in turn, dissolved into her own John Standish, who was not her own. She saw him with a woman on his arm, a woman who turned and waved a crumpled sheet of paper in the air.

Pearl went where she must, saw what it was necessary for her to see and summoned memories which could never have been hers. She had become something other – living a life whose echoes returned from a place into which she had never sent them. She saw again a crooked man, shoulders sloping downwards. She saw a crowd of faces staring upwards, as though she floated in space, and how could this be unless she looked through other eyes or travelled back along a line to a place it was impossible for her to visit? She was a baby, crying for the breast but the breast was smeared with blood, scored by a mark which would never fade away. Yet her hands reached out, opening and closing but holding nothing. And the white shapes of faces against a large darkness and herself, high, raised up, elevated.

Other scenes, too, hardly less dark yet lit with a kind of glow. Still she travelled backwards, from a fierce light into a sudden darkness, warm like a summer sun; and through and across that sea she sailed into a self which was not herself and yet was a self she grasped, a different being and yet as bright as ice scraped from a green-white window, bright as the shining slice from an open door, golden on the night-time snow.

A mist formed, dissolved and re-formed as something seeped steadily through her body, unlocking the secret chambers of her brain, flowing through memory, releasing desire, flooding her with hope. She saw the future, as it seemed, but could no longer distinguish it from present or past. It was as if the dark berries which she had brushed past on a winter's walk, crushed underfoot on an autumn day, exerted their authority and offered their ambiguous gifts.

The cathedral loomed ahead of her, drew her onwards as though there were a power in it born of the limestone which formed its skeleton. She walked and ran and skipped and dragged her shoes through dust and mud and hard-ridged stone like furrows to its great doors which hung, the folded wings of some giant bird of prey. Some part of her recognised this for mere fantasy but that part had no power to intervene. She felt a ripeness ready for the harvest, a strength which seemed to blossom out of weakness. Yet something had snapped inside her. Deep within some tension had been eased.

From time to time she came fully to her senses to find herself alone in an empty room, with, far away, the summer sound of birds. Once a fly exploded into an urgent threnody as its wings beat to shreds in a spider's web. She had a thirst which closed her throat but had no strength to rise, still less to descend the stairs or draw water from the well. Her days and nights were a blend of fevered sleep and wavering visions.

She was back at Mousehold, though this time no familiar figure was beside her. And as she stood and felt the heat burn to her very soul, so she heard a sound and watched a scarlet light begin to flow towards her. It moved along the ground, a wavering necklace of rubies, glinting against the ochre of a land sucked dry of moisture and grace alike. She was the sudden centre of flames, which seemed to wave like ribbons in her hair. She was a bride who wore not white but deepest red and carried in her hand a spray of fireflies. She knew that she was watched. There was a man with a crooked shoulder. His clothes were dark, his skin a parchment white, a magpie of a man who turned his head from side to side as though searching out glitter for his nest. And far below, in the distant cool of cathedral cloister, a man who waited for her life to end. The fire was all about, as though it worshipped her as queen. A black-edged star of cinder fell into her hair, its bright heat crusted with pure jet. She made no move to brush it away and could feel a burden lift from her as gorse bushes turned from yellow to crimson and the blackened grass transformed into a sea of blood.

It was as she lay thus in a tangled weave of sheets that she dreamed a man had entered her room. He carried in his hands a goblet which he elevated above her head, speaking softly in a voice she could not hear and a language she could not decipher. He looked down at her but though she could have reached out her hand and touched him she could not distinguish his features in the darkened room. Then an arm slid beneath her neck and lifted her head. The goblet was pressed cold upon her lips and cool water, which smelled of dark earth, trickled into her mouth until her throat opened and the copper-tasting coldness slowly entered her. And as she drank, ever more eagerly, choking a little so that the cup was withdrawn, and then again, desperately but more slowly now, she strained to see who this might be but lacked the energy even to concentrate on so simple an act and, finally, sank back into the eider pillow and felt his arm withdraw. Already, as he withdrew, he had become her lover, smiling back at her, with a smile she well remembered.

Within the hour a sudden pain shook her and her back arched. Her stomach muscles, too, seemed to lock and the pain pulled her down into the bed. Had she, perhaps, pricked her finger on a wild rose and allowed the spores of lockjaw to work their way like tendrils along her spine? She lifted her head for a second, only to have it forced down again by a tremor which flowed through her body. Then it was gone and she lay, her face prickling cold with perspiration as the air from a half-opened window raised the corner of a curtain and a bright flash of light illuminated the darkened room. Then it was back, as though a huge invisible hand were pressing down upon her, only to release her a long minute later. And so it continued, ebb and flow, fullness and emptiness, until, at last, with a long sigh, like the sigh of death, she fell back into sleep in a bed now wet with more than the sweat of fever, stained as it was with a red so deep it was close to black.

Nor was the fever broken. It was another crisis that had passed, so that she was still in a limbo of consciousness when she felt her limbs bathed with a soft cloth and the sheets unwound from her limbs and withdrawn. She revelled in the flow of air across her, like the clear water of a stream. Indeed she felt as though she were being cleansed, washed quite clean, within and without, like a child by its mother. She submitted without demur to the firm hand which moved her first one way and then the other, which withdrew the sticky sheets that seemed to tear from her body as a bandage does from a wound, and then, later, replaced them with fresh ones which smelt of the summer air and not of the grave. There was the sureness of touch of a physician, a healer of broken bodies and bruised souls, and she surrendered without question, she who had no option but to obey.

Then she was asleep again, having swallowed more water with an edge of bitterness which made her run the tip of her tongue along her teeth. It was as though she had bitten into the kernel of an unripe plum or taken as sugar what in truth was salt. Her dreams now were gentler, though. She no longer twisted and turned like a worm on a fisherman's hook. Nor did John Standish float arm in arm with another. She no longer looked at the slowly turning floor of the cathedral far below and longed to plunge down, to become part of its moving pattern. Instead she was at home. She held her mother's hand or walked along through woodland paths. She looked across the great bay which seemed so like the ocean but at whose furthest edge, before the true wildness of the sea, a protective arm and beckoning finger of land drew people to a dream itself part fevered sleep and part true hope.

Then, at last, on the sixth day, though she could not have told whether it was the sixth or sixtieth, she woke. The curtain fluttered in the breeze. The heavy buzz of bees blended with the dry rattle of crickets. Beside her, on a low table, was a half-filled glass of water. At her neck was a crisp white sheet and she knew, with sudden and perfect understanding, that she no longer carried a child and that it was she who had been born rather than that other who she would never know and who would never suckle at her breast.

She was changed. She lay for a while like one who had fallen from a great height, testing each limb and each sense in turn. But it was not her bones that were broken. The changes within her were more subtle than that, and more final. There was a terrible clarity. Six days without food made her so sensitive that the sounds which she heard seemed magnified, while the light which flooded the room quite dazzled her. Her fingers tingled. There was a hunger so intense it seemed external to herself, and a thirst which the half-filled glass of water could not slake. Indeed, in drinking it her hand shook so that it spilled on the sheet, a grey stain flushing the white linen.

Perhaps the changes in her body, combined with hunger and thirst, had created the images which she had seen in her restless sleep and which now seemed just beyond recall. The healing process is anyway one of forgetting. We remember the fact of pain but not its substance. We bear the scars but, stare at them as we may, can never quite people them with agony. Language is no less; the same dead tissue which hints at the experience may yet conceal it. The magic of speech is to deliver the world into our possession but we compromise to communicate and in that compromise is our tragedy as well, perhaps, as our exultance. Silence alone does not betray and Pearl was silent now, searching through her memory, reaching for something which stayed stubbornly beyond her reach. There was an emptiness she could not fill, but there was also a new strength building cell by cell.

And when she thought of John Standish something had changed. The forced link between them had been snapped, a key had broken in the lock. There was no way now to open the door again. Why, then, even now, did she cling to the thought of him? Love can transmute into hate with a suddenness which the alchemists would envy: but Pearl did not hate. It was beyond her capacity. Yet there had always been a determination in her, and though womanhood had passed a gentle hand over the troubled waters of her spirit there was in her a need to force issues to a resolution. As once she had restored to her mother the scarlet letter Hester had thought to discard, so now she thought again to confront this man with his responsibilities. Though what might those be, now her claim upon him had been voided in the flesh? And what was the document she had seen, and who the woman? There was, she realised, a kind of coldness in her speculation which suggested that he had been driven from her heart but, as she lay, still weak in body and in spirit, even now the thought of him quickened her pulse.

Then, as she watched the dust turn slowly in the shaft of light which angled across her room, she heard the sound of an approaching horse, dull and distant at first, where the path was velvet with moss, and then sharp as that path gave way to the flagstones of the stable yard. She had no power even to raise herself in the bed and hence none to reach the window and see who her visitor might be. Perhaps it was that same weakness which made her fear the worst. It is true that she had never seen the crooked man except in the shadows and she could scarcely imagine Lawyer Simple riding one mile let alone three; but she knew herself the marked victim of conspirators and must expect their attentions now she lay with no recourse or defence. And what of that raven of a man who had spread his wings and turned his threatening features to her in Opie Street? Was he about to reach a claw into her bosom and tear out the still beating heart to win his prize? Was he, indeed, the crooked man?

Whoever was below must be attending to his horse, for she had not detected the click of door bolt or the squeal of hinge. Then she heard him walk across the yard. What now? Should she be murdered in her bed? But even in her weakness she could smile at her own fears: did she not have friends enough that one should have chosen to visit her? But who? Not William Prynne who travelled only by cart or trap, having long since learned most horses had stronger wills than his own. No, nor yet Standish, for he would never risk to see her again. Nor, she realised suddenly, was the list of friends so long, after all.

Below she could hear the kitchen door open and close. A clock struck the hour as though to welcome the intruder. Ten.

Then silence. Whoever had entered was still in the kitchen. Sorting through the knife drawer, perchance.

She was not afraid. She lacked the energy even for that. Instead she waited and watched the golden dust turn lazily within the sharp-edged beam of light. Outside, crows called raspingly to one another and, further off, a cuckoo sang its two-note defiance.

He was on the stairs. Then he was at the door. He knew his way, then, knew where his victim lay. The handle turned, slowly, gently, as though not to disturb her, and then the door opened, equally slowly, cutting across the shaft of light from the window. It was a brave woman, a brave person, who did not clench her knuckles and Pearl's fingers were curled, her hands white and shaking when, through the doorway, came a man she had not thought to see. He came and stood, with gold flecks of dust twinkling round his head.

'Master Hawkins!'

'Mistress Prynne! Pearl! Mistress Prynne!' He could not seem to decide which name might serve for the occasion.

'But how could you know . . . what has . . . what I . . .?'

'Pray do not exert yourself, Mistress Prynne. All will be explained. I have some water for you' – as he did – 'but would . . . could . . . is it possible . . . a little food?'

Suddenly, as though the word itself had the power to summon appetite, she was reminded that she was not merely hungry but desperate for food. 'Yes, oh yes, I am . . . I do . . . I would . . . like some, thank you.'

'Then rest yourself and I will prepare something.'

'But I must . . . What has happened to me? Why are you here?'

'Explanation or food. You may have both and welcome but one must have precedence. Which is it to be?'

'Explanation. No, food. No . . .'

'Rest a while. I shall be back in a moment and will satisfy you on both grounds.' He turned to the door but then halted and turned again. 'Pearl! Mistress Prynne!' But words were ever inadequate tools and with no further comment he turned a third time and closed the door, sending the lazy dust in slow spirals.

She let her head fall on the pillow, aware of a sudden and complete feeling of safety. She had thought this man of no consequence and yet each encounter proved him more necessary. Nor had she failed to notice the intimacy of his address to her, but she could not resent it. And what was his Christian name? He had told her. Daniel. What more apt for one who daily lived in the lion's den?

He was as good as his word, returning in a matter of minutes with some eggs scrambled on a plate and with a glass of milk besides. Pearl struggled to rise but lacked the strength. No matter, since he put the plate and glass on the bedside table and reached both his hands beneath her arms to lift her gently against the pillow before handing her the food. Then he and she both realised that she could not even lift the fork to her mouth. Without remark he began to minister to her as a mother to a child and did not stop until she had finished both food and drink. Then, pressing a clean kerchief softly to her lips, he laid her gently down again.

'And now, explanation. In short, you were poisoned.'

'Poisoned!'

'Yes.'

'But how, and how could you know this? How come you here? I do not understand.'

'The poison was in the well water.'

'The well!' She remembered the taste. Saw herself raise the cup to her lips. 'How do you know this?'

'He who did the deed was seen.'

'Seen? By whom?' She found herself repeating every word.

'By one who watches you. He is called Charley.'

With difficulty, she prevented herself from repeating this, too. 'This may not be.'

'And you say so, but it was so.'

'But how should he find you?'

'By looking.'

'But . . .'

The clerk placed a hand on her arm.

'He has followed you, I fancy, more than once and has seen us together. There is more to him than you would imagine. He sought me out and told me of one with no hair who sought to harm you. And we know who that might be.'

'So it was . . .'

'I came. The door was unlocked. I found you in distress.'

Pearl felt suddenly overcome with shame. He placed his hands on hers and looked into the eyes of one who would look anywhere but at one who knew her deepest secret.

'The distress, I hope, has gone and with it all memory of its cause.'

She turned her face to the pillow, a bitter tear forcing its way out of an eye.

'You are weak. Another day and this will be but a memory, a shadow of a memory.'

'How long . . .' she turned back to him, '. . . was I ill?'

'Some few days. I would guess you had not drunk deep, though the fever had you in its grasp. Having no skills I could only watch and tend to you. But as I sat below and wondered at your fate I discovered a book, old and cobwebbed, and in that book found described a remedy.'

'The book,' whispered Pearl to herself.

'It was yours?'

'No. Not mine. Chillingworth's.'

He paused and shook his head. 'Then there is a curious providence in this world for, desperate as I was for your recovery, and anxious for your sake not to seek a stranger's help, I followed the recipe and turned apothecary. With what fear and doubt you might imagine for I knew not the cause and therefore not the remedy, except that remedy in general was promised in that book. But within the hour I sensed a change and berry and herb had plainly wrought their magic.'

'But how could you desert your duties?'

'There has been much coming and going in Opie Street and I had but to mention sickness for my employer to be glad to banish me.'

'Master Hawkins.'

'Daniel, and I hope.'

'Daniel. How can I thank thee?' she asked. 'Thou hast saved my life.'

The lawyer's clerk looked down at her and smiled to hear a you become a thee quite as though the potion which had restored one life might work its alchemy on language too and hence redeem another life besides.

'Charley, I fancy, has that distinction.'

'He, too, and I shall seek him out.'

'Thou wilt have little distance to travel for he has not left this place, save to summon me. Had thou but the strength to stand by yonder window thou wouldst see him at his post. He is a gentle soul, nor capable of raising his hand against anyone, but he would permit no further harm to befall thee.'

'But it is thou I must thank, too. Though I have been ensnared in dreams and visions I know full well the service thou hast done me.'

'It is little enough.'

'But how could thou have served so long in Opie Street? It is not in thy blood to act as assistant to such a man as he. He is as different from thee as night to day.'

'And yet not so different, after all.'

'But why did thou not denounce him? Why not carry the story to a magistrate?'

'Because I may not do so.'

'But why?'

'Am I not my brother's keeper?'

'And he were thy brother, perhaps.'

'Then I must tell thee plain. He is. He and I are brothers.'

'Never!'

'He is the elder. Many years since we were lawyers together, scarcely out of the Inns of Court. He committed a crime. I knew later that he did so for the conspirators who now threaten thy life. I discovered him. Blood is a powerful bond. I urged him to leave before he be found out but he had ever great influence on my mother who pleaded with me to protect him and secure his position. He cared nothing for her but she doted on him. Her health was frail . . .'

He broke off and glanced at the window, as if even now they might be overheard.

'These are so many excuses, I know. He had done a wrong and others suffered for it, but I kept my peace and at his urging made alterations in a document which might otherwise have done him ill.'

He looked at Pearl, her head sunk deep in the pillow, making his confession, as if to a minister or even St Peter himself. What he spoke now he had never spoken before and she knew he sought her absolution.

'I was young, then, and my mother's distress was great.'

If he looked for understanding from this frail young woman he did not look in vain. She smiled up at him and reached out a pale hand. He grasped it eagerly.

'No sooner was the cloud lifted from my brother than he began to exert his power over me. Though to reveal my counterfeit would be to bring about his own arrest, yet he perversely threatened me with it for he knew that the double blow would prove fatal to our mother. So he persuaded me to alter another document to serve his purpose and once he had that – unconnected, as it was, with his own case – he had me in his grasp. My mother, our mother, died and by degrees I was no longer brother, partner, lawyer, but keeper of the outer room, clerk and occasional forger. Yet he must tolerate a certain amount from me for he knows that over the years I have become more reckless of my own safety. It follows that he does not enquire too closely where I might be or what I might be about.'

'Have there been those who suffered for what thou hast done?'

'There have. Yet none, 'til now, but those who are as sharp in their ways as he. I have refused to become confederate in robbing the widow's inheritance and have but matched my own skills against those of others in this city who would seek to take all the grain into their own granaries. Even in thy case I thought it were but another dispute among the rats over a morsel of cheese. But when thou didst come to Opie Street I saw thou wert no rat and the moral world was reborn of that instant.'

'To have lived with this, and for so long, must have been a great burden.'

'The back bends until you can no longer expect to look others in the eye. Yet must I say I have frustrated other schemes of his. Where I have refused to do injury to those not of his pack he has turned elsewhere but I have used my skills to hinder him. He suspects me, no doubt, but has no proof positive to find me out. And thus I have sought to still my conscience.'

'Can goodness come from evil?'

'Thou art recovered because I followed a book of spells.'

'Ay, and a book which once belonged to the devil himself.'

She smiled once more and squeezed his hand. 'It is thy better nature that has betrayed thee into this morass and I have cause to know how good that nature is. Thou did perchance what thou had little choice but to do.'

'No. I could have acted otherwise but what the consequence might have been I may not know. The law, however, I do know. It is for the strong and not the poor and weak, and to tell the truth I find it difficult to believe that I have corrupted, on those four or five occasions, a system whose corruption here is bone deep. But, enough. It is thy recovery to which we must bend our strength. And thou do but eat as thou hast done and thou wilt be recovered in a day or two.'

And it was so. Yet in those few days of dream and fantasy and revelation she had come a distance in her understanding. Every voyage a lesson: every life a truth.

Chapter Eight

There is a moment in all stories when an inevitability seems to build and that moment is both one for which we look and one which we dread. We need the last brush stroke, the note which resolves the chord. But it is also a door slamming shut, a sound which reverberates backwards through the text. Were there no other possibilities born out of such lives than this one? The child runs into the path of a galloping horse. Can we not reach out a hand and restore her to a safety we have conspired in denying? Yet there is a theology to story: life eternal, resurrection. Open the book and the child starts into the lane once more. Life as recurrence. A promise broken may be renewed. But still the horse's hooves thud dangerously close.

It was then, when all options seemed closed down, when all possibilities seemed exhausted, that Pearl found a purpose, recognised, perhaps, that she was living her mother's life a second time but in a different world and at another time. It was then that she seemed to gather her random thoughts and her torn and aching body and direct them to a purpose. That she did not understand that purpose and could not have named it had she been asked, has no bearing on the singleness of mind which now shaped itself not into a thought, still less a coherent plan of action, but, say, a way of being, a manner of conducting herself which might lead to revelation and a studious clarity. And yet if true clarity may only blaze in the last times, flicker in a sky so bright that it forces the eyes to close, yet it burned there, too, in her mind. For she was on the very verge of understanding that there was not one to be exposed, claimed, surrendered, but two. One now, one in a past which was no more past than any past ever is. Two children engendered, but only one to survive. One father whose gentleness was a fault; one whose remoteness might yet prove a sin.

Every life is a myriad of paths not taken, of glances unremarked, words unuttered, lovers not embraced, thoughts and memories left in forgotten corners. Because we act does not mean that we understand. Sometimes we act in order to understand. The longer we live the more, perhaps, we perceive how little there is we comprehend.

Though Pearl could see no resolution to her problems, no escape from the maze which she had entered unaware, a resolution was at hand for the story was hastening to its end, though she could scarcely have guessed at the events which would lead to its conclusion. Certainly she could not imagine that drama must first give way to farce once more before the threads of the tapestry could be pulled at last into place and so reveal the pattern they would form.

The day was such as had never dawned before, for the Swan Inn had come to Caistor, much as Burnham Wood had come to Dunsinane and with the likelihood of somewhat similar consequences, as it seemed to Pearl. This was the first excursion outside London any of William's drinking companions had taken and the journey by stagecoach had already convinced them of their mistake, not least the cat, which had incautiously hidden amongst the baggage, no doubt thinking, thereby, to avoid that ever-present boot which seemed as much a part of life to him as the bacon fat which fell on the floor and the sun which rose in the sky. The combined weight of those fattened for many a year on roast beef, pork fat, goose, sausages, blood pudding, eggs and the hundred other delicacies of the establishment, washed down by Deptford's best, proved too much for both coach and horses which jointly refused further progress before they had cleared Epping until another coach shall have been summoned and the passengers reassigned to the mutual benefit of wood, springs and horseflesh. Said passengers were at last discharged in Norwich, to the relief of all involved, though principally, one suspects, the beasts of burden who learned what so slight a word as 'burden' might be expected to encompass.

The last miles were completed with the assistance of Widgery. His horse, apparently, was stronger than those which pulled the Norwich stage, that or more persuadable by Widgery's foot. Loading the passengers in and out of his cart was another matter. The hostess of the Swan had a hard enough time negotiating the almost level floor of her inn; raising her above ground level, even in separate portions, was a virtual impossibility. But ingenuity, will and a certain level of desperation eventually prevailed. The owner of the Deptford Ale Company, meanwhile, had finally to be persuaded to abandon the keg of beer which he had already carried a hundred miles, though not before drinking several pints of the brew.

This travelling circus arrived at lunchtime. Despite a long journey it had plainly not lost its sense of timing. Pearl, who was spending a few days with her relatives, her head a whirl, her body in confusion, ran into the garden, surprised to find how pleased she was to see her London acquaintances again.

'It's the niece,' shrieked Mistress Nibbins, cackling loudly, despite her evident discomfort at finding her body distributed rather too casually among the boxes and people around her.

'My friends,' shouted William Prynne, an affectionate greeting considering the fact that he had quickly established that no ale was on board the wagon, merely its living symbol.

It is true that Pearl's cousin failed to join in the general merriment but even she could hardly suppress a smile.

'Prynne, my dear,' asked Mistress Nibbins, in a voice

somewhat between a squawk and a scream, 'what is that smell, pray?'

Everyone stopped for a moment, like a pack of hunting animals, and sniffed the air. None affected to detect anything, except Pearl who understood the problem at once, having had the advantage of a brief stay at the Swan.

'It is fresh air, Mistress Nibbins. Fresh air.'

'I never heard such. And is this what we must breathe every day?'

'Have no fear, my brother has ways with fresh air which will no doubt be to your satisfaction,' added Nancy with some acerbity, having not welcomed news of the imminent arrival of this carnival.

There now ensued the process of removing from the cart that which had been placed therein with such difficulty a bare two hours before, and though this time gravity was a friend rather than a foe the task was a difficult one. Eventually boxes were discovered and placed one upon another until a staircase of sorts had been constructed, down which there descended these potentates from another land.

Only then did Pearl realise that their visitors included young Sam, who had remained hidden behind his employer until she rose unsteadily to her feet and clipped him painfully round the ear, and equally young Jack, who descended last and backwards as though he would as soon be leaving as arriving.

'So you are all come. And who, pray, is left to serve your customers at the Swan?'

'The Swan, my dear, do not exist for to serve the convenience of customers. Whatever can have given you such an impression? If I am disposed to offer a little in the way of restoratives to those as appreciates them that is entirely at my convenience which since I am here and not there it ain't. Convenient.'

'Of course.'

And so they trooped inside, Mistress Tubbs following her nose, having little choice in the matter, while her husband followed his wife, having as little choice himself. She was arrayed in such a costume as might have become a duchess if but the duchess had lacked a little in judgement and subtlety. He wore a cloak which seemed to carry its own history by way of stains which recalled many a meal and perhaps its aftermath and though his nose lacked the projective energy of his wife's, yet it appeared lit from within by some fuel which never seemed to fail, glowing redly in fair weather and foul. Sam came behind, burdened down by a trunk which seemed half his height, followed by Jack, looking not ahead but behind. Last of all came the cat, enticed, no doubt, by the smell of cooking which had begun to purge the freshness of the air.

The whole army encamped in the parlour where the table was laid for the meal, the whole army less young Sam and Jack whom Mistress Nibbins banished to the kitchen, much against the wishes of cousin Nancy but to the advantage of all others, the parlour being small and the guests being quite otherwise.

Somehow each found a place which corresponded to that which he occupied at the Swan, quite as though the world were no more than an extension of that establishment and, indeed, they had barely settled when William called 'Ale!' and barely a moment or two had passed before young Sam struggled out of the kitchen carrying pewter tankards of such. There followed that moment of spiritual communion which Pearl had witnessed in London as all lifted the tankards to their lips and tilted their heads back to the heavens. Again the hollow sound of metal being placed decisively on wood and a few further moments before a general sigh.

'Mistress Tubbs,' said Pearl, breaking the silence, 'you were kind enough to introduce me to London. I hope you will permit me to be your guide to Norwich.'

'Goodness, child, and you have been here but a few months. Is Norwich so small that it is possible to encompass it so soon?'

'Not all, I grant you, but those places which are held to be its finest sights.'

'I am not a one for churches, I should warn you.'

'Were we not married in one?' asked her husband, somewhat vaguely.

'So we were, my chuck. So we were. And shall be buried in one or thereabouts, I dare say, but such places should be kept for best. Overuse may make them lose a certain charm.'

'Nonetheless, the cathedral, Mistress Tubbs,' she urged, pausing a second as she did so, for she realised suddenly that she might be committing herself to go where she had no desire to venture. She need have had no such concern.

'Cathedrals, my chuck, is but churches bred for size. They make me dizzy with all that height up above. Give me a good low ceiling I can touch.'

'There is inns,' observed her husband, half a statement, half a question.

'Inns?' replied William, his face glowing. 'No city in the country, saving your own, has more nor better, nor more welcoming, nor more convenient, nor with warmer fires, nor with better ale, saving your own, nor . . .' He would evidently have gone on until lunch was served had his eye not espied another armada of tankards, white sails fluttering, advancing towards him. Mr Tubbs' wayward eye, too, caught sight of the returning fleet and, bidding farewell to its companion, watched its approach. Since he had until then, as she supposed, been looking at her, Pearl was perplexed to find herself still addressing, as it were, his disinterested eye. Even so, propriety made it difficult for her to look away, although she knew she merely conversed with herself.

'My friends,' said William Prynne, getting with some difficulty to his feet, perhaps on the assumption that the same manoeuvre might prove impossible a little later in the afternoon. 'My friends.' His face beamed. Had it beamed any more they would have had need to shield their eyes.

'My friends . . .' he paused.

They all leaned forward, urging him on, if only because their own tankards were raised expectantly before their mouths.

'Words . . .'

They swayed forward again.

'Words . . . my friends, is nothing.'

There was a pause and then, overcome by his own eloquence, their host collapsed.

'Nothing,' they all replied, as though that indeed were the toast, and as one swallowed the ale. Then tankard after tankard was banged down on the table as though the meeting were being summoned to order, as in part it was, for the sight of Jack, backing into the room, steam, as it seemed, coming from the top of his head, announced the arrival of lunch, a ceremony which, as Pearl well knew, all present treated with true reverence.

'Mistress Nibbins,' said cousin William, 'though you are all our guests and though it falls to me and would be my pleasure to carve the beef yet, knowing your skills with the knife, it would be a pleasure to see you wield it.'

Mistress Tubbs instinctively pulled her chair back from the table and put a protective hand to her face.

'Most advisedly,' replied Mistress Nibbins. 'Give me but a knife and hot flesh and I could not ask for more.'

Pearl felt her appetite disappear. To her left a woman mountain wielding steel, to her right the unmoving eye of the beer master. Yet these she counted her friends, and, certainly by contrast with others she had met, they were full of life and took pleasure in every moment. The last months had seen enough pain; a little comedy might serve its turn.

Nancy, who spoke so slightingly of the Swan and its denizens, had laboured the night before and all morning to prepare the feast of beef and fowl and vegetables fresh from the garden. These now began to disappear like May frost, while she sat at the head of the table and smiled to see so many smiling faces, shining with grease no less than pleasure. Hers had been a house where contentment had stood in place of pleasure since the *Hope* had foundered those many years before but though there was still a sadness deep within her heart the laughter was itself like wine to one who had never tasted wine herself. When, later, one of the guests reached for one of her dead husband's clay pipes and even her brother, by then long surrendered to beer and company, moved to prevent it, she first shook her head to arrest him and then nodded her approval to the guest.

Meanwhile, however, the meal continued. Sam and Jack moved backwards and forwards, one more backward than forward.

'Mistress Tubbs, is the fowl to your taste?' enquired her host.

Mistress Tubbs, having at that moment contrived to stick a chicken bone sideways in her mouth in her eagerness to strip all remaining flesh from it, was not well disposed to speak. Nonetheless, sensible of the proprieties, she endeavoured and as a result sent out through her mouth, wedged open thus, a kind of mist of chicken, gravy and peas. And since she turned her head in distress at this, or perhaps simply to demonstrate to all her unfortunate condition, managed as a result to spray all about her with a sampler of her meal.

Her companions accepted the baptism with good grace and would have continued with their meal had not Pearl noticed their guest's alarm.

'Mistress Tubbs. Are you in distress?'

The lady in question nodded vigorously.

'Do you have something stuck in your throat?'

Again she nodded, this time with such exaggerated violence that even her husband assigned both of his eyes to her, having before been content to rest only one on her suffering.

'What, my chuck, an obstruction, is it?'

She would have nodded again but that her scarlet was beginning to shade into blue. The table erupted as each guest proposed solutions, some of which would require equipment not likely to be found around a common home, others pushing back chairs endeavouring to invert the unfortunate lady until this should effect a solution. Upending Mistress Tubbs, however, being beyond the powers of the assembled friends, she might well have expired had her husband not struck her a blow on the back with a vigour that might have stunned a runaway horse. The bone shot out of her mouth with such velocity that for a moment all present were in danger.

'It is, indeed,' replied Mistress Tubbs, quite as though nothing had intervened between question and answer, 'but it were a pleasure to see such . . . fields.' Invention, it seemed, had waned, nor was Pearl surprised who had heard her complain earlier of 'nothing but grass from Epping to Norwich'. But if invention had failed, appetite had not, for she reached out for another chicken leg, plainly not at all disturbed by her experience.

'Pearl, my dear,' said Mistress Tubbs, cheeks glistening with a subtle dew of perspiration, 'how do you like our England now you have seen more of it? Does it suit you as much as the snakes and cold and lizards and naked men with their knives and such?' She smiled sweetly, no doubt believing that she had balanced the negatives and positives in about equal proportions.

'There are snakes, as you say, and cold and blizzards, too. I never yet saw a naked man, though, with knife or without. And, yes, I like it well here. I liked London, where all were so busy and time seemed to rush, and I like Norwich, where none seem busy and time reaches out from dawn to dusk at just about a proper speed.'

'And are there entertainments here? Are there bears? Are there public . . . occasions?'

'I am new here. But there are places to walk and places to see.'

'Are there, chuck?' replied Mistress Tubbs, eyeing the custard.

'The jam pudding, my dear,' observed cousin William, raising an eyebrow.

'I will get it.'

'My dear . . .' The objection was not pressed and Pearl willingly rose and hastened to the kitchen where a large saucepan bubbled on the fire. Nancy followed behind and together they lifted it onto the table. Inside were two long puddings wrapped in muslin. Together they hooked them out with a fork and placed them on a platter. Steam dampened Pearl's hair.

'Where's the privy?' asked Mistress Nibbins. 'Beer does have this effect upon me.'

She was directed to the garden beyond, where a simple outhouse served the function she required, and with such dignity as she could muster proceeded through a doorway built for rather more slender forms. Indeed there was a moment when it seemed that architecture might defeat need, but flesh is malleable and with a little effort may be made to flow around doorpost and over sill.

Back at the table the arrival together of pudding and fresh ale was greeted with a joint sigh of satisfaction so loud it was almost a cheer and there was a general scraping of chairs as room was made for the anticipated expansion of stomachs.

Pearl herself had not adjusted to the English bill of fare and failed entirely to understand their love of suet and flour steamed into gelatinous logs. Nor could she appreciate the desire they evidenced to pour large quantities of milk, yellowed with eggs, over everything placed before them, but this they proceeded to do with very evident satisfaction.

'Mistress Prynne,' said Master Tubbs, lighting his pipe with a taper from the fire. 'How are things with you?' Since only one eye swivelled in her direction she was unsure if she had his full attention but few, she realised, could ever have that.

'All is well, sir,' she replied, who knew things were far from that but had no wish to spoil the enjoyment of the day.

'And is all settled of a legal kind – lawyers, in my experience, being second only to cockroaches as vermin that cannot be got rid of but serve no purpose except occasionally to fall into beer barrels.'

All round the table looked anxiously into the tankards before them.

'It is true that I am having . . . that there . . . It seems there may be others with a claim to the Hall and to more than that as well.'

'My dear,' said Nancy, 'why ever did thou tell us naught of this? My brother shall see to it at once.'

'Into beer barrels,' repeated the brother, a look of some concern upon his face.

'He is a man of business,' continued Nancy, 'who has some dealings with lawyers and will doubtless put all to right. Wilt thou not?'

'I shall, indeed,' he replied, and then, after a second, 'What?'

'Thou shalt accompany Pearl to her lawyer and secure that which is hers, thou having experience of lawyers and the world, as she does not.'

'Lawyers,' he said, contemplatively, 'are such as I have ever endeavoured to avoid. It is true that I have had need to deal with them but as a breed they are not to my taste. They are as lilies of the field, except they lack their beauty and perfume. Who hast thou had dealings with, cousin?'

'With a man called Simple.'

William Prynne stopped and looked across at her with some alarm. 'Simple?' he repeated. 'Now there be a rogue. I am not a one to speak ill of another but Simple is as sly, dangerous, self-serving, hypocritical, pompous, avaricious and deceitful as any man who swore an oath to uphold the law.' He paused, as though to be sure that he had unloaded a sufficient supply of adjectives. 'And I can't say fairer than that.'

'I have met another man who has the same opinion and I doubt not with yet more cause,' said Pearl, needing no further confirmation of the villainy of one she had come to know as an enemy.

'There'll be other lawyers, I dare say, my dear,' observed Nancy, putting an arm around her shoulders.

'In my experience,' said Mr Tubbs, his eyes separately surveying the assembled party, 'they are like rabbits. One day two, the next four, and so on until one day the whole world shall be lawyers disputing whether this be Tuesday and who may own the air we breathe.'

Air, though, by this time, and whoever might own it, was in short supply in a certain cottage in Caistor as clay pipes were smoked by William Prynne, by the owner of the brewery and by his wife, each holding the delicate stems like a swan's neck between the fingers of a giant.

'The privy is a mite small,' assayed Mistress Nibbins, as she made her way from the kitchen towards the table. 'I always thinks that privies should be ample. What say you, Mistress Prynne?'

Mistress Prynne, having no views on this matter and being more than a little embarrassed at having her opinion solicited, searched for words but found none.

Cousin William, meanwhile, sat back in his chair, his mouth wide open and his eyes tight shut. Master Tubbs similarly slept, though one eye remained ever alert lest some cutpurse might seize his chance. Mistress Nibbins, preferring food and drink to sleep, dedicated herself to extending the meal until it should become less an occasion than a way of life.

The meal might well have shaded thus into a common sleep had there not come a knocking at the door, both loud and insistent.

'Hold. I shall be with you directly,' shouted the hostess of the Swan, under the impression, it seemed, that that was where she still was.

Nancy, however, having already moved to open the door for their urgent guest, relieved her both of the responsibility and the near impossibility of negotiating her way out of her chair.

'Is Mistress Prynne within, pray?' enquired an anxious and somewhat tousled man, somewhere, as it seemed, between thirty and forty years of age and wearing a jacket which seemed to have more lavender than grey about it. 'It is most urgent.'

'Master Hawkins,' exclaimed Pearl, coming to join her cousin at the door, 'whatever can it be that brings you here in such a flurry?'

The same gentleman looked doubtfully at the older woman, as though judging whether he could share his intelligence with her, and then, abandoning all caution, blurted out his message.

'I have told him all. I have issued my threats. I have told him that he and his conspirators must be on their way or I shall reveal everything.'

'Master Hawkins! Is this wise?' asked Pearl, taking him by the arm.

'Wise? Wise? I know only that it had to be done and it is done and I am glad.'

'Sir, I know not who you may be but plainly you are a friend to Pearl and so I beg you step inside. The doorway is no place for a conversation.'

'But we must be on our way.'

'That is as may be but you will please me, sir, by stepping inside.'

'Pray do so, Master Hawkins,' added Pearl gently. 'Thou hast ridden a way.'

And so this lawyer's clerk, nervous as a young colt, was led inside and into a room so full of grotesques that he turned and would have made his escape forthwith were Pearl not standing between him and the door and smiling encouragement.

'Dear friends,' Nancy called out, and with such an edge to her voice that those asleep returned to consciousness while one guest's eye came into momentary alignment with its companion, 'this is a friend of Pearl and hence of us.'

The clerk looked anxiously about him, who was both unused to company and to such as these, as who would not be?

'He has been a great help to me and is as honest and kind a man as I have ever met,' testified Pearl.

Such a fulsome compliment transfixed its subject with embarrassment so that he scarcely would have known where to look. The company, for their part, rose magnificently to the occasion, throwing out various indistinct but welcoming comments and waving vaguely in his direction with pipes, tankards and, in her cousin William's case, a silver-headed cane.

'He is clerk to Lawyer Simple,' announced Pearl.

There was a sudden silence and Mistress Tubbs spat in the direction of the fireplace and might well have hit her target had the cat not chosen this moment to venture past.

'But he is not of his camp. Indeed he had just done a brave, and as I fear, a foolish thing.'

'It had to be done and it is done . . .' replied their guest, turning his hat round in his hands as though he would wear its brim away.

He was interrupted by the chair which cousin William thrust beneath him so that he sat down abruptly, leaving the rest of his sentence above his head.

'You shall tell us all, sir,' the same cousin insisted, 'as soon as there is ale in your stomach.'

'I do not drink, sir.'

There was another silence, more complete than the last. Mistress Tubbs prepared once more to expectorate and the cat made its defensive arrangements, heading swiftly for the kitchen door.

'A little tea, sir.'

'Most kind.'

Her cousin busying herself in the kitchen, Pearl resolved to share with her friends the details of her situation. Sitting herself beside her new-found friend, whose nervousness in such company she could fully understand, the more especially since she saw that he was transfixed by the Gorgon eye of the maker of Deptford Ale, she explained the events of the recent months as well as she might, though omitting that which touched her most closely.

Like the audience of some street entertainment they gasped, expressed shock and surprise, and then burst into applause when the clerk emerged as hero, the part of heroine being played by she whom they all had grown to love.

'But, sir,' at last interrupted Pearl's cousin, 'are you not in great peril? Will these villains not seek you out and hunt you down?'

'I do not care if they should,' he replied, and with such simple goodness that all applauded again, forgiving, it seemed, the villainy to which he had himself admitted. 'And besides, they know that I have placed documents in the hands of others such that if something were to befall me their doings should be known.'

'My friend, and I hope I may so designate you,' said Tubbs

with a deal of solemnity, 'there be such things as vengeance, and people as will wreak it.'

His wife gave out a little shriek of alarm.

'But you are safe here,' observed cousin William.

'And my lads, my dear lads,' said Mistress Nibbins, gesturing towards young Sam and Jack respectively, who had just renewed the supplies of ale, 'is well known for sorting out those as is the cause of trouble. In my . . .' she hesitated, '. . . profession' – a word she spoke with great dignity and passion – 'there is occasions now and then when there are persons who would benefit from having their arms broke or their heads a little knocked about, and my lads is always happy to oblige.'

'Mistress Nibbins,' objected Pearl, 'there will be no need for that.'

'I am not so sure,' said the clerk, a little nervously and in a manner not quite that of the hero they had applauded but a moment ago. 'There is one, at least, in that conspiracy who would not hesitate at murder.'

Again a shriek from Mistress Tubbs. She was plainly so alarmed that she almost placed a hand on her husband's arm, coming to her senses only just in time.

'Mistress Prynne,' said the clerk, with some seriousness.

'Pearl,' admonished his young friend.

'Pearl.' He spoke the word with some difficulty and not a little reverence. 'Pearl, hast thou forgotten how they sought thy life?'

This time Master Tubbs did feel himself seized by his wife and looked down with every sign of astonishment at what he seemed to feel was an arm he had never seen before.

'It is true.'

'But what, pray, should we do now?' asked the former clerk, uncertain, suddenly, of the wisest course.

'We shall go to Opie Street before he should have time to make further conspiracy,' said Pearl, clear at last as to how she should act and clear also that action was required. Enough of delay. She had looked for advice to the wrong source, had set aside her determination at love's behest. Now she would hesitate no longer. Meaning lay in action. She would track the phantoms to their lair.

'I'm for that,' said Master Tubbs, as though anxious to do anything which might free him from the hand which gripped him hard.

'Not you, sir, but Daniel and I.'

'Daniel and thee?' questioned her cousin. 'Into such danger and all on thy own? This may not be. We are an army,' he asserted grandly, sweeping his arm around the table at a group of potential officers and troops such as would have made any general weep. 'We will mass our forces and close upon the enemy.'

Another shriek from Mistress Tubbs, who evidently had an endless supply, was lost in the general banging of tankards and shouts of enthusiasm. However, ale being what it is and the difficulty of transporting such a crew having already been established, the dishevelled army never did march towards Norwich. Pearl and Daniel Hawkins in a pony and trap set out alone to join in a battle which must at last solve the problem of an inheritance and settle the future of a young woman who had decided that she would wait no more for fate to decide it for her.

'Are we acting wisely, Mistress Prynne?'

'Was that not the question I directed to thee but a moment ago? What answer now?'

The wind blew in her hair as the pony broke into a fast trot.

'As to wisdom, I have no knowledge,' replied the clerk, wild-eyed, his jacket flapping like that of a scarecrow in a field. 'Or perhaps I have been too wise for too long. Has the time come for some foolishness?'

Pearl, who had not been guided by wisdom overmuch in her twenty years and was not inclined to be so now, especially when it came to those who sought to take her life, was determined that, wise or foolish, they would challenge their enemy on his home territory and let the consequences take care of themselves.

'It has, indeed,' she shouted, and, though they rode towards danger, both did so with smiles on their faces.

Pony and trap were now on rather firmer ground and they had fallen into a steady rhythm of hooves on stone and moss. So much seemed to have happened in such a short time that Pearl was quite bewildered. Her life had been turned inside out. She had learned she had a weakness she would never have suspected, discovered in herself that at which she would have wondered in another. Now she rode to confront enemies she had not seen, except the menacing Simple and his dark companion, with no knowledge what the outcome might be and with a knight beside her dressed in lavender – though, she noticed, for the first time, with a resolute jaw and a clear eye. The transformation in him, indeed, was remarkable and, as she watched him pluck a fly from the pony's haunches with a gentle caress of his whip, she realised that at some moment contempt had been exchanged for toleration which in turn had made way for respect, reliance and even – and, yes, the thought was clear – for admiration and affection.

Opie Street was as it had ever been, short, narrow and closed in upon itself. Though birdsong had accompanied them upon their journey, no bird flew here nor did people stroll along it to admire its buildings, large and imposing though they be. None came hither who had no business to conduct and none came whose heads were not cast down when first they entered or when they later left. There was a kind of scuttling which characterised those who came to Opie Street. Some carried papers tied up with red ribbons; some shook their heads as though unable to understand or still more to believe what they had been told. Tears were not unknown on Opie Street. Ladies often held kerchiefs to their noses and men likewise. It was as though some cloud had decided to rest here and shed its rain on all who entered in.

There are none in sight, though, when Pearl and her companion step down in the sawdust scattered to deaden all noise. Look up and down the street: no movement is to be seen. It is not surprising, of course, that they stand for a moment outside the chambers of Lawyer Simple, having reined in the pony and descended from their war chariot, thinking on what they must do, for Simple himself requires that they break the silence of Opie Street. Voices will be raised. Issues will be laid open. Dust will be blown from papers, cobwebs be swept away. And questions will yet have answers. But though answers be what we seek they are not always those we would hear.

At last they stir themselves and climb the three stone steps to the double doors. He looks at her and she at him and then together they join their efforts and push the doors which swing inwards on stiff hinges. A breeze raises a thin spiral of dust behind them which quickly settles back again. There is the slow ticking of a clock. It is nearly five. In a moment the mechanism will stir and a bell will be struck to mark the ending of another Opie Street day in which, with luck, nothing will have been accomplished, but he who dwells within will have earned another sovereign or two to join those many others in the bank around the corner.

Again they look at one another for strength before striding on towards the inner doors, dark, solid, forbidding. Instinct makes Daniel bend a knuckle to knock but he stops himself in time and, grasping both doorknobs at once, pushes.

The doors swing open without a sound. They step within the gloom and he turns to close them once more.

Outside, the clock dutifully strikes. No one stirs. The great leather chair is turned away from them, facing a bookcase from which no book has ever been removed in living memory. The table, though, is not as Pearl last saw it, nor the rest of the room. It is bestrewn with papers. So, too, the floor. It is as though someone has thrown handfuls of letters and deeds and documents about his head and cared not where they might land. An ink pot, too, has been upset and ink flows over several sheets of paper by its side. Violation. All has been overturned.

But what of the principal, what of him whose office this is, the guardian of the mountains of paper, chief prevaricator and, as she has learned, chief conspirator? What of him who had planned to take her life? Her companion strides forward, walking on the papers as though they are stepping stones in a stream. Grasping the high-backed chair in his hand, he pulls it around. And as he does so a gasp is followed by a swift backwards pace. The chair swings back and forth for several moments before squeaking to a halt. At last her companion steps aside and she sees, even in the gloom of this inner room of a gloomy house on gloomy Opie Street, a man, his head to one side, his eyes open, who appears nonetheless to sleep. Except his sleep seems likely to be prolonged, for, from his chest, just below the lapel of his jacket, itself as black as the spilled ink, there projects the handle and part of the blade of a knife. So are his questions halted, so the search for answers which he valued not at all is done. He has evidently decided to try his hand at silence for an eternity or so. Everything is still. Not he alone, it seems, has been stopped. There is no movement.

Pearl and her companion stand quite still, side by side now but not touching, quite separate, each contained within and by their own thoughts, until, after what seems several minutes but which surely cannot be as long, a sound begins to fill the room, faint at first but growing until it appears to occupy the whole of this dishevelled space. Pearl looks about her in alarm and it is some moments before she realises the source. It is the one-time clerk and present hero, Daniel Hawkins, whose desperate sobs so disturb the peace of death. He reaches out a hand, blindly, and it must needs be blindly when his eyes are full of tears. She steps towards him and grasps that hand. It is several moments more before he begins to control himself and the sobs subside.

'My dear, dear Master Hawkins, I know this is a great shock. I too have never been so close to such violence, but this man was thine enemy whose death thou lamentest so hard.'

'Mistress Prynne,' replies the one-time clerk, 'this was indeed my enemy, as thou sayest. But this man was also my brother.'

'Thou hast told me so but I still cannot believe how this may be.'

'It may be because God ordained it so. Thou hast seen him as he has become and as he has now received his just deserts for what he has done. But there was another who preceded him who was my companion as a youth. Then he and I were as one. We shared all and there was none who ever loved each other as did we. A single thought would pass between us without words. If he were beaten for some fault then tears would flow from my eyes and the other way about.'

'Then what . . .'

'All changed. As I told thee before, there was one whose company he kept. He would go to meetings in a room in Tombland, nor would he tell what befell him there. But he changed by degrees until he and I were strangers. I do but remember what we once were, who later were no more than enemies. It were those years that returned to me a moment since. The tears were not for him who sits in yonder chair but for him who ran through the fields beside me and climbed apple trees in Cathedral Close. I cry for what I was myself.'

Pearl squeezes his hand and with difficulty suppresses a sympathetic tear of her own.

'But what has happened here? Who has done this deed?'

'As I would guess, his confederates, or rather one in particular. They had relied on his abilities in burying deep what they would not have others know. He had lost those abilities, or at least his power over one whose skills were the basis of that power. Nor were they content with taking his life. There was something further they would lay their hands upon and I fancy I know what that might be. They have not found it nor could they do so since I have removed all documents of the kind they sought.'

'But they will be after thee,' says Pearl with a growing sense of alarm.

'Perhaps, but I think not. They survive only in the shadows. Like so many cockroaches they exist in the dark and the dirt. Stir them into the light and they run about and may be crushed underfoot. This murder will send torches into every corner. They will be scuttling for cover as we speak.'

But are they? A second later there is cause for doubt for the outer door opens suddenly and, as it crashes back, so a swirl of wind enters a room which has felt no breeze in many a year. Papers fly in the air and the chair on which the once threatening Lawyer Simple sits swings round with a noise which would terrify at noon on an August day in the light of the sun. Here it freezes the blood, the more especially when the movement throws its occupant forward so that the body slumps onto the desk and the eye which has fixed many a poor unfortunate is pierced by a metal spike on which customer's accounts are impaled. The sound is like that made by a jelly when it falls at last from the mould, a kind of sucking followed by the impact as head hits desk and the spike appears through the back of Simple's skull like a shining finger.

Daniel puts his arm around Pearl to shield her from what he perhaps thinks must be another assault; but none enters. Perhaps the door opened only to make way for a soul's departure. If so its journey must have had but one destination if justice should at last have come to Opie Street. And so the moment passes, but protective arm is not removed from protected shoulders for alliances may be bred of more than fear and friendship out of more than need.

The days that followed were a blur. Pearl was called before the magistrates and required to give her account, not only of that day but of her previous dealings with Lawyer Simple. This she did with such simplicity yet such clarity and passion that they nodded among themselves and wrote words on paper as though this were in itself to contain and understand the past. The villains were not hard to identify since several men had fled the town and there were documents, that a former clerk had saved from those behind which his brother had once sat in his great chair, which identified conspiracy and fraud alike. Pearl did not pass on the confidences of her new companion with respect to his own activity as scribe and forger but he declared them himself. Some sought his indictment but Pearl returned to the Guild Hall where magistrates sat and so moved them with her account of his repentance and of the power that his brother had exerted that they forbore to act against him.

The miscreants, however, were not to be found, though the tracks of their escape were easy to detect. They had followed the path taken by their colleagues full twenty years before and made haste to the coast, though this time not to Yarmouth but to Cromer. From there they set sail for the low countries where the trail soon disappeared. Whether they lived as other rebels had amongst the dull canals of Holland or whether they had taken ship across the dark Atlantic none could say. These were days when disappearing was a necessary art and there was neither will nor means for justice to follow.

As for Daniel Hawkins, he now laid aside his borrowed name and became Simple himself. In thrusting the dagger into his brother's chest the murderers had, wittingly or not, transferred, too, all ownership of property and money to the brother who survived. And though he set himself to make restitution to those he might have harmed through his confederacy in crime, yet afterwards he remained a wealthy man with property of his own. His first expenditure, however, was on Opie Street. He tore the heavy curtains from the windows and painted everything in white until the eyes dazzled. Beyond the door he had boxes with flowers set along the wall. His front door he coloured lavender and the sawdust was swept from the street so that he could hear the sound of footsteps and carriages as they passed a door which was now more often open than closed. And within, to welcome those who might venture in, a young man who looked somewhat older than his years, a man whose face was a little flattened but who smiled at all those who came there. His title was clerk, though he did no more than cheer those who passed him, but his name was what it ever was: Charley. Each night he walked the three miles back to Colney, for he would not be separated from the world he knew nor from one who lived there who we can say he loved, for what may love be if not such devotion.

One day, some weeks after the events which brought death to Opie Street, Pearl once again stepped into a place that could have had nothing but dark memories for her. Yet the transformation was such that she had no thought of the past. Indeed she smiled to see how earnestly her friend had wrought such changes in street, house and office. Nor could she do anything but smile once more when Charley took her by the hand and drew her in, such was the pleasure he took in pointing out his surroundings. There were no papers, no heavy tomes, except one smart row, dusted and cleaned and clearly awaiting daily use, no forbidding portraits. There was no dust, no air of prevarication and contempt, no shadow, no clock to strike despair in those who saw their lives slipping away in the law's delay. Charley took up her hand and gently raised it to his head.

'Charley! And art thou well here in thy new abode?'

He made no reply but drew her through into the inner room whose door was open to the light. As his new employer jumped to his feet, sending a very small pile of papers to the floor, he withdrew, though not without looking behind him smiling as he did so at one whose life he had saved and from whom he would not be parted longer than he might. After a moment more he closed the door behind him and Pearl turned back to greet her clerk restored as lawyer, a stranger transformed into a friend.

She saw what she had known but never permitted to enter her heart: that this man was true, not unhandsome, either. With the shadows gone he stood proudly yet modestly enough and looked her in the eyes, as she in his. The years separating them seemed of no account. He drew her to a chair and urged her sit.

'I have somewhat to ask thee, Pearl. But before I do there is a document I must show. I had thought to commit it to the fire for it must pain thee but since it touches thy life I have resolved that thou shalt know the truth.'

So saying, he walked to the desk, the very desk on which she had last seen Lawyer Simple lie in death, and, taking a key from his pocket, opened the top drawer. Inside, it seemed, was a single sheet of paper. He turned and clutched it to his chest, as though uncertain even now that he should part with it. After a second, though, he walked across to her and placed it in her hands. It was a letter, written in a spidery hand, and she could see from the signature, full of loops and flourishes, that it had been written by the man who had been struck dead and whose body she almost felt she could see stretched before her. But what she saw next seemed to stop her heart in its beating for it was addressed to one John Standish.

She read the letter in some bewilderment, for she saw from the date that it had been written when she was still on board the *Revenge*, with a week to travel before landfall. But what she read was the cause of more dismay than bewilderment for it gave the news of her impending arrival and of her cousin William's intent to send her to Norfolk on the *Nancy Jane*. It reminded Standish of a duty which it did not specify and instructed him to leave a woman whose name it forbore to identify. It said no more than that but it was enough.

'A spider's web may be attached to several branches. Standish's father was a friend to him who was not thy friend. Conspiracies may pass from one generation to another.'

'But why?'

'Who can tell? There is property here, and money, too. And there may be other secrets yet. Thou hast spoken of finding secrets of a sort in the cellar. Who knows if this be but one part of what may be there? To understand is to be one of them. All I do know is that they have striven to gain possession of that which is thine. Perhaps, indeed, there is the motive for they have lost much and perchance they lay the blame for that at thy mother's door. Her they may not reach, except that through Chillingworth they did, destroying what she valued. But thou wert within their grasp. Perhaps there is no secret. Perhaps revenge is their subject and their object, too, and thou wert sent across the ocean to suffer just the fate they planned for thee.'

'But why . . .'

'No doubt they thought to terrify thee, first. A man with a crooked shoulder in the night-time, a figure from thy dreams, and thou alone. And if not that then a mess of documents and deeds to swallow thee and spit thee out. And all the time a means to ensure delay.'

'But . . .'

'These were thorough men. They have had many a year to make their preparations. If thou should have escaped their traps and still pressed thy case they had one extra ace to play, one last means to break thy heart.'

She looked at him, a thought beginning to shape itself in her mind. He nodded.

'They sought to break thee with thine affections and, should that fail, then, marriage.'

'Marriage,' she repeated, as though in a kind of trance.

'Should thou have married thy parson . . .'

She half raised her hand as though to ward off the thought.

'All that thou owned,' he continued, 'should have become his and if his, theirs. And once theirs there would be no further use for thee. Thou wouldst be in a room and they alone would hold the key to all doors save one.'

Pearl sat in silence, staring into her own heart. She had seen evil and taken it for good, as her mother had done before her. Was there no gain in wisdom, then, with the passing of the generations? She had surrendered that which was spurned, as had her mother. She had traded her freedom for nothing but a fancy. Was she no more than the past's echo, the repetition of another's story? Betrayal there had been, but by another or by herself?

'Do not blame thyself. These were adepts at their trade. And besides, this is all behind thee. The documents are clear. The Hall and more is thine.'

'I do not wish it.'

'It is thine.'

'It has a history I cannot face. I do not wish to face. But there is another I would wish were mine.'

223

'Another?'
'My mother's home. The home of her mother, too.'

I say the plotters were fled but one was not, for scarcely a few weeks had passed before he presented himself at her door. John Standish, his clothes awry and his eyes wild, stood before her in the evening light, his face bearing a livid scar and one arm hanging useless by his side. They stood staring at one another as though confronted by some mystery. Then Pearl stepped aside so that he could enter. They stood once more when she had closed the door, unable, as it seemed, to know who should speak or what should be said. Then she led him into the kitchen and indicated a chair. He shook his head.

'I may not stay.'

She nodded, mutely.

He paused again, and looked around the room, though for what he could not have said.

'I had to see thee before I went. I have done thee wrong.'

'Indeed.' She had found her voice.

'And now I have done another wrong and sacrificed my mortal soul.'

'How so?'

'There is a man.'

'A man?'

They were silent again.

'I have fought with him who menanced thee.'

She looked at him as at a stranger. 'I do not understand.'

'How much dost thou know of what has passed?'

'Little enough.'

'I was under instruction.'

'Instruction? Who are you that you must obey others?'

'I am my father's son and thought I did a son's duty.'

'Were it duty to bring ruin to a stranger who relied on your . . .?' She could not speak the word.

'I was told only that I must befriend thee . . .' Then he stopped. 'No. I was told that if opportunity presented itself I should rid them of a problem.'

'To kill me.'

'No. I refused to do ought but tell them how things were with thee. They thought to do no more than wait out the time. I am sure of it. I was never privy to their plans. But I . . . it was never planned that I should . . . My life, Pearl . . .'

She stiffened and he stopped. He continued.

'My life has been without true purpose. There was another to whom promises were made.'

'So.'

'Hear me out. I come to make full confession. There was another but when I first saw thee all other thoughts flew away. They had planned for everything but not for this. I was turned all about and scarcely knew what I should do or where my loyalties should lie.'

'To yourself, it seems.'

'There is nothing thou couldst say which I have not said to myself and there is nothing I can say that will justify . . .'

'There is not. And were you . . .' Pearl hesitated, 'were you told to . . . when you and I . . .'

'When they saw that I would not lift my hand against thee they merely required of me that I should play my role in keeping thee within their grasp.'

'And how should you do this?'

'I owe my father everything. He has secured all I have and I thought obedience my chief responsibility. I was wrong.'

'How should you do this?' Pearl repeated, staring intently at this minister turned villain.

There came no reply.

'So.' She relaxed, as though now she should have heard the worst there was to hear. 'There is no truth in you, John Standish. These were wolves and you threw me to them. But worse, far worse than this, you betrayed me in your very heart. I turned to you who needed help and love and it were counterfeit you offered.'

'No. No. It is not true.'

'Then you do not know yourself.'

'And in proof of this I have done thee one last service.'

Pearl shook her head in despair and disbelief.

'I have chanced my mortal soul to deflect a blade that was levelled at thy heart.'

'How so?'

'At the last there was one who thought to rid himself of thee as he had of Lawyer Simple. He and I fought the day of Simple's death. I bear the wounds.'

'And is it gratitude you want?'

'I did what I must, I believe. He no longer cared for the property or the secrets which it held. It were enough that thou had thwarted him. We met. We argued. He told me whither he was bound and we fought. Thou need have no more fear of him.'

'And you, John Standish?'

'Must be away. There is nothing left for me. I have done thee great wrong and if I suffer now then there is justice in it. But I did love thee.'

'There is no thee and thou for us, nor do I believe you. Words cost nothing. I have heard them before, remember. My mother once . . .' Then she was silent. 'Goodbye, John Standish. May God forgive you.'

'And thou, dost . . . do you forgive me?'

'I have closed that book and shall never open it again. Look to yourself. The fields are still full of those who would search you out.'

'But, Pearl . . .'

'Say no more.'

'The child. What of the child?'

Pearl paused and looked at this man who had once meant so much to her.

'There is no child,' she said, deliberately. Then, for no reason she could have explained, not least to herself, her tone softened. 'There is no child, John.'

He looked at her, bewildered. 'I do not understand.'

'No. You do not. But I say again, there is no child.'

The two stood in the kitchen of that dark house, with a clock ticking their lives steadily away, as the last threads which held those lives together snapped, silently, one by one.

That night Pearl sat with her diary. The rush of events meant that she had written nothing of the events at Caistor or Opie Street, or of her time with the magistrates. Indeed, she no longer felt the need to inscribe her thoughts at all, preferring to live rather than to report. So, instead of continuing her narrative she took her quill and drew a wavering line across the page. But beneath it she wrote lines which she had stitched on a sampler many years before in a distant cottage, at her mother's knee. And when she had written them out, in a clear hand, she spoke them aloud to herself and any other who should chance to hear: 'The days that are past are gone for ever. Those that are to come may not come to us. The present time only is ours. Let us therefore take the moment for our own.'

As she finished so she returned in her mind to that time, so long ago, when she had stitched what she could not yet understand and stood on the edge of a mystery that would only be resolved by time and by knowing the pain which is inseparable from life's true adventure.

She placed the quill in its holder and, before snuffing out the candle, slowly closed her book.

Epilogue

Within a further month a circle was closed. Pearl was back where her mother had run and laughed and cried as a child. The motto above the doorway was stripped of brambles and cobwebs. Rooms were cleared and cleaned, the damp driven out by fire. To the rear of the building nettles, cow parsley and wild roses were raked and burned and the river, long hidden, revealed so that she could sit in the sun and watch swans and kingfishers, moorhens and ducks glide and swoop and flutter against the evening sky.

On the hill above was the Hall which she had abandoned, sold to her friend who was Simple in name but not in nature. Of an evening he would ride down to the further bank and converse with her across the glittering stream or cross over the stepping stones to watch as she painted the scene, her canvas propped against the stump of an old elderberry tree.

One evening, as housemartins crossed and re-crossed the open land along the river bank and the first bats flew in tight patterns by the barn, he directed his horse to the far bank. The first shadow of night was gathering to the east but behind him the sun flared as it touched the breast of the hill. There had been rain two days since and the river had not yet fallen again to its autumn shallows. Still he chanced the stepping stones and to any who watched appeared to walk on water as he set his feet where habit told him safety lay. He knew nothing of Chillingworth's winter plunge, many years before, into those same waters, a plunge without which he would not be walking thus miraculously. Had the cold but clutched that twisted physic tighter about the heart, had a branch which spun in obedience to wind and current only struck him harder, he would have perished that night and so no fated romance would have been followed by no desperate flight and two souls would not have become as one, nor two bodies either. And but for that there would be no such person as Pearl and no story to be told. Everyone's story is everyone else's, too, for there is no self unless it be breathed into existence by another, no, by two separate selves who for a moment of time believe themselves within the same account.

For the most part, too, every tree and brook has been seen through other eyes than our own and hence their meaning changes with the years and with perspective, too. There are those who remember a tree as witness to a first kiss and never fail to smile when they look at it. There are others who remember a parent strip a branch to form a cane to beat obedience into a rebellious heart. So we are to one another. Pearl remembered the tears shed by her companion when he saw his brother dead, tears which none but he could understand. And had her own mother not once felt love for the very man she thought the source of all her woes? Then again, had he not at last repented and offered her the chance to live again, to unpick the pattern, unroll the woollen ball back into a skein, undo time, unmake a sin? Or was it vengeance, after all, which he bequeathed?

Daniel called to her from mid-river. She looked up. He seemed to stand in a pool of molten gold. She waved and smiled to see him thus surrounded by a mirrored sun. He stepped carefully across and soon stood on grass already silver with dew. Somewhere in the distance a dog barked, though so far away that the noise became absorbed into the general sounds of an autumn evening. He was not dressed for riding.

229

There was a formality to his appearance as though he had come on some errand. And so he had, who had not asked the question which he had prepared himself to ask at Opie Street. He was nervous, too, who had sat many an evening in just this place and beside this young woman, who now began to pack away her paint and brushes.

He stood and looked down at her painting. It showed a young woman, so like herself that it could surely be no other. But at her breast, in scarlet thread, was a single letter which seemed to pick up the light from the setting sun and glow with such brightness that all else seemed dull besides.

'Thou hast tried thy hand at self-portraiture and the likeness is true, as it seems to me.'

Pearl looked up with a frown on her face. 'It is not me. It is my mother.'

'Then mother and daughter are as one.'

Pearl smiled to herself, as should she not who had come to recognise both the truth and the falsity of this.

'Yet what is that mark at her breast?' he asked, pointing a finger at the emblem which shone with such strange and subtle light.

'That is the sign of her goodness,' she whispered.

'It is unusual, surely.'

'No, not as thou might think. And yet thou art right, for there is none but she who can turn sin into redemption, not in this world at least.' A tear had come unbidden into her eye.

'Do not cry, Pearl,' said her companion with some alarm. 'There are those here who love thee with such constancy as might rival a mother's love.' He said it with urgency and then blushed at his zeal.

Pearl looked up sharply. Somehow she had known this moment must come. A wave she had seen form out at sea was about to break upon the beach.

'I am one such, Pearl. I know there are years which separate us . . .'

Pearl raised a hand to stop him. On the hillside above them the sun had all but disappeared. Together she and the man who struggled to confess his love stood and watched as deep orange dissolved into a soft grey mist. Then, as the final wash of colour disappeared it was as if time itself had been suspended. No clocks struck here, as in her former home they had. The bats flew in their cabalistic patterns, as they doubtless had for centuries, unaware of what dramas might be enacted beneath them. A breeze rose from the river sending autumn leaves tumbling across the grass while, one by one, stars began to appear, cold and distant.

Pearl at that moment was well named for there was a kind of pale silver sheen to her face in the glow of the harvest moon. It was as though this whole display of nature's severe beauty were but to create a setting for this moment. Creation was in the balance. She had a decision to make. She had come so far. She had seen so much. She had begun to feel a new power and a new sense of purpose to her life. When she sat at her easel and held her brush like a plumb line against the sky she felt that she in some degree invented the scene which she saw. Something entered her being which transfigured the world and the eye which saw it.

She had travelled alone and though she would not have prevailed had not another come to her aid, was she to surrender her freedom to another's care? There was love, to be sure. She could not doubt the truth of that. He was to her what she was to him, nor did she require his earnest attempts to translate his feelings into words. Her hand was in his, had sought it out, indeed, quite without her knowledge. But in her ear she heard a whisper, low and elusive, yet clear enough. It was not to be confused with the rustle of aspen leaves nor yet with the distant sound of water flowing over stones. It was her mother's voice she heard, speaking her name but as one does when a child ventures too close to the fire. Yet he whispered, too, and with no less love or urgency.

Pearl was born for the future. There would come a time when her paintings would perhaps hang in the light of fires which were not her own, when her name would be spoken of by those who never knew her, save through those paintings, even though there were few women who were honoured then for the skills they possessed or the virtues they embodied. As she stood with another in the light of the moon on a September evening it was that future, or perhaps merely that fantasy of a future which hung in the balance. There were perhaps future generations of women who held their breath as she prepared to give her answer to the question which at last that gentle man, dressed in a pale lavender turned grey by the arrival of night, had brought himself to ask.

Many years later, when at last, in a distant land, Hester died, her daughter felt a sudden pain, a regret that they should now never meet again in this life and that her mother should have mourned so long for a lost daughter. But in truth she was lost no more. She was found and in finding herself had completed a story begun so long before in the Norfolk hamlet to which she now returned and in which she lived with great happiness. But did she read the account of her mother's death and then pass the letter to another, who stood beside her and kissed away her tears, or did she fold it neatly and, quite alone, place it within a box against tomorrow?

Reader, she did not marry him. Or so it is said. But who can be sure? These are distant days of which I speak and history and story but two letters separated. For myself, I like to believe that such souls as these did indeed find in each other the answers that they sought. And if what we wish is not always what may be, well, why do such things as stories exist under God's good heaven?

Every voyage a lesson: every life a truth.

Note

In my earlier novel, *Hester*, I explored the life of Hester Prynne before the events which Nathaniel Hawthorne describes in *The Scarlet Letter*. In *Pearl* I suggest a possible fate for Hester's daughter. Hawthorne sends Pearl out of his book with his blessings. She is, he implies, to become something more than an echo of her mother but we know nothing of what lies in wait for her. Once she leaves the text of *The Scarlet Letter* she exists only in the form of other texts, letters, along with a few 'articles of comfort and luxury' and 'beautiful tokens of a continual remembrance, that must have been wrought by delicate fingers, at the impule of a fine heart' which reach Hester from another land. There is even hint of a child, but nothing is certain. Nothing in *The Scarlet Letter* ever really is.

A year after his first novel Hawthorne published *The House of the Seven Gables*. After the solemnities of *The Scarlet Letter* he plainly felt the need for humour and reconciliation, even if there is still a smell of brimstone in the air. It is that spirit I have tried to capture, though once again I have not tried to imitate Hawthorne but to write with a flavour of the 19th century doing its best to understand the 17th century. Hawthorne, however, is secure from whatever sins I may commit. Writers are in a sense without morals. They steal from history, from their lives and from one another. I have stolen from Hawthorne. All I can say is that while I was in his house I stood amazed at what he had made and in the end could only steal the shadow, not the thing itself.

Incidentally, for those who wish to seek it there is an Opie Street in Norwich. It was not called that in the 17th century. It was known then as Devil's Alley. The very appropriateness of such a home for Lawyer Simple, however, precluded its use. Fact fitted fiction all too neatly. So, ahistorically, Devil's Alley became Opie Street but since history is a branch of fiction I am not disposed to worry overmuch. If you do choose to go there, however, it is best to visit in the daylight hours for I am told that at night the street sign has been known to transmute and Opie Street become Devil's Alley once again.

Perspectives

A handbook of Christian Responsibility

M.A. Chignell

Edward Arnold

First published 1981
by Edward Arnold (Publishers) Ltd
41 Bedford Square, London WC1X 3DQ

Reprinted 1982

British Library Cataloguing in Publication Data

Chignell, M.A.
    Perspectives: a handbook of Christian responsibility
    1. Christian ethics
    I. Title
    241   BJ1251

    ISBN 0-7131-0614-X

Acknowledgments:

My warmest gratitude to many friends, but especially to Barbara Windle,
without whose expert and meticulous help this book would never have
been written, and to Doreen Sides, whose interest and competent typing
of the manuscript has been an encouragement to us all.

M.A.C. March 1981

The Publishers wish to thank the National Council of the Churches
of Christ in the USA and Thomas Nelson, New York for permission to
use verses from the Revised Standard Version of the Bible, copyrighted
1946, 1952 © 1971, 1973.

Set in 10/11 pt Century and printed in Great Britain
by Spottiswoode Ballantyne Ltd., Colchester and London.